Chase Harlem

Elise Burke Brown

The Little free Library —

Welcome to the

mayhem!

Elise Burke Brown

Text copyright © 2025 by Elise Burke Brown

Cover Illustration © Nat Mack
Distributed by Simon & Schuster

ISBN: 978-1-998076-78-9
Ebook: 978-1-998076-79-6

FIC022040   FICTION / Mystery & Detective / Women Sleuths
FIC022090   FICTION / Mystery & Detective / Private Investigators
FIC022000   FICTION / Mystery & Detective / General

#ChaseHarlem

Follow Rising Action on our socials!
Instagram: @risingactionpublishingco
Tiktok: @risingactionpublishingco

In memory of William Gerald Beecham, Sr., my PawPaw and my hero, who taught me how to tell a story. I hope this one makes you proud.

Chase Harlem

Chapter 1

Them There Eyes

New Orleans, LA

There are three things a woman needs to be happy: good friends, comfortable shoes, and a reliable taser.

Daryl Wayne—former bodybuilder and current big finance embezzler—didn't know about the last item on the list. If he had, he probably wouldn't be screaming obscenities while waving an embarrassingly small knife at me.

As he took a step toward me, I knew I could use my years of self-defense training to disarm him with a blow to the inside of his elbow, then incapacitate him with a jab to a pressure point on his neck, before using his own momentum to pin him to the ground and lock his arm behind him. But that seemed like a lot of work for a Monday. So, I simply avoided his knife hand and tased him in the neck. He landed on the hot asphalt in a convulsing heap, smelling slightly of burnt flesh and mostly of urine.

I kicked his tiny knife away from him. "Honestly, Daryl, you shouldn't add attempted assault to your list of crimes. Stabbing me won't prevent me from talking to your bosses. They're the ones paying me, remember?"

Daryl worked in the finance department of one of the biggest businesses in New Orleans. A few weeks ago, he approached his board of directors with "evidence" of embezzlement and fraud. I'm not sure it was part of his plan for the board of directors to hire me to investigate the matter further, but he played along pretty easily at first, providing me with everything I needed to accuse his work rival of embezzlement. The whole thing smelled fishy to me, and my little profiler brain knew Daryl couldn't be trusted. So, I gathered some evidence on my own. It turned out Daryl Wayne was the one embezzling, and he was attempting to use me to frame some other fella at the office. Our little confrontation was the result of my letting Daryl know, in the politest way possible, that I would not be manipulated.

Clearly, the conversation had not gone well.

Once I was sure Daryl was unarmed, on the ground, and would not be getting back up to attack me again, I pulled out my phone and called the New Orleans Police Department's non-emergency line.

After two rings, Geraldine picked up with, "NOPD. How may I direct your call?"

"Hey Geraldine," I said, "it's Chase again."

"How may I help you, Chase?" Geraldine claims I'm one of her favorite people, but that's not saying much because Geraldine says that about everyone.

"Do you have a unit you can send out to the Buster's on Conti Street?" I asked. "This guy just tried to stab me with a *ridiculously* small knife."

"Oh *ho-ney*," she said, her thick Louisiana accent emphasizing the "h" in a way only a true Southerner could, "did you tase him?" Geraldine knows all my tricks.

"Yes, ma'am."

I heard her shuffle through the phone, and I'm sure she was leaning in to whisper, "Did he piss 'imself, too?"

"Yes ma'am, he did."

She sighed. "Briggs and Chandler are the closest unit to you. You know Briggs ain't gonna be happy 'bout puttin' that man in his car."

Not a surprise. I've never known Briggs to be happy. In fact, Briggs is probably clinically depressed and should not be allowed to patrol the streets. Of course, I didn't tell Geraldine that. I just said, "Thank you, ma'am."

"And Chase, you know those fancy new phones like you got, they all got an S.O.S. alert on 'em. Maybe next time a man tries to stab you, you oughta think about using that. You got folks you can trust to help you out if you need it."

I looked at the piss-poor pile of Daryl on the ground and couldn't help but curl my lip. "It's not really an S.O.S. problem, Geraldine. Like I said, it was a really small knife."

When people think of my city, it's the smells of beignets and crawfish, the sound of a saxophone playing on the corner, and the vivid pastels and bright colors of the French Quarter. Me, I know better. After finally finding parking nearly a block away from my tiny apartment— which functions as both my office and living residence—I took the long trek down St. Peter Street. I was nearly overwhelmed by the smells of chicory roast and rich chocolate croissants as I passed by Spitfire Coffee, but I forced my tired mind to focus instead on the few people meandering around me. New Orleans is exciting, magical, an adventure waiting to happen, but it's also haunted by one of the highest murder rates in the nation. There's an underlying danger, even in the early morning. My years of training won't allow me to relax without a couple of drinks, and I've learned not to drink when I have cases to solve.

It was a Tuesday morning in the beginning of November—a few days after my small incursion with Daryl. Halloween had only recently passed. So, I was still having to watch my step to avoid the signature plastic beads littering the streets. We locals take our Halloween festivities very seriously. I'd been lucky enough to snag a couple of small cases that would pay the bills, just as things were beginning to cool down after the holiday craziness.

On that particularly crisp autumn morning, I was just getting back to the office from a long night of casing an older lady. She was suing one of the local restaurants because she claimed she'd slipped on their supposedly wet floor and broken her hip. Yet, somehow, she still managed to make her weekly ballroom dancing class. If her hip was hurting her, she certainly wasn't showing it as she swung around the dance floor with a smorgasbord of retirement-aged men, not to mention the youthful dance teacher—who had a way of swinging his hips that made me forget what his face looked like. She hadn't left the dance studio until nearly midnight, which is 3:00 a.m. in post-seventy-year-old time, and she wasn't alone, which meant I had to follow her home to take more pictures—not the most fun part of my job. To make a long story short, I had plenty of pictures and was quite sure the lawsuit would never go to court.

As I made my way to my building, 911 St. Peter Street, I was feeling pretty good about my job and was looking forward to the hefty paychecks I'd receive once I turned in my hours. Sure, I was far past the point of exhaustion from pulling an all-nighter, but overall, I was feeling good.

The last thing I expected to see was a fifty-something-year-old guy standing just outside the courtyard entrance to my building, wearing jeans and a black hoodie zipped up to his chin. As he paced a small circle on the cement outside the courtyard gate, his left hand fiddled with the zipper on his hoodie. Even from my place on the corner, I saw that he needed a shave. His harried expression and the way he kept examining his wristwatch told me he'd been waiting for quite some time. He stepped toward the door again, his hand shaking as he pressed the buzzer. Call it my "detective instinct," if you want, but I was positive he was ringing for my apartment, number 6. I was also positive that this guy was hiding something under his hoodie, and it probably had to do with some unresolved trauma from his childhood, likely something to do with his father—

I shook my head. Reprogramming my brain after years of profiling criminals was no easy feat. I still had trouble not over-analyzing perfectly harmless strangers on the street sometimes.

"May I help you, sir?" I asked him, walking the rest of the way up to him and the door.

He jumped at the sound of my voice, and if it wasn't the surprise of my stealthy approach that startled him, it was probably my grungy all-nighter appearance. "Are you Detective Joanna Harlem?" he asked. He had heavy, severe eyebrows that angled down on their outermost tips as if they were weighed down by wisdom. His eyes were small but compassionate and made me think he was the type of man people trusted immediately. In fact, the way he carried himself, with his shoulders curled forward slightly, made me think he also carried the weight of many people's secrets.

"It's Chase Harlem, Private Investigator," I corrected him. I love the way that sounds. What I didn't love was the look of total bewilderment on the guy's face when I said it.

"I'm sorry?"

I sighed. It was too early, and I was too tired to be polite. "My name is Joanna Chase Harlem. I'm a private investigator. It's different from being a detective—detectives are cops, and I don't have a badge. My clients, colleagues, and people I find generally annoying call me P.I . Harlem, my friends call me Chase, and my mama calls me Joanna. Nobody, absolutely nobody calls me Jo, Joey, Jojo, Jodi, Anne, Anna, or any other stupid nickname you might manage to extract from the name Joanna. I've shot people for less."

His heavy eyebrows raised slightly, and his eyes twinkled with amusement, but I could tell he was still confused about something. He cleared his throat. "I expected you to be ... well—"

"Forty?" I finished for him. It was the typical reaction. Even though I'm over thirty years old, I can still pass for a young'un'. Plus, I was standing there with my coffee-colored hair in a high ponytail, no makeup on, wearing a New Orleans Saints hoodie with faded blue jeans and a pair of bright red Chuck Taylor All-Star Converse—my trademark sneakers. In hindsight, I appeared pretty unprofessional. Truth be told, the whole ensemble was my usual look. Since I'm my own boss, I've made Converse, jeans, and an old T-shirt a part of my company dress code. Since my company consists only of me, I never have to worry about those pesky rule-breakers.

The man nodded in response, and I knew I had to do something to instill confidence and wipe that look of confusion off his face. I took a deep breath and explained, "Look, I've been working all night, and I've got clients waiting for information, so I'm not gonna stand here and list my credentials for you. You can take me as I am or leave me alone."

Instilling confidence is not really my thing.

"No, I believe you," the man answered with a smile, all hesitation leaving his face. I might be better at instilling confidence than I thought.

There was an awkward silence in which he continued to smile, and I tried to figure out the meaning behind his smile. I didn't rush it. Truth be told, I relish awkward silences. I don't know why. Does that make me one of those socially awkward people who don't understand social cues? Probably. Okay... definitely.

After deciding his smile was neither patronizing nor nefarious, I asked, "And you are?"

"My name is Henry Nolan," he answered, shaking my hand in greeting once again, as if this whole encounter hadn't been awkward enough already. He had a decent grip, but soft hands—definitely not a working-class guy. His thick eyebrows drew closer together as if something had occurred to him. "Are you the same Harlem who teaches the free women's self-defense class down at the Baptist Church?"

I dropped his hand and stepped away. It was true that I taught that class, but many of my students had boyfriends, husbands, or run-of-the-mill stalkers who did not need to know about their whereabouts on Tuesday nights. I didn't know this man, and even if he seemed harmless enough, I wasn't about to risk putting one of those women in danger after working my butt off to keep them safe.

"I don't know what you're talking about," I said.

"Some of the women in my church attend, I believe. I'd be happy to spread the word about the class if—"

I turned away from him and toward my courtyard door. "You need to leave. I don't know what you're talking about."

He must've noticed his mistake because he quickly changed the subject. "Daryl Wayne told me you could help me with something."

That stopped me. "Daryl Wayne?"

"Do you remember him?" Henry asked.

"Nope," I lied. Of course I remembered Daryl. I'd just tased him two days ago and still had to go by the station to fill out the police report.

"He told me you were an excellent investigator, so I was hoping I…" he stopped as the courtyard gate swung open, and the awkward teen who lives in number 5 came scampering out, down the stoop, and onto the sidewalk between us. She held an unlit cigarette in her hand, which she hid behind her back when she recognized me. She gave me a quick nod before shuffling away down St. Peter Street.

"Mornin'," I called after her. I briefly wondered where a kid like that would be going, other than high school, on a random Tuesday morning in November, but quickly reminded myself that the neighbor's kid was none of my damn business. I turned my attention back to Nolan, who was shuffling his feet again. "May I speak to you in private?" he asked.

"Sure thing," I said. I pulled my keys out of my camera bag and unlocked the gate, allowing Mr. Nolan to enter before me. He stepped through the entryway and into the small, French-style courtyard, complete with black iron chairs and a fancy fountain that hadn't worked since before I moved in. I stepped past him, leading him straight back from the gate and to the door of my 360-square-foot apartment. I opened the thin, double French doors and motioned for him to step in ahead of me.

That turned out to be a mistake. As soon as Nolan stepped into the room, a tiny creature darted across the brick-laid floor in a blur of white fur and scampered up the poor man's leg before landing on his shoulder, chittering into his ear.

"Dammit, Louis!" I shouted, yanking the albino ferret off Nolan's shoulder before striding across the tiny room that served as my living room, kitchen, and office space to return him to his cage. I shoved him through the metal opening of the cage, secured the door behind him, and commanded, "Stay in your cage."

I quickly turned back to Nolan, frozen in my doorway, his eyes wide in shock and possibly disgust.

"Sorry about that," I said. "He's a Houdini when it comes to breaking out of his cage."

"I see," Nolan spoke slowly, like he was still processing the situation.

"He belongs to a client," I explained, pointlessly. That was mostly true. Louis had belonged to a client, but when I went to the client's apartment to collect my due, I saw the ferret mostly hairless, emaciated, and clearly scared of everything that moved. In lieu of the paycheck I was owed, I took the mustelid. I'd planned to give him away to a good home once I got him healthy again, but I'd grown attached to the little guy.

Nolan simply nodded.

"Follow me," I said. I directed him to the corner of my apartment, far away from my cluttered kitchen. My office was really more of a closet under the stairs where I'd managed to shove a desk, two threadbare office chairs, and an empty filing cabinet. It was relatively neat today compared to what it usually looked like, and after moving a few things around, I was able to uncover one of my two chairs so the man could sit. After he had, I plopped down on top of my desk in front of him.

It was at this point that he began to rummage through his leather man-bag—you know, those purses men carry, except they don't call them purses—and I silently wondered whether he was about to pull out a gun and try to shoot me in the face. I know I'm paranoid, but you have to be a little paranoid to make it in my line of work. Besides, this guy said Daryl Wayne sent him, and Mr. Wayne and I were not exactly what one would call old friends. Worse, I realized my gun was in the camera bag I'd let slide onto the coffee table as I'd shoved Louis into his cage. It wouldn't do me a heck of a lot of good there, now would it? I guess that makes me stupid, but according to my personal philosophy, so is everyone else.

Either way, Mr. Nolan didn't pull out a gun and shoot. Instead, he pulled out a copy of a local newspaper and handed it to me. The top story was about a football player whose body had been found at a Halloween party in the Big Easy. The footballer's girlfriend had been found dead of a drug overdose on the same night. Usually, murder isn't really news in New Orleans, but since this football player happened to be Eli Goldman, LSU's starting quarterback, the newspaper had made an exception. In case you didn't know, college football is its own religion in the southern states.

"Yes." I nodded after the man didn't speak. "I've heard of this case. Do you know something—"

"You need to know that this—in the picture—is my son."

There was the clincher. I glanced at the newspaper. The photo spread across the front page was of Eli Goldman and his fellow athlete, Jeremy Lackey, who had been at the masquerade, too. Rumor had it Lackey was the last person to see Goldman alive, which made him the primary suspect.

"You mean, the football player is your son?" I asked, stupidly.

"That's right."

I stared at him in confusion. It didn't make any sense for Henry Nolan to be Eli Goldman's father. After all, Goldman's dad had been doing interview after interview since his son's death, and he looked nothing like the man sitting across from me. After a moment of confusion, my sleep-deprived brain finally forced my slow mouth to ask the obvious question: "You think Eli Goldman is your *son*?" I had to be sure I wasn't hearing things.

Mr. Nolan shook his head. "No. Not him."

Ah, that made more sense. "Jeremy Lackey is your son?" I asked.

"That is correct," he answered. His tone was level, making it annoyingly difficult to interpret.

Something still wasn't making sense. "But his name is Jeremy *Lackey*."

"We don't share a last name," he said, simply. "We don't share much of anything. It's a complicated story, really, but—"

"Look, Mr. Nolan," I interrupted, "whatever your story, it doesn't matter." I had managed to avoid any cases having to do with violent crime for the entire two years since I'd set up shop in New Orleans, and I wasn't about to ruin my streak.

Mr. Nolan started to argue, but I held up my hands to silence him for a moment so I could explain. "I know the police detective working this case, and I can assure you he'll figure it out just fine without me." I wasn't just saying that because said detective happens to be my best friend; he really is good at what he does. Almost as good as me.

"I want you, P.I. Harlem."

11

"I don't—"

"Daryl confessed to me the truth of your business relationship," he said, interrupting me again. "I'm positive you remember him despite what you say. Surely, it's not *every* day that someone pulls a knife on you." I thought I saw him smirk, but I was running on too little sleep to know for sure. "Even so, I am impressed that you didn't brag about your ... altercation. I feel most people in your position would have, especially since I'm here to offer you a job."

Yeah, I was still salty about the whole knife incident, but this conversation was just too weird.

"Daryl confessed?" I asked. I needed clarification because I could not wrap my head around Daryl ever confessing anything to anyone.

To answer my question, Mr. Nolan unzipped his hoodie to reveal a white clerical collar, and I mentally berated myself because I *knew* he was hiding something under that hoodie. I never would have guessed the clerical collar, though.

"You're a *priest?*" I asked, quickly re-assessing everything I'd said to the man during our exchange and hoping I hadn't been a total jerk in the short expanse of time I'd known him.

"Surprised? I thought you were an investigator," the priest remarked. He said this with the same unreadable smile he'd had in the hall. Smiling priests apparently make me nervous.

"You have a son!" I pointed out, though I had to admit—given my day job—that I should have guessed he was a priest. I mean, he was a relatively attractive, fifty-something-year-old man without a wedding ring; he was wearing a jacket zipped up to his neck in the New Orleans humidity and not using it to hide a firearm; he knew about the women's self-defense class I teach at the church. Plus, he had those trustworthy eyes and that secret-sharing stance I'd noticed on the street. "Wait, how do you have a son?"

"The same way as everyone else. I wasn't always a priest. I didn't even know about Jeremy until he was five years old, and I was well into the priesthood. I served a short term at the Catholic Church in his hometown, or else I might never have known him at all. His mother had gotten married, and I had no place in his life."

"Harsh."

"It's all part of God's plan." He said it like a man who never got the chance to live with the consequences of his choices. He wasn't bitter, exactly, but there was a hint of sadness. "Now, P.I. Harlem, will you help me?"

"Why me?"

"I needed to find someone to help my son. I'm sure you're aware of the fact that he's the primary suspect. They haven't arrested him yet, but it's only a matter of time. I think he's a smart kid who knows when he's in trouble." He paused, pulling at his collar before looking anywhere but at me. "My son has never asked for my help before, but this time, he did. Then, just when I was beginning to doubt my ability to help, Daryl confessed. He told me about you." Father Nolan's kind eyes met mine. "Whether you have faith or not, P.I. Harlem, I believe God sent me to you. Will you do this for me?"

"Mr.—Father Nolan, I'm not trying to be rude. Really, I'm not. Once upon a time, I would have sold my own grandmother to snag a case like this one," I admitted. "But the NOPD detectives are more than capable of handling this case without me. And like I said before, I know the detective in charge of this. He'd cut off his left arm before he'd let an innocent kid hang."

The priest was silent for a moment, obviously considering my stance. Perhaps he was even reconsidering hiring me. His final answer, however, was unchanged. "I admire your honesty, and I'm now even more certain that my hiring you is God's will."

"I'm sorry," I said, rising from my chair. I'd noticed Louis had escaped his cage again and was surreptitiously slinking his way across the living room area and back over to the kitchen, probably planning to steal an apple from the counter. In three strides, I managed to make my way past Father Nolan and scoop the fuzzy creature into my arms. He immediately started to nuzzle under my chin, making a noise that sounded suspiciously like a purr. "I don't take violent cases," I informed Father Nolan. "You'll have to find someone else."

Father Nolan sighed. His chair squeaked as he leaned toward me, but he didn't speak. He closed his eyes, and I honest-to-goodness think he said a silent prayer before looking back up at me. "P.I. Harlem, my son is innocent," he said, his deep voice soft and full of conviction.

"I'm sure he is," I reassured him.

The priest looked up at me from his chair, his dark eyes looking into mine with something like pleading, and I felt like my stomach had dropped into my shoes. "You can't let an innocent man stand accused of murder, can you?"

Damn. He'd looked into my eyes and found my weakness. For a moment, I thought I was going to be sick. The image of a corpse hanging lifeless in a jail cell flashed before my eyes. The moment expanded into a never-ending loop. The room felt like it was getting smaller, and it was hard to breathe. My mouth felt dry, and bile rose into my throat. The only thing that kept me standing was the steady rhythm of Louis's heartbeat as he sensed my anxiety and nuzzled his fuzzy little head into my jaw. I closed my eyes, took a breath, counted to four, and sighed slowly. After doing that a few more times, I was finally ready to look into the priest's eyes. "No. I cannot."

He nodded, staring at me like he thought I might shatter into a million pieces, and honestly, I couldn't blame him. "So," he asked, "you'll take the case?"

I shrugged, scratching Louis behind his fuzzy ears. "I don't see any other choice." I was surprised to note that, once I'd agreed, the tightness in my chest seemed to vanish.

Father Nolan nodded. "You won't regret this," he assured me. "I *trust* you, P.I. Harlem. In time, God will give you the strength to trust yourself."

I suppose a rational thought pattern would have led me to wonder how this priest could afford my hourly wage, but due to a lack of sleep, my capacity for rational thought was nearly depleted. Instead, I was now Elwood Blues in a black hat and shades, blasting the Blues Mobile over the drawbridge on a mission from God. Needless to say, I took the job.

Father Nolan and I talked for about fifteen more minutes. He didn't have a lot of information to fork over; the cops working the case were keeping a tight lid on everything. I took notes and agreed to call him as soon as I knew something.

Chapter 2

A Beautiful Friendship

What happened next is too boring to recount in a lot of detail. I fed Louis the ferret and called my client—remember, the insurance folks I mentioned—a few minutes after the priest left, which was around 8:00 a.m. The insurance folks and I agreed to meet at three o'clock that afternoon to exchange money and info.

After that, I tried to sleep, but my never-ending battle with insomnia wouldn't allow it. The fact that my brain liked to play out scenes of torture and death before my eyes was a major contributing factor. I finally pushed myself off my futon mattress and took five long steps to the top of my stairwell. There, my cheap, sixty-six-key keyboard sat. I played through all the sheet music I owned. I'm not a particularly talented pianist, so it takes a massive amount of concentration for me to play even the simplest of songs, but that's why it works to calm me. I settled in, my fingers gliding slowly across the plastic keys as I emptied my soul into each fathomless chord, falling deeper and deeper under the spell of the music. The melodious strains shrouded me, sheltering me from any thought of the outside world as my pulse slowed to meet the intricate jazz rhythms.

I was finishing "Don't Cry Baby" by Madeleine Peyroux when I finally began to feel grit beneath my eyelids every time I blinked—a sure sign that sleep was imminent. I stood up from the stool in front of my keyboard, turned, and lunged onto the futon.

I slept for five whole hours. It was *magical*. I didn't even have any nightmares, which would have made my federally mandated therapist happy.

When I woke up, I took another shower and avoided the mirror as I changed into my fancy work clothes—an Irma Thomas T-shirt, jeans, and Converse. Next, I printed some incriminating pictures of an older lady along with some notes from the Daryl Wayne case, grabbed a snack, met up with my employers, got paid, filled the gas tank, and blah blah blah—you get the point.

At exactly 7:00 that night, I headed to First Baptist New Orleans. It was one of your typical Southern mega-churches. It featured a youth center and a large gym, which offered a wide array of fitness classes. When the church secretary—my good buddy, Geraldine—suggested to the preacher that they hire me to teach a self-defense class, he scoffed. So, I offered to teach the classes for free. Southern Baptist preachers love when things are free.

"Hey there, honey," Geraldine called as I entered the gym area. Being in her sixties, Geraldine was supervising the younger women as they laid down mats for class. She made her way over to me and whispered, "I hope Officer Briggs wasn't too nasty to you the other day when he came to pick up the man with the knife."

"No more than usual." I shrugged, crossing my arms in front of me. Geraldine would lunge in for a hug as soon as she sensed an opening, and

I was not a hugger. "His partner, Chandler, was nice enough for both of 'em."

"He's a good young man. A little dull, but good."

I looked out across the gym as more women entered. I spotted Maria Burke across the room and waved her over. The petite brunette trotted across the floor, braids bouncing, as she moved like a Disney Princess prancing around with her forest pals.

"Hi, Chase," she greeted me. "Big class today."

It was, indeed. The class had started small—just me, Geraldine, and Maria Burke—but had grown quickly. By this November, I will have been teaching for over a year, and classes were usually between twenty to twenty-five women. I had my regulars, of course, who I always kept a closer eye on.

I nodded. "Yeah. It's not bad." I shifted to face her fully. "Look, do you know if your grumpy husband is working the Eli Goldman case?" Her husband was Detective Matt Burke, my work-obsessed best friend.

"Girl, yes," she said, rolling her eyes. "And he won't tell me a thang about it. He knows how much I'm banking on my old team winnin' the national championship this year. I need to know who's gonna be leadin' my tigers now that Goldman is dead."

My nose scrunched involuntarily at the mention of college football. "Isn't the season over?"

"Over?" Maria squeaked. "Girl, how do you live in the South and not know anything about college football? We still have the playoffs and National Championship in *January*. How are we gonna win without Goldman?"

I shrugged. "I'm not a fan. Sorry."

Maria raised an eyebrow. "Why are you asking about the case, then?"

I turned toward the gym full of women and ordered, "Everybody, find your spots and start stretching."

"Oh, no." Maria grabbed me by the elbow and turned me toward her. "You're not shutting me out like you do with Matt. What's up?"

"I can't really say."

Maria's eyes lit up. "Someone's hired you to solve it, haven't they? It's your case, too." She'd always been too smart for her own good.

I nodded, and she squealed. "This is fantastic! You and Matt can work together."

"If Burke—erm, Matt—wants to work with me, maybe."

She rolled her eyes again. "You two are ridiculous. You're best friends, but half the time y'all act like you hate each other." Clearly, Maria has trouble understanding what "friendship" looks like to law enforcement officials.

At that moment, I notice one of my regulars, Bianca, coming through the gym doors. She's only been late once before. I smell trouble.

"Lead stretches for me, will ya?" I threw the question to Maria over my shoulder as I crossed the room to Bianca.

Bianca was a full-bodied woman, taller than me, with tight curls cascading down to her round shoulders. Her skin was almost as dark as her chestnut hair, and to me, she looked like a model for an expensive makeup company. She was putting her bag down on one of the bleachers when I approached, and she flinched when I called her name. She turned toward me and flashed a brilliant smile that didn't meet her eyes.

"Hey, Chase," she called. "You good?"

"Always," I answered, keeping my voice low, cautious. Bianca was one of my girls, and I didn't want to scare her off. "You?"

"All good here."

"How's your sister?"

"She good. Real good. Kids are a handful, though." She laughed, but it was forced, and it reminded me of the sound my papa's geese would make when the water in the pond got too low.

"Good thing she has you around to help out, right?"

"Yeah. Course she do." She shuffled from foot to foot as she spoke.

I was already smaller than her, but I lowered myself to the bleacher and looked up at her. "You know, if it's too much on her to drop you off, I could always come pick you up for class."

"No, uh, that ain't necessary."

"It's no problem. Her place ain't far from mine." A couple of weeks before, Bianca had come to class with bruises. After a brief conversation, I cut class short to help move Bianca out of the apartment she shared with her waste-of-oxygen boyfriend and into her sister's place.

Bianca turned her head, eyes studying the floor. I stayed quiet, waiting for her to say what she needed to say. After what felt like ages, she murmured, "I ain't stayin' wit' her no more."

I feigned surprise. "Oh, that's cool. Where are you staying?"

She finally met my eyes, and she looked so scared I thought my heart might break. "I moved back in with Tarant." Oh, the waste-of-oxygen was back. "I'm sorry. I know you don't like him, but—"

"Hey, hey," I shushed her, standing to take her hands in mine. I made sure she was looking me in the eyes before I continued. "I don't judge, Bianca. Safe space here." It wasn't what I wanted to say. I wanted to drive her back to Tarant's and do exactly to him what he'd done to her a few weeks ago, but court-appointed anger management classes had taught me not to solve all my problems with punching.

"He's just been real nice here lately, you know? He apologized and bought me flowers—like how he used to be." Of course he had, because abuse is a cycle—something easy to see when you're on the outside looking in.

"Isn't that what happened last time?" I reminded her as gently as I could.

She sniffed. "He ain't never apologized before, not like this."

I took a breath, sorting through all the things I couldn't say, knowing that if I said the wrong thing, Bianca might walk right out those doors and never come back—losing the strongest support system she had. "Just—just promise me that at the first sign of trouble, any little thing, Bianca, that you'll call me. You got my number."

She nodded and gave me a shaky smile. "Girl, you know it."

"And remember, the best self-defense is—"

"Being aware and being prepared so you can remove yourself from danger as quickly as possible."

It was the best I could get; I had to start class.

After I taught a couple of basic techniques to escape holds, I paired the girls up to practice. I purposely paired up with Bianca. She was confident, and by the end of class, her fear of my judgement seemed like a distant memory. It was still hard to watch her go, though. As always, I had to remind myself that I can't save everyone.

Chapter 3

Trav'lin' Light

After an unnecessarily exhausting class, I decided to grab a bite to eat and check my email. What better place to do that than The Gambler?

The Gambler is a little bar and grill located on the corner of Bourbon and Saint Peter Street. At first glance, it looks like a pretty sketchy place, and that reason alone keeps the tourists at bay. Inside, well, the place still looks pretty sketchy. It has the look of an old-time saloon mixed with a speakeasy that might have hosted Al Capone back in his heyday. It also has the benefit of free Wi-Fi, cold beer, and fantastic Cajun cuisine—none of which exist in my apartment—so it remains a great place to take my antique laptop and do research or check emails.

You'll soon realize that my favorite thing about The Gambler is the people who work there.

First, there is Domino, the bouncer who always stands at the front door to greet everyone with his massive bulk.

"Hey, big guy!" I greeted him as I walked through the door.

He grunted in response from his seat next to the enormous bar.

"How've you been holding up?"

He shrugged. He never answered that question.

Domino is the biggest, most intimidating man I've ever seen in real life, and I have been to a professional wrestling match before. Seven feet tall, Paraguayan, and covered in tattoos—the man could bounce a rhino if it dared to enter the bar—but he has the brightest, prettiest green eyes I've ever seen on anyone. Those eyes are almost enough to make him more beautiful than intimidating ... almost. He's also terribly protective of people he likes, and by some miracle, I landed on that short approval list.

"Ain't seen you in a while, little Harlem," Domino said as I sidled up beside him. He always calls me "little Harlem"—I'm not sure why. Maybe he knows of a bigger Harlem somewhere out there?

"Yeah, I've been working on this case," I told him. "Some old lady was trying to cheat her insurance company." I didn't mention the whole taser incident because it would have seemed like I was bragging.

"Catch her?" he asked me.

"You know I did," I said with a laugh. "How are things going around here?"

Domino answered with another shrug, which I translated to mean things had been pretty boring, and thumbed toward the tables. During the weekends, The Gambler is packed with locals, but on this particular Tuesday night it was nearly abandoned. There were only about four or five guys, all regulars who knew better than to talk to me, so I knew it'd be a good night to get some work done.

"How's the new guy?" I asked. By "new guy," I meant the man who had come into the bar a few weeks before and put on a show that had me laughing just remembering it. He was one of those obviously fashion-sensitive guys but not so obviously a card shark. He sharked the reigning poker champ who had been working at the bar for as long as I could remember. Of course, he was hired immediately.

He called himself Ace Maverick—ridiculous pseudonym, I know, but I didn't pick it—and had he wanted, he could have used his steely-eyed, strong-jawed good looks to become a Hollister model. A somewhat skinny Hollister model, but a Hollister model, nonetheless.

"He's working out okay. Deuce hates him," Domino answered.

"Deuce hates most people," I pointed out. The "Deuce" who Domino was referring to was Deuce Marlboro—if you haven't noticed, nobody who works at The Gambler uses their real name. Deuce was the bar's on-staff server, bartender, and backup bouncer. He also enjoyed playing pool with anyone who entered. His twin sister, Dice Marlboro, was also a server and the former poker champ at The Gambler. And that, in a nutshell, is the main reason that Deuce didn't like Ace; the guy sharked his sister and took over as the house poker champ. Oh, and the bet was that if Ace won, Dice would have to kiss him. Ace won, and Dice kissed him. Deuce is a very overprotective twin brother.

"Well, I'm sure Deuce will warm up to him, eventually," I said, my voice laden with sarcasm. Just for giggles, I added, "He warmed up to me, after all."

Domino smirked. The truth was that Deuce *had* warmed up to me—maybe a bit too much, but I'm not complaining. I mean, I'm pretty sure he's some kind of criminal, but he's hot and relatively harmless, so I'm not complaining.

I passed Domino and entered the room, sliding my hand across the rustic wooden bar that crowded the downstairs area before making my way up the stairs. There were even fewer customers scattered about the upstairs balcony—bringing the total number to nine, including myself, a number which doubled that of the four-person staff. The boss, who I knew simply as "Boss," was behind the much smaller upstairs bar, as usual. He was one of those older men who you'd easily recognize as a badass—a Clint Eastwood type. His thin, wrinkled lips puckered around his ever-present toothpick like it was a lemon, and his squinty eyes seemed to look at everyone, yet at no one.

Dice was serving beer to a few guests on the balcony. She was about my height, with the same hazel eyes as her brother. She always wore colorful eyeliner that usually matched her hair, which changed color every other week. This week, it was dark violet with bright lavender streaks. Looking at her, you might think that she was just another punk-pop chick with a nose ring. You'd be wrong.

I spotted Deuce and Ace playing pool at a table closest to the bar, tension radiating off them like steam on New Orleans asphalt in the summer. It explained why everyone had chosen to sit outside, even in the cool weather—far away from the two men. I took note and made my way across the bar and out to one of the iron tables on the balcony. I sat down and tried to relax, taking in the sights and sounds of my city as jazz music floated up from somewhere below. My relaxing moment was cut short when a crash and shout of pain exploded from the pool tables—Deuce had broken a pool stick across Ace's chest. Ace was going to get himself killed if he wasn't careful.

I rolled my eyes at the over-dramatic men and pulled out my laptop, immediately opening to an article about Eli Goldman's murder.

Dice had run inside to make sure Ace had not *already* gotten himself killed when Deuce looked up and noticed me. He threw what was left of his pool stick on the table they'd been playing at and made his way over, plopping down in the chair beside me and sliding his arm along the top of the seat behind me.

"Considerin' a career change, ma chèrie?" he asked, noting the LSU article I was perusing on my laptop. That's another thing: Deuce was a Cajun hottie, meaning a hottie *with an accent*. He was also about 6'2" with jet-black hair, big doe-eyes, and some serious fight moves. Now do you see why I frequent The Gambler?

"Thinking I might try out for the team," I joked.

Deuce laughed and let his arm drop just enough for his hand to graze my shoulder. I didn't mind. He smells like mangos, which I find suspicious, considering he works in a bar that serves Cajun cuisine.

"You'd definitely give 'em hell," he said.

"It's what I'm good at." Not meeting his eyes, I casually asked, "Did you kill Ace?"

"Nah, he'll live." Deuce didn't make it sound like a good thing.

"You know, he could have you arrested for assault."

"He's too into my sister, but if you wanna see me in a pair of cuffs, ma chérie, I can oblige."

This invite was enough to make me look up and meet his gaze. He was in a flirty mood, but heck, so was I. I batted my eyelashes in the most ridiculous way I could manage and said, "I do have a pair of cuffs in my office."

"You're working the masquerade murder case, aren't you?" Dice asked, suddenly behind me. Here's the truth: Dice Marlboro is almost as good of a sleuth as I am—almost. Really, she reads people like nobody I've ever met, and despite her rocker chick appearance, she's crazy smart. As if to prove this fact, she sat a tall glass of stout on my table. I only drink when one case is finished and another is about to begin, and she knows it.

She's also really good at sneaking up on people, which I think would make her Catwoman if this were a novel about superheroes.

"Yup," I answered.

"What, you ain't got any cases of your own?" Dice asked. Her Cajun accent has never been as strong as her brother's. Sometimes it disappears completely, depending on the crowd, but I guess that's how siblings work. I know I couldn't be more different from mine.

"This is my new case," I answered with a grin.

Dice's brows rose marginally higher—a subtle look of surprise I admit I enjoyed far too much. What can I say? The lady is rarely surprised by anything.

Deuce, on the other hand, started at that. Never bothering with subtlety, his hand dropped from the back of my chair as he pivoted his body to face me. "Thought you didn't do violent crimes no more?" he asked, and bless him, I could hear the concern in his voice.

I shrugged.

"You're serious?" Dice asked.

"I'm serious," I confirmed.

The twins looked at each other, and I could sense the silent conversation going on over my head.

"Stop it," I said.

"Stop what?" Dice asked.

"Stop with the creepy twin stuff. It makes me uncomfortable."

Dice rolled her eyes. Deuce put his arm back around my shoulders and, thankfully, changed the subject.

"You know," Deuce said, and I could feel his calloused fingers playing with my hair, "I always wanted to get into the detective game. Think I'd make a good dick?"

"Shut up, Deuce," Dice said, sliding into the chair across from her brother and me. "Who's your client?"

"I can't answer that."

Dice thrummed her platinum nails on the table as she stared at me.

"Go ahead," I told her. "Say what you gotta say."

"It's just—" Dice hesitated, "this is the first seriously violent case you've had since you came here. It's murder. I didn't think you took murder cases."

I shrugged. "I have my reasons," I assured her, unconvincingly.

Dice smirked. "It's about damn time."

"What?" I asked.

"It's about damn time you put on your big girl panties and started doing what you're good at again. Your skills are wasted on insurance claims and cheating spouses," Dice told me.

I stared at her in shock before responding, "Thanks? I think."

"You know," Dice told me, "the papers have been saying that the—"

I cut her off, "I don't want to know what the papers are saying. Reporters lie, and I don't want the facts to mix with the fiction and confuse my delicate brain." I then added the confession, "Besides, I'd already read most of the print articles before I knew about the job."

Dice raised an eyebrow. "And where do you plan to get your facts?"

"I'll have the usual," I said, turning my attention back to my laptop and avoiding the question as best I could.

Deuce let out a groan beside me. "You not workin' with that couyon detective, are you?"

"Burke's not a couyon," I argued.

Deuce raised an eyebrow.

"Okay, he's a couyon," I admitted, "but so are you, and so am I. He's a grade-A detective, and I need an in."

"Do you think the NOPD's letting him work the case?" Dice asked. "It's pretty high profile."

"He's their lead detective," I said. "Of course he's working it. And I already checked with his wife."

Dice snorted. "You'd think the cop would be a little concerned about the army of women you're raising in which his wife is your colonel."

"You should really come back and help me with another class," I told her. She'd come once or twice, and we'd sparred. It was the most fun I'd had in a while. More importantly, it reminded my 'army of women' that women can be dangerous, so they shouldn't underestimate their opponents.

"We'd probably start an uprising."

"Sounds like a fun Tuesday night to me."

Deuce cleared his throat. "And how do you plan to get the couyon to work with you, eh?"

I shrugged. The answer was obvious. "With beignets and coffee."

Deuce laughed. "Laissez les bon temps rouler, ma chèrie!" he exclaimed before ordering me another stout.

Chapter 4

Just Friends

At about 11:50 that night, I shook off my alcohol consumption with the help of two cups of coffee and headed out to the Ramada on Chef Menteur Highway. Being several miles outside the heart of New Orleans, the hotel was relatively quiet. I felt like an owl hunting prey as my eyes combed the dark parking lot.

Finally, I spotted my victim. A black 1993 Honda Accord Special Edition was tucked into a corner at the back of the lot, nearly blending in with the darkness around it. There's not much to say about the car, and anyway, I was more interested in the man behind the wheel. The man who I knew never locked his doors, making it quite easy for me to sneak up on him during his stakeout, armed with coffee and beignets, and hop right into the passenger seat of his car.

I did just that. "Hi, best friend," I said to the .44 magnum revolver aimed at my eye, "wanna lower your gun and have a beignet?" I lifted the box and shook it at him as an incentive. "They're from Cafe Beignet," I told him, even though he probably recognized the box already.

Burke growled before lowering the definitely-not-standard-issue handgun and putting it back in his hiding place. "What the hell you doing Chase?" Sorry for the profanity, but what he actually said was much worse than "hell."

"Would you believe me if I said I needed a ride to work?" I asked, handing him a plain beignet—he would kill me if I got powdered sugar all over his car—from my box of deep-fried bargaining chips.

"It's midnight, your office is on the other side of town, and you live in it," he growled, but he took the beignet and ate it in two bites before reaching for the world-famous Morning Call coffee I'd put in his cup holder. That's what progress looks like.

"You'll get yourself shot one day, Chase," Burke told me after he'd eaten another two beignets.

"As long as you're the one doing the shooting, I think I'll survive," I told him.

Let me take a moment here to help you get a good picture of Detective Matt Burke. Think back to every popular noir detective you've seen in those old black and white mystery movies—picture Humphrey Bogart. You know the guy I'm talking about—that classic tall, dark, and handsome, yet mysterious, sleuth who's often found sitting alone with his scotch in some dark corner of some shady place. He has the fake "I prefer to work alone" attitude about everything. He even comes equipped with his own heart-wrenching backstory. Take all that, add a confoundingly amazing wife, put it in a blender with some New Orleans coffee, and you have Burke.

He swallowed another gulp of coffee. "What do you—is that a *rat* in your *shirt*?" Burke asked, taking his eyes off the dark hotel to stare at the fuzzy head popping out of my hoodie.

"Don't be ridiculous," I said, tearing off a piece of a beignet and feeding it to the chittering animal in my shirt. "It's a ferret."

Louis had whined at me all evening, leaving me no choice but to pack him into the pocket of my hoodie and bring him along on my nocturnal escapades. Burke, who was notably terrified by mice and rodents, was staring at Louis's fluffy white head with a look of total disdain. I guess ferrets are close enough to rodents to warrant his concern.

"This is Louis, as in Louis Armstrong," I told Burke. "He's my emotional support animal." Louis nipped at my ear in request of more food, and I tore off another piece of beignet to oblige the small creature.

Burke finally pulled his eyes away from me and my furry companion to pay attention to the Ramada. A dark green convertible had pulled into the lot, parking as close to the front office of the building as possible. "It looks like you're growing a new, better-looking head with the way he's coming out of your shirt," Burke told me.

"Ha ha," I deadpanned. "It seems the beignets and coffee I brought you, also gave you a sense of humor."

"Breakfast of champions," Burke said, shaking his mostly empty coffee cup at me.

"Anyway," I continued, "I'm here to help you with a case."

"Says who?"

"New client."

"Shut up."

"Look, Burke, I'm on a mission from God," I said it just like Dan Akroyd in *The Blues Brothers* and boy, did it feel good. Louis gave a chittering noise of support from my pocket.

Burke choked on the coffee. "What?"

"A priest hired me to look into the masquerade murders."

Burke's eyebrows shot into his hairline, and his head snapped around to look at me so quickly that I swear I heard his neck snap.

"Why do you think I need an emotional support animal?" I asked, feeding Louis another bite of beignet. "This is my first murder case in years, and after that last doozy, don't you think I need emotional support?" The joke fell flat—even to my ears. My last therapist told me that processing my trauma through humor was not always a good coping mechanism, and I could tell Burke agreed by the look on his face. I can't help that I'm only funny to myself.

Burke contemplated me in silence for another moment, which made me ask, "You wanna hold Louis?"

He quickly shook his head and turned back to stare at the green convertible. Nobody had exited the car yet, and based on the way the small vehicle was shaking, I thought they might be a while.

After a moment, Burke cleared his throat. "How's this priest connected?"

"Confidential," I said with a snort. "You wouldn't believe me, anyhow."

He opened his mouth as if to argue but then thought better of it. "Fair enough," he said with a shrug.

"I'm guessing such a high-profile case would belong to you, yes?"

He nodded, taking another swig of coffee.

"Any information you care to send my way?" I goaded him.

"Confidential."

Louis made a hiss of rebuke at Burke's rudeness, and I gave the ball of fluff another nibble of a beignet to thank him for his support.

Burke was being a turd, and I had no idea why. I was fairly sure I'd done nothing to irk him lately. Heck, I hadn't even called him in two weeks or more. So, I had to try a different approach.

"Dude," I reasoned, "you probably have, like, twelve cases right now. It couldn't hurt to let me help out on this one."

"The boss hates you," he helpfully reminded me. "She'd lose her crap if I let you consult." He did not say "crap," but I enjoy censoring him.

The current NOPD captain was Burke's former partner. She was never much help when it came to solving anything, so the powers that be decided to promote her to captain. Bottom line: the captain who sucked as a detective never liked me—possibly because I refer to her as "the Chihuahua"—and I never liked her—probably because she refuses to acknowledge the fact that I, unlike her, am a good sleuth.

"That never bothered you before," I reminded him.

"Chase—"

"C'mon, Burke, work with me here! I'll owe you one," I practically begged.

"You owe me twenty."

Louis climbed further out of my shirt, putting his tiny paws on my left shoulder and stretching the upper half of his lithe body as he warbled at Burke.

"So, what's one more?" I asked, pulling the precariously balanced ferret off my shoulder and into my lap. "C'mon, give me the details, and let me finish this one."

Burke put his coffee cup into the cup holder, freeing his right hand to massage the wrinkle between his eyes, the one right above his nose. "Chase," he said, "it's a murder case."

"I'm aware of that."

"It's violent."

"Murder usually is," I reminded him.

"You don't take cases like this," he reminded me.

"Maybe I should start."

"Didn't you come here to get *away* from violent crime?" he asked, even though he already knew the answer.

I let out a sigh and scratched Louis behind his ears before answering, "Yeah. I moved to the nation's murder capital to get away from violent crime. We both knew it wouldn't work like that."

Burke let out a long, frustrated groan, which sounded like the howl of a dying animal, and I knew I had him. "You got any idea," he asked, "how many P.I.s I got askin' for details on this case?"

"But are any of them as good as me?" I then began to twirl my fake mustache and continued, "I know how to use the gray cells, mon ami." Louis ducked his furry head into the pocket of my hoodie, no doubt embarrassed by my performance of two impersonations within five minutes.

"You know I got no clue what you're referencing when you do that."

"And I forgive you." Agatha Christie is rolling over in her grave, but I will forgive the man. "Now, are you going to let me in or not?"

The green convertible suddenly stopped shaking, and two reasonably intoxicated people got out of the car. Burke lifted his binoculars and watched after the couple as they staggered up to the office door and into the hotel.

After they were gone, he let out a sigh, putting the binoculars back in his lap and glaring out the windshield and into the night.

"You plannin' to tell my wife if I don't agree to work with you?"

"I do see her every Tuesday."

He sighed. "If I agree to work with you, will you get the hell out of here?" he asked.

"Sure," I said with a shrug.

35

"Fine. Now get out."

"One sec." I reached into my hoodie, pulled out a large manila envelope, and handed it to Burke.

He opened the envelope and pulled out the pictures from inside, using the light from his phone to see. "Ugh," he grimaced, shoving the pictures back into the envelope. "Why would you show me that?"

"That's Carlos Marcello and his mistress," I told him. "His wife would be really upset to see these. Maybe even upset enough to tell you where Carlos has been doing business lately."

Burke stared at me, his mouth open and his eyes glowing. "You know, you could've just led with this instead of letting me sit out here in the cold trying to catch this guy."

"I wanted to win you over with my charm. The fact that I'm an amazing P.I. with dirt on the criminal you're after is just an added bonus." I grinned. "So, want me to stop by the precinct in the morning?"

"Absolutely not," he said. "Captain would have a stroke."

"Fine. Meet me at the coroner's office. I need to get a look at the victims."

"You will make Dr. Han's day."

I rolled my eyes. "That man needs to get out more. Enjoy talking to Mrs. Marcello!"

"Don't you dare bring that damn rat," Burke warned as I hustled out of the passenger's seat and scrambled victoriously into the night.

Chapter 5

Easy Living

The coroner's office was cold and smelled like antiseptic. The fact that I would likely end up there one day on one of those cold slabs was far from a comforting thought, but not for the reasons you might think. I don't fear death—that comes for everyone—but I really *hate* the cold. I dug my hands deeply into the pocket of my New Orleans Saints hoodie and paced the frigid lobby as I waited for Burke to show up. It was 7:00 a.m., and I was running off four hours of sleep and coffee fumes, none of which was helping my apparently fragile nerves. I'd left Louis at home, as Burke had requested, but I was beginning to regret it, as I took in a deep breath and then released it slowly. I had no time to be afraid of the cold.

Four minutes ticked by before I gave up, marched out of the coroner's office, and called Burke from the parking lot. As soon as he accepted the call, I asked, "Where are you? It's cold and smells of death."

I could hear traffic in the background. A car honked, and Burke cursed creatively. I honestly didn't know a four-letter word could be so versatile. "I'm on my way, Chase," he growled.

"Okay. Since you're on your way, why don't you give me the details about our case."

"It's *my* case, and don't you want to see the bodies first?"

"I need to know what you know before I see the bodies," I told him. "Otherwise, I'll make assumptions, and you know what assumptions do."

I heard another car honk through the phone and Burke swore some more. I could visualize him, window rolled down and screaming into the streets.

"You should really talk to someone about your road rage," I said.

"Shut up, Chase."

"You ever wonder why I don't like riding anywhere with you? This is why."

"Do you want to hear about the case or not?" he growled.

"Of course. Please enlighten me. What do you know so far about the murder of Eli Goldman? He was LSU's star quarterback, right? Up for the Heisman?"

"I'd be impressed, but I know you Googled that," Burke said, and he was right. I couldn't care less about football, and it's always been a point of contention between us.

I continued, "His girlfriend was Regina Doyle, and she was an actress at Tulane, right?"

Burke grumbled something about tourists before answering, "Musical theater major, yeah. She had a cocaine problem—that's what killed her. Most of the crew at the party were her theater friends. Except for Jeremy Lackey. He played football with Eli."

"All that I got from the interwebs," I told him, sitting down on the hood of my red Isuzu Rodeo as I listened to him curse at more tourists blocking the streets. "Now tell me the full story, everything you know. Don't leave anything out."

"Yeah. I know the drill," he grumbled. "These six kids go to the masquerade together, like a triple date. It was at a bar on Willow Street, that all the college kids tend to go to."

"I have heard of it, yes."

"All six of 'em dressed like superheroes or something—"

"Which superheroes?"

"That don't matter," Burke grumbled.

"All details matter, Bee; fill me in."

Burke cursed some more but complied with my request. He knows my process works, even if it is tedious. "I think they were the super friends."

"Avengers or Justice League?"

Burke was silent.

"Was someone dressed as Batman?"

"No," he said, "Eli was the clown."

"So, Eli was dressed as the Joker. I'm going to guess Regina was Harley Quinn. Was there a Two-Face?"

"Yeah, Lackey was Two-Face, Chris Bryce—Regina's theater buddy—was Scarecrow, and their dates were ... Catwoman."

"They were both Catwoman?" *Blasphemy.* "You do realize that all of those characters are villains, not super*heroes,* right?"

"You do realize that I give absolutely zero craps, right?" Again, I'm editing Burke's language. "Anyway, these six kids got to their party at about 11:43 p.m., but the star couple was apparently having a real public, real nasty fight. See, Goldman was a straight edge guy, meanin' no drugs, no alcohol, no nothin. So when he found out his girlfriend had been dabblin' in cocaine, he wasn't happy. Apparently, he took what she had on her and planned to flush it at the next available toilet, but he never got the chance. We found a small, tin box of white powder on him later. Her fingerprints were all over it."

I mentally noted this information while Burke went on, "Their fight got so bad that their friends separated them. The guys took Goldman outside, and the girls took Regina to the bar. According to Bryce, he took Goldman aside and offered to take Regina and his date, who was Regina's roommate, to the girls' dorm, leaving Goldman, Lackey, and Lackey's date at the party."

Burke continued, "Chris left with the girls at around 12:15 and didn't come back.

"Of course, Lackey says he didn't see much of Goldman for the rest of the night, except at a distance. He was finally able to catch him going into the bathroom at around two in the mornin'. Lackey claims he called out to Goldman to tell him it was time to go, and Goldman said to give him a second. Goldman then stepped back into the bathroom, leaving Lackey to wait for him in the bar. A little while later, Goldman still hadn't stepped out, so Lackey went to look for him but couldn't find him. At around 3:40, Goldman's body was found in the back freezer." For a moment, my mind flashed to an old case of mine—a locked freezer and the smell of blood and stale meat. My hands began shaking and my throat constricted, so I took a deep breath and held it for four seconds, forcing myself to keep listening to Burke. "He'd been stabbed to death, several times in the back. Murder weapon still hasn't been found."

I spoke up, "So, according to his own testimony, Jeremy Lackey was the last to see Eli Goldman alive?"

"Possibly, but a lot of the staff claim to have seen a Joker roamin' around as late as 2:00."

"I need to see this body," I said.

"I'm two stops away," Burke assured me.

"Anyone with motive?"

"Lackey's the second-string quarterback. With Goldman out of the way, Lackey will probly' get his position on the team and a better payout with his NIL."

"NIL" is shorthand for "name, image, likeness." The NCAA had recently decided that student athletes had the right to sell their "name, image, and likeness" in order to procure sponsorships from big companies. For example, the University of Alabama had an athlete with the nickname "Kool-Aid." Guess which company gave him a huge NIL deal?

Of course, I knew Jeremy Lackey was the prime suspect; even the reporters were guessing that by now. I didn't say anything though, because I didn't want Burke to guess anything about my client. It would be unprofessional, for one thing, but also, I didn't want him to know that I was basically working for his prime suspect. That's just not smart, and I try really hard to be smart.

"It seems pretty simple to me," I told him.

I heard the phone click off, only to hear the screeching of wheels. I looked up to see Burke's Honda careening into the parking lot. Without slowing down, he slammed his car into the spot next to mine, switching off the ignition at the same time he shifted into park. He stepped out of the car, hair tousled, eyes still swollen from lack of sleep, and two cups of coffee in his hands.

Handing me a cup of coffee, he said, "You ready for this?"

I took a sip from the cup, which had been made exactly the way the beverage is supposed to be made—with chicory—before answering, "Lead the way, boss."

The room labeled "Death Investigation" was even colder than the lobby, and the chemical smell was nearly enough to choke me. To the right of the entrance was a wall of coolers, each intended to hold a corpse deemed worthy of an investigation. There were two metal tables in the center of the cold room.

On one table was the body of Eli Goldman.

He was face-down and covered with a sheet, but I knew it was him.

"Hey, Chase!" Dr. Victor Han called, entering the room from a small office located on the far side. He bounced his way quickly over to us, short dreads bopping up and down over his dark brown eyes. He skidded to a halt in front of me and appeared to debate something—I'm guessing whether to reach out and shake hands or hug or fist bump me— finally settling on shoving his hands into the pockets of his lab coat and nodding toward the corpse. "I guess you're here to see the big guy, huh?"

I grinned. "Don't take it so personal, Vic. I'm glad to see you, too."

"But *I'm* just here for the big guy," Burke said.

Dr. Han got the hint and maneuvered us toward the body. Without further discussion, he removed the sheet covering Goldman's torso, revealing a once muscular back littered with holes.

"He was stabbed fifteen times," Dr. Han told us.

I handed Burke my coffee cup and stepped closer to the body, bending down to get a good look at the wounds. I reached out toward one of the most prominent holes, measuring the length of the gash with my finger. "About two inches in width?"

"And about six inches in depth," Dr. Han told me.

"Standard butcher's knife?" I asked.

Dr. Han nodded quickly. "You could find one like that in almost any kitchen. I have one in mine."

"Well, there you have it, Burke. Vic says the knife's in his kitchen."

"I'm not wasting my morning listening to you two," Burke warned.

I rolled my eyes and turned my attention back to the body, pointing to the wound in the center of his back. "This the jab that killed him?"

Dr. Han shook his head, grabbing me by my arm and maneuvering me near the head of the corpse so that we were both looking down on the body from above. The doctor pointed to another stab wound, right where Goldman's neck met his shoulder.

"My knowledge of anatomy is spotty at best," I admitted, "but that looks like it definitely would've sliced through the carotid artery."

Dr. Han nodded excitedly. "Oh yeah. It was the first strike, and it was the strike that killed him. The rest of these were just—hateful."

"Whoever did this was angry at the beginning, and covered in blood at the end," I clarified.

"Definitely. The way the blood would've squirted out of this guy—whoever did this would've been covered."

"You'd testify to that?" Burke asked.

"Of course."

"This wound," I pointed again to the wound on his neck, "it was a blow from above, right?"

Dr. Han nodded, "Judging by the angle, I'd say so, yeah."

"You think the killer was tall?" Burke asked.

Dr. Han shrugged. "It's possible, but notice how the wound pulls right here, and the skin is torn." He pointed out the details, which I admit I would never have noticed myself. "It shows that the killer tried to pull the knife out at a downward angle, so he—"

"Or she," I spoke up.

"Or *she* might well have been shorter. It was also Halloween night—a night when kids wear heels and platforms un-ironically. I don't think anything we see here could tell us much about the killer physically, but Chase could probably do that profiling thing she does."

"I'm not a profiler anymore," I said too quickly. "Could the bruising around the wounds tell us anything about the strength of the killer?"

Dr. Han shook his head. "All I can tell you is that the viciousness of the blows indicates the person who killed him was likely very angry."

"And the time of death?" I asked.

"Based solely on the autopsy?" Dr. Han sucked his teeth as he thought about his answer. "The body was frozen—preserved—in a way. The body was found at 3:40, so he could have died anywhere between 11:00 and 3:00."

"We have witnesses who claim to have seen him up and walking around as late as 2:00," Burke reminded me.

"But did they *talk* to him?" I asked. "Is it at all possible that they could have seen another Joker?"

Burke nodded, then took a sip of his coffee to cover up his agreeing with me.

I turned back to Dr. Han. "What about the girlfriend?"

Dr. Han seemed startled by that. "She died of an accidental drug overdose—no notable struggle based on the autopsy."

"We sure it's an accident and not a suicide?" I asked.

"We've examined the murder-suicide angle, but the timetables don't add up," Burke said. "Besides, I'm pretty sure their final moments together were their very public fight—her text messages from that night indicate as much."

"You have her texts?" I asked.

He nodded.

"I need those."

"You'll have to accept the printouts."

"Done."

Burke's phone rang. He cursed again before stepping out of the room and leaving me and Dr. Han alone with the corpse of Eli Goldman.

After a half-second of awkward silence, Dr. Han asked, "You interested in playing D&D with us again? We'll be starting a new campaign and could really use another girl in the group."

I'd made the mistake of going to one of Dr. Victor Han's game nights. Only after I got there did I realize that they were playing Dungeons & Dragons instead of the good, old-fashioned board games I was used to. But it was sort of fun.

"I'll have to check my schedule," I told him. "And I want to be a tank this time, not just some fairy princess healer."

"You were a powerful high elf, but I'll see what I can do. We could always use another Orc."

"Orcs are cool," I agreed.

Burke slammed his way back into the room. "Gotta go," he announced, looking me in the eye. "It seems a certain Mrs. Marcello wants to talk to us after all."

"You're welcome," I told him before turning to Dr. Han. "I did him a favor—as friends do."

"Yeah, yeah," Burke said. "I gotta get back to the precinct."

"I need to go for a run today, anyway," I told him.

"You still running through cemeteries for fun?"

"Running through cemeteries? That's too morbid even for me," the coroner told me.

I shrugged. "Less morbid than leading tour groups through the cemetery. Besides, I kinda like the reminder of my imminent doom. Keeps me humble."

Both men shook their heads at that.

"Wanna grab some po'boys for lunch?" I asked Burke. "My treat."

"I get to choose the venue?"

I raised an eyebrow at his dumb question. "Why would you get to choose the venue if it's my treat?"

We agreed to meet at The Gambler.

Chapter 6

Pink Champagne

I have only a few healthy habits. Okay, so I have *one* healthy habit, and that's running. I use it to clear my head and think through my cases, allowing the consistent rhythm of my footsteps to stomp out any distractions. I've solved many a case while running through the Saint Louis No. 1 Cemetery.

That was a particularly good day for a run. It's usually so humid that running feels more like swimming, but the New Orleans summer heat was finally giving way to fall, and with it came a crisp breeze that was only partially buffeted by the stone tombs in the cemetery. I cranked up my Joe Liggins playlist and ran to the rhythm, my five-year-old Nikes slapping against the mixture of broken concrete and gravel before I turned the corner to avoid a group of tourists paying their respects to the voodoo queen, Marie Laveau. I waved at tour guide Tom, before taking a sharp turn onto a gravel walkway and getting back into rhythm.

I picked up speed when I got to the end of the gravel lane, taking a right turn by the wall to avoid some grungy college kid smoking weed and leaning on the wall to my left. I assessed the likelihood of the kid being dangerous and decided the handgun strapped into the holster over my shorts—since Louisiana permits open carry—would be enough of a deterrent. Surely, the gun screams, "Stay away from me!" to any rogue killers.

I leaped over a crack in the cement and quickened my pace, picking my knees up and feeling the burn in my glutes. My mind began relaxing as my heart started beating faster.

I listed the facts as I ran zigzags between the tombs.

Eli Goldman and Regina Doyle were a couple. I side-stepped a family of tourists and nearly face-planted on a loose stone but righted myself and kept going.

Regina had a drug problem. I ran past a stone angel and then turned to run backward, keeping my eyes on the angel and giving my calves a workout.

Both Eli and Regina died on the same night. Remembering the near collision with the tourists, I turned around and ran toward the west wall of the cemetery.

The number of times Eli was stabbed and the way his body was stored indicates a crime of passion. I leaped over a bouquet that had been laid in front of one of the smaller tombs.

Regina's death could have been an accidental overdose—or it could have been a premeditated murder. I lost my stride for a moment as the facts began to waver into theories. Righting myself, I continued steadily past a couple of stone sepulchers.

The primary suspect is Jeremy Lackey. I saw Homer Plessy's grave in the distance and stepped up my speed for the final leg of my run.

Burke had doubts about Lackey's motive. A small child stepped out from between two of the graves in front of me, and I skidded to a halt—nearly falling on my butt to keep from hitting him—as gravel shot out from underneath my shoes. He looked up at me with wide eyes and trembling lips. I figured my sweaty face, disheveled hair, and the gun probably scared him as much as he'd startled me. I was saved from another moment of silent awkwardness when his mom—or maybe his nanny—stepped around a tomb and grabbed his hand, looking at me as if I were some kind of predator. I made myself resist staring after them as they walked away, looking instead at my shoes as it slowly dawned on me that, friend or no friend, Burke would not have allowed me near this case if he'd actually believed he'd already found his man.

I lifted my hands over my head, breathing in the graveyard stench, and walked the rest of the way to Homer Plessy's grave. It was time to play to my strengths and find Burke a new suspect to hound.

I love running, but I hate smelling like sweat and death. So, after my graveyard trip, I headed back to my apartment building. Walking across the courtyard, I spotted the teenager I'd seen the morning before. She had a textbook on one of the iron tables, apparently doing homework even though it was probably too hot for an outdoor study session. She also had a cigarette burning between her left index finger and thumb.

When it comes to my neighbors, I tend to stick to one simple rule: don't make contact. It's not that I'm a snob; I just don't like people knowing my business. Besides, once they know my business, they ask me for favors. If I gave them one single week of polite socialization, I'd be getting a call every time someone's dog went missing, or some kid lost his favorite toy. I don't have time for that sort of thing. Besides, my mama always told me to hide my crazy, and I've got way too much of that to keep hidden.

However, the kid didn't look over thirteen, and the cigarette was far from flattering. So, against my better judgment, I said, "You should stamp that out."

She looked up at me—the shock apparent in her eyes. "I'll get right on that," she said with a smirk and took another puff.

Before I could stop myself, I'd reached across the table and snatched the stick from her lips, tossing it on the ground and stamping it out in one swift second.

She spouted a couple of uncreative words, to which I replied, "Stop being such a cliché, kid. Especially a bad cliché. You'll be dead before you're thirty."

"What do you care?"

I shrugged. "I ain't gonna watch some kid kill herself in my courtyard."

After saying my piece, I turned on my heel and continued across the courtyard, earphones protruding from my ears and eyes on my door.

"Hey," the kid called out. She either had no grasp of basic body language or didn't care that I had more important things to do.

I thought about ignoring her and letting our conversation end, but something in her voice made me turn back around. "Yeah?"

"You're that detective, right?" the kid asked. She was pretty, with a heart-shaped face, light umber skin, and light brown eyes. She also tried to hide that pretty under baggy clothes, frizzy hair that hung in her face, and seven layers of what looked like voodoo necklaces of all lengths stacked around her neck.

"Private Investigator," I told her.

She raised a fuzzy eyebrow. "You any good?"

I shrugged. "Good enough to pay the bills."

"You ever, like, find people?"

Well, that was a loaded question. Here's the thing: I'd worked a few missing person's cases in my time. They rarely end well. I wasn't about to heap tragedy on some strange kid, so I simply said, "If they want to be found."

"What if they don't?"

"Huh?"

"What if they don't want to be found?"

I shrugged. "Probably best to leave 'em alone."

"What if someone, like, paid you?"

"Don't you have school or something?"

"Don't you have work?" she shot back.

"I do, actually," I said with a wink. "Best get on that." I then walked past the kid and into my apartment, trying to ignore the lost look in her eyes that I often see when I look in the mirror.

Chapter 7

Do Whatcha Wanna

I got to The Gambler about half an hour before Burke showed up, and I spent the extra time doing important research. And by "important research," I mean I checked out social media, successfully cyber-stalking Regina Doyle and all her friends and followers to try and determine which of them might be a drug dealer.

While researching, I also went ahead and ordered two of my favorite po'boy sandwiches, one for me and one for Burke.

"Whatcha researching this time?" Dice asked, looking over my shoulder.

"Maybe I'm just checking my Facebook. You ever think that?"

"Nope."

I sighed. Of course, the purple-haired girl knew me too well. "I talked to Burke."

"Yes. That's why you got the two barbecue shrimp po'boys."

"Maybe I was just hungry."

She raised a skeptical eyebrow. I was beginning to think she had some kind of psychic powers.

"Okay, so yeah. Burke should be here in a few minutes. Until then, what do you think of this guy?" I held the laptop up so Dice could see the social media page I was investigating. Chris Bryce, the same Chris Bryce that Burke mentioned was at the masquerade, who was also one of Regina's best friends. That was clear based on the pictures on his page. Reggie, as she was called on social media, was in the majority of them. As I mentioned before, Reggie had been a pretty decent leading lady in most of Tulane University's musicals, while Bryce resigned himself to being a costume designer.

The real question here, however, was whether or not Chris Bryce had a motive for killing Eli Goldman, and based on my most recent theory, that boiled down to whether or not he was Regina's drug dealer.

Naturally, I asked the girl with the psychic—though possibly imaginary—powers, "Does he look like a drug dealer to you?"

Dice raised a pierced eyebrow in my direction. "And why would I know what a drug dealer looks like?" she asked.

"I thought you knew everything."

Dice grinned. "Good answer. Let me see." She picked up my laptop and started scrolling through Chris's page. Based on his pictures, he was a good-looking guy—tanned skin, short-cropped hair, a bright smile, dimples, and was nearly as tall as Goldman. It was no wonder women seemed to flock to him.

After a moment, Dice stopped scrolling and pointed to a picture. "That his girlfriend?" she asked. The screen showed a picture of Bryce at a bar with a pretty, ebony-skinned young woman with braids.

"That's Regina Doyle," I said.

"The dead girlfriend? The dead girlfriend of *Eli Goldman*?"

I nodded, then pointed out another picture just beneath that one. "That's Candace Moon, the girl Bryce took to the dance the last night Regina was seen alive." The photo featured Bryce standing between

Candace and Regina, his arms wrapped around each woman's shoulders. Bryce and Regina were both smiling into the camera, but Candace's eyes were on Regina. Candace was, in a word, cute—with long raven dark hair, dimples, and hazel eyes. But Regina had an other-worldly beauty. Her skin was flawless, and her smile lit up her entire face.

Dice clicked on Candace's name beneath the photo and went to her page.

"Her relationship status says, 'It's Complicated,'" Dice pointed out.

"And his says 'single,'" I told her.

"He also has way more pictures of other girls on his profile," Dice said.

"You mean he had way more pictures of Regina."

Dice pointed a finger at me in confirmation. "Doesn't seem like a one-woman kinda guy."

She tried scrolling through Candace's page, but it was set to private. Only her profile picture was displayed along with a few other school pictures, and her profile picture was of her and Bryce. Dice pointed out this little detail before saying, "She's definitely more professionally-minded than he is. I mean, her profile is private, and she only posts about school functions. Even the pictures she has up only show stuff for school. She wants to be employable. That doesn't seem like something a drug dealer would be too worried about."

She quickly clicked back to Bryce's page and started scrolling through his pictures again. Every photo seemed to be of him at some party with his arm around a young woman, and quite often, that person was Regina Doyle. "Him, on the other hand," Dice pointed to a particularly unflattering picture of Bryce in a room surrounded by blacklights, his teeth glowing bright with his eyes looking dull and glazed, "he goes to a lot of parties, but that might not mean anything. He's clearly wasted in some

CHASE HARLEM

of these, but that doesn't prove drug use." She scrolled through a few more pictures. "Honestly, if he is a drug dealer, he's good at staying sober enough to keep it out of pictures."

She handed the computer back, and I quickly returned to Regina Doyle's page. Her feed was filled with depressing comments along the lines of "praying for your family" and "Rest in Peace." I scrolled down to her last post. It was a picture of her and Candace getting ready for the party on the night she died, Candace posing like a cat, claws out and staring into the camera, while Regina took the picture with one hand, holding Harley Quinn's baseball bat over her shoulder in the other hand. She had no idea it would be her last night alive.

You can't save everyone. I shook my head at the reminder.

"You said you're looking for a drug dealer," Dice interrupted my internet stalking, "so is that part of your profile?"

I rolled my eyes. "I'm not a profiler anymore," I reminded her, annoyed that my drunk self had once over-shared with her and Deuce about my time working for Big Brother.

She shrugged. "Just because you don't work for the FBI anymore doesn't mean you can't use the same methods."

I felt my chest tightening as I glared up at her. For one dark moment, I debated telling her the truth—that our beloved federal investigators "tried and true" methods don't always work. Sometimes, those methods create profiles that point to the wrong people—the innocent people—and those people face a future too terrible to fathom. The ache in my teeth from clenching my jaw too tightly alerted me to my rising blood pressure. Slowly, I took a breath and let it out. Dice knew a lot, but she didn't know about this. She couldn't.

55

Instead of telling her to screw off, which isn't a nice thing to say to someone you like, I said, "I don't have enough information to create a profile yet. Even if I wanted to."

"You made some good guesses about me on New Year's Eve."

My ears burned, and I couldn't meet her eyes. I'd had too much to drink, yet again, and Dice asked me to "read her" for fun. I'd managed to remind her and Deuce about how hard they worked to keep their family together despite having parents who couldn't care less. I also, apparently, tried to deduce what type of abuse finally drove them away from their family for good. What really sucked is that I'd been right about all of it, and Dice didn't talk to me for a couple of weeks.

"I'm sorry," I said.

Dice flipped her purple hair and got back to the topic at hand. "What all would you need to do a full profile—like, an accurate one?"

I felt my eye twitch with irritation. "Depends on the crime. Usually, autopsy reports, crime scene photos, and witness testimony."

"Gotcha," she said. I could tell she wanted to ask me something else, but I was saved by Burke entering the restaurant and making his way over to our table.

Dice smiled, waved at Burke, and danced away to get my order.

"You got stuff for me?" I asked as soon as he sat down. Normally, I'd give him a chance to get situated, but Dice's questions had me on edge. I knew she was just curious about my process, but the past was the last thing I needed to be thinking about at the moment.

Burke rolled his eyes and let out a grunt as he slid a manila file folder across the table. "You know how much trouble I could get in for sharin' this with you?" he asked.

"You know how much me glancing at this could help you?"

He did, and his silence spoke to that.

I thumbed it open to find an eight-by-ten photograph of Eli Goldman's corpse lying on the floor of an industrial freezer, blood pooling under his back as his lifeless eyes stared up into nothing. His clown makeup made it eerier, the red lipstick stretching beyond the corners of his mouth, making it appear inhumanly wide and grotesque.

A yellow number marked a place on the floor where the blood had been stepped in, and I flipped the photo to find a smaller close-up of the blood, the perfect pool disturbed by a smear and what appeared to be a boot print.

I looked up at Burke, and he answered my question without me having to voice it. "Print matched the boot of the kid that found 'im."

Great, so it was useless.

I took a breath and flipped past the crime scene photos and the autopsy reports, and straight to the printouts of Regina Doyle's text messages. The parents must have given the cops consent to go through her phone because the first few pages of texts were lined up like screenshots instead of the typical printouts emailed by phone companies. There were texts with "Mom," "Dad," and a few other college friends and family members, but most of the texts were with "Romeo," which I assumed meant Goldman. I tried to ignore the tragic irony of the nickname as I read through their heart-eyes and kissy faces.

On November first at 1:56 a.m., she'd sent her last text: "I'm sorry baby. I'll do rehab...We'll make it work...I love you..." Her Romeo never responded, and I knew he never would.

I flipped through the other printouts until I finally came to pages from the cellphone provider. These were a little more difficult to read because they just showed the numbers, not the names she'd programmed into her phone. I spent a few minutes matching up the transcripts. It was easy to match the Romeo texts to his number, and it looked like nothing had been deleted. Most of the other message threads could be matched as well. That's when I noticed something.

"Hey, Burke, look at this." I put the papers on the table between us and pointed to the issue. "There's this one lengthy text thread on the cell provider's printout that's not in the screenshots."

"It's a 407 area code," Burke said.

"That's Florida, right?"

"How should I know? I'll have my guys trace that number and see who it belongs to." He pulled out his phone to send the necessary emails.

"Think they'll work fast?"

"They never have before."

I looked back at the transcript, examining the last text that was sent to that number. "According to this, the last message she sent to this 407 number was on November 1st at 1:45 a.m. It says, 'Thanks for your help, but I don't think we can see each other anymore.'"

"Think she was cheating on Goldman?"

"I think it's far more likely that the kid behind this mystery number is her drug dealer."

"Makes sense. It'd explain why she deleted the texts."

"Unless someone else deleted them."

Dice chose that exact moment to bring us our po'boys, and Burke returned his phone to his pocket, insisting he'd call the tech guys later to speed things along. I, too, put my laptop away and started chowing down. For a moment, we chewed in companionable silence.

Burke looked around the dingy little pub. "You know there's a bar down the street that was featured on the Travel Channel," he told me, picking a barbecue shrimp off his sandwich and taking a nibble.

Having nearly finished my own sandwich, I picked a shrimp out of his and finished it off, ignoring his statement as best I could.

"I'm just sayin'," he continued. "They have a plaque and everything."

"What's your point, Burke?"

"Chase, this place is kinda sketchy."

I laughed out loud, nearly choking on my shrimp. "Oh, this place is *stupendously* sketchy! I'm fairly sure everyone working here has committed a felony at some point."

"So why do we eat here?" Burke deadpanned.

"I fit right in," I said with a wink. "Also, the food is awesome. Did you know they won the po'boy festival three years in a row?"

"The festival is not a competition, Chase," he reminded me.

I rolled my eyes. "Well, if it were a contest, they would've won. Face it, Burke, the food here is awesome, and the service is hot."

As if to prove my point, Deuce chose that moment to slide into the booth beside me. "Bonjour, ma chérie," he greeted me with a kiss to the cheek, sliding his arm around me, "ready to ditch the couyon and get outta here wit' me?"

Burke glared at him. "Haven't I arrested you before?"

Deuce shrugged. "Wouldn't be surprised. What does surprise me is that Chase brought you in here."

He turned to me, tightening his arm around my shoulders and brushing his calloused fingers up my arm, before continuing, "Ma chérie, I thought better of you."

For the record, these two do this every time Burke and I eat at the bar. Sometimes, if alcohol is involved, there's even profanity. It's the world's most arbitrary pissing contest.

"We're working on a case," I reminded Deuce.

"Oh yeah." He turned back toward Burke. "Eli Goldman?"

Burke glared at me, and I shrugged. He knew I wouldn't be unprofessional enough to tell Deuce any details about the case, but the fact that the probable former criminal knew about me working on the case was enough to annoy Burke.

"That ain't really your business," Burke told him.

"You think Lackey did it?" Deuce asked, unperturbed by Burke's obvious annoyance. "I mean, he do got a motive."

"How do you know that?" Burke asked.

"He's second string, an' it's all over the news 'bout the whole NIL thing. 'Sides, he's kinda a bastard in his interviews."

I interjected, "Just because someone's a bastard doesn't make him a murderer."

Deuce smiled. "That's true. In fact, most of the murderers I know are really friendly people once you get talkin' to 'em."

"I find the fact that you say that with a smile to be very disturbing," I said through a large bite of Burke's sandwich.

Deuce laughed before leaning closer to kiss me on the temple. "I could come by your place and disturb you some more if you're up for it."

"I'm not telling you where I live, Deuce," I groused. "You just admitted to being friendly with murderers."

Deuce raised an eyebrow, and I could practically feel him studying me. For a moment, he looked sad—well, maybe not *sad,* but definitely some level of disappointment. Then, the moment was over, and his flirty smile was locked into place. "What makes you think I don't already know where you live, ma chérie?" He slid out of the booth and headed back toward the pool tables.

"That's creepy!" I shouted after him.

"Why do you hang out with that couyon?" Burke asked.

I threw a French fry at him. "The same reason I hang out with you, couyon."

"And what reason would that be?"

"Free entertainment. I'm keeping these texting transcripts. Now, let's go solve the mystery and save the day."

.

Chapter 8

He's My Guy

The football player—a.k.a. the illegitimate son of my client—was spending his "don't leave town" time in the Bourbon Orleans Hotel, one of the most expensive hotels in the city, located, as the title implies, at the corner of Bourbon and Orleans. I was just glad Burke found parking because he was already in a bad mood after I'd made him listen to jazz standards on the drive over. Is it my fault that the man chose to live in the jazziest city in America? My point is, unavailable parking might have driven him over the edge, and unavailable parking is a pretty significant trait of my city.

We walked into the luxurious lobby and straight to the elevator, which I wouldn't have noticed had I gone alone, because I was too busy staring up at the million-dollar chandelier.

"This is *fancy*," I sang. "Tell me your department's not footing this kid's bill just to make sure he stays in town or something."

"I got no idea who's paying for it," Burke grumbled. "I'm just glad it's not me."

He knocked on the door of room 211, and it swung open to reveal a copper-skinned young woman with reddish-blonde hair standing on the other side. She had the look and body of a cheerleader, and had I been someone who enjoys the ladies, I might have been too distracted by her to notice the wrecked hotel room behind her.

"Good thing you're not paying," I mumbled to Burke. "There's no way they're getting that deposit back."

"Yeah?" the cheerleader called to us. I was guessing that this was Tanya, the girlfriend Burke had mentioned.

"Ms. Herrera," Burke spoke to her, completely ignoring my pointed statement, "I'm Detective Matt Burke from the New Orleans PD, and this is Private Investigator Chase Harlem. She's consulting with me on the case. We were hoping to speak with Mr. Jeremy Lackey if he's available."

Tanya Herrera crossed her arms and stood her ground. "He's already answered all your questions." Note to self: tell the client that a girlfriend snarking to the cops makes him look suspicious.

"We just have some loose ends to tie up," I cut in. "The sooner we talk to him, the sooner you both get to head back to LSU."

"You mean, he's been cleared?" she asked.

"I'm hoping to do just that," I told her honestly.

She hesitated for just a moment before agreeing. "C'mon in and have a seat. Jeremy's at the pool. I'll go get him."

She ushered us through the door before grabbing her purse and heading out, presumably down to the pool to get the athlete in question.

"You shouldn't have told her you were hoping to get him off the hook," Burke told me, but he didn't seem angry.

"It got her moving, didn't it?"

Burke moved to the far corner of the room where two chairs had been turned over and quickly began straightening them. One was a traditional black office chair, and the other was a cushioned burgundy monster that looked like it belonged in one of the many antique shops on the strip.

I moved right behind him and helped him get the wooden desk off the full-sized bed closest to the window and resettle it next to the cracked wall.

Burke motioned for me to choose a seat. I chose the office chair, throwing my feet up on the desk for effect and admiring my sleek new shoes. He sat in the antique burgundy monster.

"You really don't think he did it, do you?" Burke asked me.

I shrugged. Truth was, I *hoped* the guy didn't do it.

Burke studied me momentarily before asking, "He don't fit your profile?"

I wasn't surprised by the question this time. Of course, Burke knew I'd been an FBI profiler—it's how we met. I was sent to New Orleans to create a profile for a particularly grisly murder. I must have done a satisfactory job because as soon as I ended my time with the bureau, Burke called me and suggested moving to NOLA. That said, I still didn't like being reminded of my past.

"I don't do that anymore," I reminded him, trying hard to keep a growl out of my voice.

Burke sighed. "That's too bad. Weren't you top of your class?"

"Didn't make my profiles any more accurate."

"It's not an exact science," Burke reminded me. "Now, you plannin' to answer my question?"

"Do *you* really think he did it?" I asked.

"Haven't met him yet." So, he was reserving judgment until then. See, I told you Burke was a pretty good detective in his own right. Not as good as me, but I won't hold that against him.

The door opened, and all six feet and five inches of Jeremy Lackey entered the room. He was dripping wet in his blue and green swim trunks, which hung so loosely on his trim hips that I was afraid we'd get a free show. He was the picture of young male athleticism—a walking Adonis carved right out of marble, and I could tell he knew it. He swaggered—yes, literally *swaggered*—across the plush green carpet and deposited himself dripping wet on the full-sized bed closest to us, kicking his bare feet up and lounging back with his muscular arms, cradling his curly head. As I stared at him, I tried to find any hint of his priestly forebear, but I couldn't spot a single similarity. Maybe Father Nolan once had those same blonde curls, but I just couldn't bring myself to imagine it.

"'Sup?" Lackey greeted us both after he was comfortable. He pushed his name-brand sunglasses on top of his head. They disappeared completely into the jungle of his hair.

"Mr. Lackey." The distaste in Burke's voice was not completely obvious. "I'm Detective Matt Burke from New Orleans PD, and this is my consultant, Investigator Chase Harlem."

"I know you," he said, looking over to me like he had just noticed my existence.

I lowered my feet from the desk and spun around in my chair to face him. "You do?" I asked. I was truly surprised.

Lackey nodded. "You're that private investigator the priest hired to get me off the hook."

Well, poop. Burke's head snapped toward me so quickly that I think I heard his neck crack.

"I'm not at liberty to discuss my clients," I told him. "However, I can assure you that I'm here to solve a murder, not get anyone 'off the hook.'

Not that you're on a hook, Mr. Lackey. That would imply that you're a suspect."

"You mean I'm not a suspect?" he asked.

And, yeesh, he was an idiot.

"You're a person of interest," I informed him. Yes, I know it means the same thing, really, but it's what cops are supposed to say to keep their suspects from skipping town.

Lackey rolled his eyes. Clearly, nobody had told him that annoying the detective who considered you a "person of interest" was a bad idea.

"We need to ask you some questions about Mr. Goldman," Burke told him.

Lackey let out one of those annoyed noises that landed somewhere between a groan and a whine. "I already told you all I know. He found the drugs, he and Reggie argued, me and Chris tried to talk to him. When he wouldn't listen, I decided to enjoy the party with Tanya, while Chris kept tryin' to reason with him. Chris is cool like that, but even he had to give up eventually. He took Reggie home, and I saw Gold hanging out at the ballroom around 2:00."

"By 'Reggie,' I assume you mean Regina Doyle?" I interrupted with the stupidest, most obvious question I could think of asking. I was hoping it would get Lackey to slow down and think things through. It was clear that he'd told this story so many times that he had it memorized. If he had more information, I would have to weasel it out of him. Luckily, I'm a pretty decent weasel.

"Yeah," he confirmed in his most "it's obvious" tone. "Her friends call her Reggie."

He was still speaking of her in present tense. Fact noted. Moving on.

"So, you two were pretty close friends, I take it?"

"We go back all the way to high school," he explained. Then he stopped to smile at some secret memory. "She's the only reason I passed English. We had to read Shakespeare, and I could never understand a word, but Reggie knew how to help. She just got it, ya know? All that theater and artsy stuff, and when she was on stage, even in high school, she acted like a star."

Lackey sat up quickly, pulling a phone in a waterproof case from the pocket on his swim trunks and turning it on. He took a moment to pull something up before tossing the phone to me. "Check this out," he told me. It was a video of Regina Doyle singing "Live Out Loud," a song from a little-known Broadway musical. Her voice was strong but not strident, and she hit the notes with ease as if it were all a game and not a performance she'd spent hours perfecting. She was enchanting, full of life and fun. It was easy to see how she had so many friends and why she'd been Tulane University's starlet. My heart began to ache. All that talent, and now she'd never grace the stage again. I closed the video and handed the phone back to Lackey.

"She's amazing," I told him.

He nodded. He didn't look so much like a used jock strap anymore. He looked like a little boy mourning the loss of his friend. "I was the one who introduced her to Gold."

"Gold," being Eli Goldman, I was sure. Did this kid have a nickname for everyone?

"How would you describe their relationship?" Burke beat me to the question.

"They were perfect for each other, ya know," he continued. "At least, they would've been, but she couldn't handle the pressure. She'd do up to two musicals at a time and was never just a dancer or whatever; she always got a big role. Add being the star athlete's girlfriend to the pile, and anyone could understand why she might want something to help with her nerves—anyone except for Gold."

"Pot helps with nerves," I told him, and no, I am not drawing that from personal experience. Any type of smoke makes me nauseous, and I'm just fine with my booze. "Cocaine's an apathy drug. It adds energy and lowers inhibitions. Not great for stress."

Lackey glared at me. "So maybe she needed some energy. She was busy."

"You think Gold was too harsh on her—that he should've cut her some slack." I didn't bother to pose it as a question because I honestly didn't want him to answer. I knew the answer would be stupid. For the record, I was right.

"Well, yeah," Lackey admitted. "Everyone thought so. Gold's a stuck-up tight-ass who thinks he's better than everyone. You know he once reported a teammate for growing weed? He reported it and nearly got the dude expelled. They suspended him for three weeks, and it almost lost us a rivalry game. Half the team was ready to kill him over that."

"Weed is illegal," Burke reminded him, "and I think you mean that Gold *was* a stuck-up tight-ass."

The color drained from Lackey's already pale face as he seemed to realize that he'd said too much. Insulting the guy you're suspected of murdering is not a good plan.

Meanwhile, I was trying to figure out how to break the news to Father Nolan. "I'm sorry, sir, but your biological son is an idiot who likes to sound guilty" didn't seem to flow just right.

"Look," Lackey continued, his tone far less feisty, "Gold and me didn't always see eye to eye, but we were cool. He was my teammate; he was my bro. I wouldn't kill him."

"Do you know who would?" I asked. "Maybe the player he got suspended?"

Lackey seemed to think about it for a moment. Then he shook his head. "Stanson's still on campus. He was nowhere near that party. Besides, he's over it. Team comes first for guys like Stanson. You gotta forgive and forget if you wanna play the game."

"Doesn't sound like Gold put the team first when he reported Stanson," I pointed out.

Lackey shrugged. "He paid his dues." I assume he was implying some type of hazing ritual that I didn't want to know about.

Instead, I asked, "Do you know Regina's dealer?"

Lackey shook his head. "Nah. Stay away from that stuff. Messes up your game." After a moment, he added, "Candace might know. She's Reggie's roommate."

Burke was about to ask another question when Lackey cut him off, "Look, I got a big party to get ready for, so if we're done here…"

"Your buddy just died, and you're planning a party?" Burke asked.

Lackey shrugged and spouted, "When in Rome, you do what the Romans do. When in New Orleans, you party." He then turned to me. "You can come, if you want. You're pretty cute. The father didn't mention that, but I guess that's not really his area. It's at the Blue Nile on—"

"Frenchmen Street, I know," I cut him off. I thought about telling him that I don't date idiots but didn't want to be rude, so I just told him maybe while Burke said no for me, and we left the pretty boy alone in his disgusting hotel room.

"I hate agreeing with your gambler boyfriend, but he's right about Jeremy Lackey," Burke said as the elevator doors closed behind us. "He's a bastard."

"Still doesn't make him a murderer." I added, "And you know Deuce is not my boyfriend."

Burke grunted, which I translated to mean he agreed. I translate most of Burke's grunts into agreements, which is probably why we get along so well.

"So, that priest who hired you knows Lackey," Burke mentioned as the elevator continued to move.

I nodded. Burke knew I couldn't tell him anything about the relationship between my client and Lackey, so he didn't ask even though he wanted to. His curiosity didn't surprise me. What did surprise me was him reaching out and pressing the stop button on the elevator. I thought people only did that in movies. He turned and looked at me.

"That complicates things, Chase," he said.

I tried to shrug the statement off with a sound that resembled a "Pfft!" followed shortly by a "Naw!"

Burke's serious expression, however, did not falter. "It don't look good that your client is somehow supporting our primary suspect."

"He's not supporting the meathead," I argued. "And I thought Lackey was just a person of interest."

Burke lifted his hands and quirked his lip in a characteristic shrug. "*I* didn't say that, *you* did."

I knew where he was going with this, and I didn't like it. "Do you actually think that Jockstrap is smart enough to have planned and committed a murder and staged a suicide?"

"He's our only suspect."

"You can't have a suspect without evidence. It's unethical."

"He has a motive."

"So does his pothead teammate, that Stanson guy."

"Lackey said he's still on campus."

"So? Find out if Lackey's right. Check the story. Don't just assume."

"I'm obviously going to check the guy's story, Chase. This ain't my first rodeo." I was annoying him, I could tell.

"Besides," I added, "Lackey's supposed motive is flimsy at best, and you know it. If you didn't, I wouldn't be here."

"Millions of dollars from NIL is not a flimsy motive."

"If he's suspected of murder, no company would risk granting him millions of dollars."

Burke growled—knowing that I was right. "Who has a better motive?" He was fishing. He knew I didn't like to reveal my theories until I had all the facts, and *I* knew that my client's relationship with Jeremy Lackey could get me blocked from helping Burke with this case.

I had to give him something, so I said, "If *I* had been selling Regina Doyle cocaine, and *I* found out her straight-edge, snitch of a boyfriend knew about it, I would be scared—maybe even scared enough to kill."

"You think it was her dealer?"

I shrugged. "It's what makes sense to me."

Burke seemed to think about it for a moment before nodding. "That don't exactly give me a suspect," he pointed out.

That was when I knew for sure what he wanted. "I'll go over the evidence again," I told him. "I can't make any promises—it's been a long time since I've handled something like this—but I'll try patching together a profile."

Once Burke had agreed, I reached forward and pressed the button on the elevator panel to get things moving again. We had come to a truce for now, but if I didn't find Burke and the NOPD some evidence attached to a new suspect soon, I might have to find another backdoor into this case.

"Hey, here's a question," I began when the elevator doors had opened, and the two of us stepped out into the lobby, "how did the staff not notice the dead body in their freezer before the wee hours of the morning? I mean, I find it hard to believe that anyone could stab someone to death and then shove the body in the freezer, and literally nobody noticed."

"You got a point there," Burke admitted. "But why would anyone working there kill a football player?"

I shrugged. "It's a long shot, but leave no stone unturned, right? Let's pay them a quick visit and ask around." Honestly, maybe my drug dealer theory would pan out at the club. I mean, it is possible that Reggie could have gotten the cocaine from a worker at the Willow, right? Maybe I wasn't leading Burke on a wild goose chase.

He reluctantly agreed to drive with me to the Willow. We still had a few hours before they opened for the night, so maybe we could catch some of the workers from the night before.

Chapter 9

My Melancholy Baby

When we pulled up to the Willow, it was to find a mostly empty street surrounding the concrete building. The Willow is far from the largest bar in New Orleans, but it is one of the best-known hotspots for college students because it features marginally famous musicians performing live music. It also has some of the best drink prices in town, which makes the Willow the ideal place for poor kids who are also trying to afford an education.

As soon as we walked in, I could tell the staff was planning to have a live band perform that night. One worker was cleaning the long oak bar to the right of the entrance, while another was checking the lights on the sign spelling "Jimmy"—a staple of this particular party palace. A third worker was setting up the stage on the far side of the large dance floor, and they had brought out the metal rails to separate the crowd from the performers.

"Oooo, I wonder who they've got tonight," I spoke aloud. "We should really check that out, Burke. They have good jazz sometimes."

"Chase, it's right after Halloween," Burke reminded me. "Nobody's gonna be playin' jazz, when all the college kids want is stuff they can dance to."

"Um, people can dance to jazz," I defended my favorite musical genre.

"Not college kids."

"Right, they only do the dances that resemble procreation rituals."

"Why you gotta say stuff like that?"

"I only speak the truth, Burke."

He reluctantly sighed and changed the subject. "Let me handle this."

He stepped ahead and led me to the door behind the bar, where we crossed the threshold into a cramped corridor. To the right, I could hear the hum of running water and dishes being washed, so I assumed that led to the kitchen. Burke stepped to the left, and I followed him down a lime-green hallway to a lavender-painted door and into a small office where a skinny, middle-aged African American man sat at a large desk. The man wore a blue and white striped button-up shirt that he had buttoned all the way up to his collar. He was meticulously cleaning a pair of horn-rimmed glasses on his green tie that clearly clashed with his previously described shirt.

While he was distracted with his cleaning, I took the opportunity to glance around his office. It was tiny, the large desk and olive-green filing cabinets taking up most of the room. Despite its cramped space, the decrepit office chair, the desk that'd probably come from the thrift store, and the linoleum floor that had definitely been left over from the 70s, the office was immaculate. The account book, receipt book, and laptop were stacked on the desk, each one sitting at right angles. I was fairly sure that I could have put on some white linen gloves and wiped my finger across any surface in the room without finding a speck of dust.

Based on my initial observations, I guessed that the guy was an undiagnosed obsessive-compulsive who was also color-blind.

The thin man replaced his glasses and rose to his feet when we entered the office. "May I help you?" he asked, clearly confused.

Burke flashed him his badge and said, "Good afternoon, Mr. Lillard. I'm Officer Matt Burke. We met the other night."

Mr. Lillard shook hands with Burke and nodded nervously. "I'm sorry I didn't recognize you, sir. I, uh, I met a lotta detectives recently." His big brown eyes shifted from Burke to me, and he extended his hand toward me.

I shook his hand and introduced myself.

Burke told him, "We have a few questions about what happened here the night Eli Goldman's body was found."

"I-I uh, already gave my official statement to the police," he said. "I don't, I don't know what else to say, but I-I'd be happy to, um, to help you folks." The poor guy was obviously scared out of his mind. Murder is always bad for business.

"We just wanted to ask you a few questions about your staff," I told him. "Are any of them new here?"

Mr. Lillard shook his head. "No-no. They've all been here nearly a year, well 'cept Corbin. Corbin's only been here about four months."

"Have any of them shown any marked changes in behavior lately?" Burke asked. "Maybe they've been jittery or irritable more so than usual." All of these would be signs of drug use. Burke was being smart.

Mr. Lillard thought for a moment, his eyes glancing up toward a corner of the ceiling as if that were where he'd find the answer. Finally, he shook his head decisively. "No, not that I can recall. They all seem normal as ever."

This conversation was going nowhere fast, and I was beginning to get annoyed. Therefore, I did the best thing I could think of and got to the point. "Do any of your employees have a history of buying, selling, or doing drugs?" I asked.

Mr. Lillard looked shocked and appalled, his jaw nearly hitting the floor as his eyes bulged out in my direction. "I-I ain't gonna hire no druggie," he said, and though the look on his face was evidence enough, I could tell by the way his voice raised two octaves that I had offended him.

"What P.I. Harlem means is," Burke growled through gritted teeth, "do you suspect any of your staff of having any involvement in drugs or knowing anyone who might have any involvement?"

His questions didn't help. Mr. Lillard shook his head more vehemently, and my patience broke.

"Thank you for your time, sir," I said. "I'd like to interview the people you had working for you last night."

"They ain't all here." He was quick to answer but not rude. Good. He hadn't been too offended by our questions.

"Then I'll interview the ones who were here and wait around for the rest," I informed him. I then turned on my heel and walked out of the freakishly clean office, down the tiny green corridor, and into the kitchen where the cook was prepping the stove, a runner was checking supplies, and another was washing dishes. "Who in here was working on the night Eli Goldman was killed?" I asked.

They each turned to look at me, and after a moment, a young guy washing the dishes raised his hand timidly.

"We got some questions for you," Burke told him, walking up behind me and flashing his badge.

The young dishwasher nodded and wiped his soapy hands on a dry towel before following Burke and me to the bar area. I immediately hopped up on a stool and indicated that the youngun' should sit on the stool beside me. He did so, timidly flipping his flax-colored hair out of his pale gray eyes and lacing his fingers on the counter in front of him. He had a few little hairs rising from his boyish chin, and his two front teeth were bigger than the rest and stuck out slightly.

"I would offer to buy you a drink, but I'm not sure you're old enough for it," I joked.

He let out a nervous chuckle after he realized that I was in fact joking.

Burke came and stood at the counter across from the dishwasher. "It's Corbin, right?" he asked. Of course it was Corbin. He was way too young to have worked there for a year or more. Honestly, the kid couldn't have been over twenty-one.

Corbin confirmed the question with a nod and a gulp.

"What happened that night?" I asked, keeping my question as general as possible in hopes of bringing him out of his shell, as the saying goes.

Corbin gulped. "I, uh, I f-found the body," he admitted.

Geez, no wonder he was nervous. Poor kid was probably traumatized. He must've been pretty hard up to come in to work so soon after a night like that.

"That must have been a terrible experience for you," I made the obvious statement in my most comforting voice. I hoped I sounded sincere because that kid needed some sympathy. "I'm sorry you had to go through that."

Burke didn't even try to do the comforting thing, which is good because he sucks at that more than I do. He just hopped right in with the first question: "Our coroner's best guess is that Mr. Goldman was killed around 2:30 a.m., so the body would have been in the freezer for over an hour before you found him at 3:40 a.m. Why did nobody notice sooner?"

Corbin gave a shaky, nervous shrug, and I seriously considered offering him a beer. Geez, the kid was about to shake himself apart, but he did finally answer, "We don't usually have to check the freezer. Boss is pretty good about having exactly what we need ready to go, but the crowd was bigger than usual that night because it was an LSU bye week, and I had to get some more shrimp for the gumbo. If it hadn't been for that, we probably wouldn't a found him until the next morning."

"Wait, you freeze your shrimp for your gumbo?" Now it was my turn to be both shocked and appalled. This was New Orleans, for crying out loud. NOLA folk don't skimp on our gumbo.

"Only if we run out of fresh shrimp, which, like I said, don't happen a lot."

"So, what you're saying is that you were the first and only person to check the freezer that night?" I asked for clarification.

He nodded. "Yeah, I mean, it's outside on the loading dock, so no one else ever goes out there unless it's Artie going on his smoking break."

"Who's Artie?" I asked.

"He's one of the bartenders," Corbin told us. I could tell by his snide tone that he was not overly fond of Artie.

"I take it he's not a good bartender if he's outside on the dock during business hours," Burke stated. He must have noticed the same tone I had.

"Well, he's Mr. Lillard's cousin or somethin', so he does, like, whatever he wants," Corbin grumbled. "He goes out there for smoke breaks all the time, and it's not, like, cigarettes he's smokin', m'kay?"

So, the boss's "no drug" policy didn't extend to his cousin partaking in Mary Jane—interesting double standard.

Burke and I shared a look, and that was all we needed to communicate our mutual understanding.

"Is this Artie guy here today?" Burke asked.

Corbin shook his head. "He hasn't been here since the night Goldman died."

This kid was just brimming with interesting information.

"Do you think you could show us the freezer before we go?" Burke asked, and I felt my stomach sink. I had to remind myself that it made sense to examine the crime scene—it might help me get into the killer's head, so to speak, and understand why he hid Goldman's body in a freezer instead of literally anywhere else.

"Um, I guess so, sure." Corbin slid off the barstool and led us back through the door, down the cramped ugly hallway, into the kitchen, and through a back door. Behind the bar was the concrete loading dock Corbin had described. A large garage door allowed for the loading of food from the trucks directly into the kitchen pantry. On the far side of the garage door loomed a padlocked metal door that I was sure would lead to the industrial-sized walk-in freezer. I tried to calm my thundering heart by focusing on the fact that this was not an old ivory freezer stuffed into the basement of a butcher's shop. It was nothing like that.

"Is that padlock always locked?" I asked Corbin, finding any detail I could to focus on.

He shook his head, and his limp hair swished. "The boss put it on there the morning after we found Goldman's body," he told us. I guess Mr. Lillard didn't want any more bodies ending up in his freezer.

Instead of leading us across the concrete dock to the freezer door, Corbin stopped right in front of us. It took me a second to realize that the poor kid's feet had pretty much frozen to the pavement. I know it's a cliché, but that boy was frozen with fear, and I couldn't blame him. After all, I was counting to four as I drew in each breath in order to stave off a panic attack, but at least I work a job where I know I'll see dead bodies. Working as a dishwasher, this kid would never have expected that kind of experience.

I looked at Burke, who gave me a look that screamed, "You're the nurturing female. You handle this. Use those female powers." Realizing that I was giving in to a centuries-old stereotype and forcing myself to put Corbin's fears ahead of my own stale panic, I reluctantly placed my hand on Corbin's shoulder.

"We'll take it from here, Corbin," I said. "Just hand Officer Burke your key, and we'll let ourselves in."

The kid didn't even hesitate. He passed over the tiny metal key and booked it back into the kitchen. Burke walked across the dock and unlocked the padlock, taking the lock off the handle and opening the door for me to enter. I take great pride in the fact that I only hesitated for a moment before stepping across the threshold and into the frigid air.

Just a few years prior, walking into a cooler would have reminded me of one of the many reasons I had permanently moved back to the humid American South. I've always *hated* cold. Once upon a time, it made me angry, but anger was not the emotion I felt when stepping into the freezer that day.

It was dark in that freezer, and for one terrifying moment, I was back, trapped in a box that smelled of blood and death, the pain in my gut long since forgotten as it slowly sank in that no one knew where I was, and I'd die alone in the cold. I felt dizzy as my stomach began to churn, and my fingers trembled, not just from the cold. I'm pretty sure that the inside of that freezer is what actual Hell is like—cold, dark, and utterly hopeless. I've always hated the cold more than fire, anyway.

Then Burke flipped on the light, filling the tiny room with an orange haze. I wasn't alone in a tiny box. I was *standing* in the cold with Burke, who was breathing, living, and *real*. I took a deep breath, pinching the inside of my elbow to remind myself that I was alive. The dizziness dissipated, and my fingers stopped tingling, but my stomach continued to churn. I tried to take in the chilly interior as quickly as possible. There was about a three-foot-wide, eight-foot-deep space to stand in the cooler; the rest was covered with shelves of frozen foods. Burke pointed to the metal floor in front of me. "He was laid out in the middle right there, his feet near the door and his head on the far side. It was obvious he'd been dragged in here fast," Burke told me.

I stared at the ground, and for a moment, I saw it—Goldman's frozen body staring up at me, eyes wide and empty, tears frozen to his face, lips blue. Blood pooled around him spreading even as a watch, flooding the area and drawing ever closer to my shoes. Another life I hadn't saved. I sucked in a breath, trying to calm my heart, but the air smelled of copper, and I gagged at the taste of blood. I couldn't breathe, couldn't think. All I knew was that I was cold and needed to get out-out-out! I stepped back, ramming into Burke, my feet slipping on the frozen floor, and I fell, the image of Goldman's frozen corpse there in front of me, his frozen eyes following me as I scrambled backward, sliding across the cold floor on my butt. I tried to breathe in, but it felt like my throat had closed up—no air could get to my lungs. My vision swam with black spots that looked like millions of ants encroaching on a picnic, and it was cold ... so cold.

Then I was outside on the concrete slab, Burke kneeling in front of me, hands hovering far enough away not to scare me but close enough to reach me if I became frenzied. He said something I couldn't understand. The New Orleans heat, even in November, was welcoming, and I closed my eyes, trying again to breathe deeply. I managed to suck in a short breath, held it for four seconds, and released it as slowly as I could, then repeated the process until my chest loosened up and my heartbeat slowed. I could hear Burke saying my name, but I took several more breaths before opening my eyes again to the bright New Orleans light. I was *not* trapped, I was *not* cold, and I was *not* bleeding out.

"I'm okay," I said, embarrassed by how not okay I sounded. Burke reached out to touch my arm, and I immediately pulled away, shoving myself against the outer wall of the restaurant. "Don't touch me," I hissed. I took another deep breath, closing my eyes in a vain attempt to dispel the shadows. I waited until the tightness in my chest lessened, then said again, "I'm okay." It sounded almost believable that time.

"I'm sorry, Chase," he said. "I didn't think about—"

"Don't," I cut him off, shaking my head. I tried to smile, but I'm sure it looked more like a grimace. "Being stabbed and tossed in a freezer is a horrible way to go. I should know."

I meant it as a joke, but judging from Burke's flinch, I'm pretty sure it fell flat.

"Too soon?" I asked.

Burke shook his head. "If this is too personal—"

"It's not," I lied. It hadn't been personal, really. But anyone sick enough to kill someone the way Goldman was needed to be put away for good.

I closed my eyes, but the image of Goldman's corpse and staring eyes flashed before me, and I quickly looked back up at Burke and said, "He was dead." I meant it to be a question, but my voice was too shaky for any inflection.

Even still, Burke knew what I was trying to say and answered, "He was dead well before he went into that freezer."

I nodded. It was comforting, somehow, to know that he hadn't died there—that he hadn't spent his last moments slowly bleeding out on a frozen floor, wondering if anyone would miss him. I took another breath before rising shakily to my feet. Burke reached out and cupped his hand around my elbow to keep me steady, and I didn't jerk away from him this time.

"Sorry," I said.

He squeezed my elbow. "Don't *you* start," he growled, but there was no anger in his voice. "I should've thought about it first."

I shook my head. "Normally, I'd have insisted on seeing the crime scene. I just—"

"I know," he cut me off.

"I hate the cold."

"Can't blame you for that."

I took another breath and counted. My chest was still a little tight, and I was tired. Otherwise, the panic attack had passed.

"You wanna talk about it?" Burke asked.

"Hell no," I told him, quickly extracting my elbow from his grip and standing at my full height.

I took another breath before changing the subject. "You think that Artie guy could've lifted Goldman into that freezer?"

"Maybe," Burke grumbled. "We'll have to meet 'im first. I'll get an address from Mr. Lillard while you go thaw out in the car." It was an olive branch. Burke needed another suspect, and I had given him one.

"I want to interview him with you," I told him.

"Of course you do." He tossed me his keys.

"Don't leave me out in the cold." Keys in hand, I headed for the car. I needed to work this drug dealer angle, and the only way I could do that was to find the drug dealer.

Chapter 10

I've Got the World on a String

After leaving the Willow, I rode with Burke back to the department. As I've mentioned already, I don't like Burke's boss, so I decided to walk to my office apartment and let Burke deal with Captain Chihuahua alone. I had no real reason to stay with him anyway, and I did not want to get bitten. Besides, the fresh air would do me some good after the whole freezer incident.

As I walked, I did my usual paranoid gumshoe strut, keeping my left hand on the concealed weapon in my purse and watching for creeps, while developing a suspect list of my own in my head. Thinking over cases always helped me keep my "murder face" intact to prevent people from approaching.

As a single lady living in New Orleans, it's important to have a good "murder face" to scare off the hooligans, and if you don't have one, it's a pretty easy thing to develop. All you have to do is walk with purpose and think unhappy thoughts. People will move out of your way—usually, they move out of your way quickly.

I finally made it back to my place around 12:45 p.m. I entered through the gate, made my way across the courtyard, and walked into the dingy place I call home to be greeted by an over-exuberant Louis, who scampered up my leg and onto my shoulder as if I'd been gone for a week instead of a few hours. I gave him a scratch behind his ears before crossing the length of my downstairs space and over to the kitchen with Louis balancing on my shoulder. I opened the cabinet above the sink and pulled out a can of ferret food before walking over to his cage and dumping the contents of said can into his bowl. Louis chittered at me happily before letting me lower him into his cage for his meal. I didn't bother to close the cage door behind him.

After making sure Louis was taken care of, I looked around my small downstairs living area. It was a mess, and as much as I hate to clean, I knew it would help me think things through. I started in the center of the room where my couch and homemade coffee table sat because the mess in the kitchen scared me. I grabbed the orange and blue fleece throw I've had since college and draped it over the back of the lumpy yellow sofa I'd rescued from Goodwill. I picked up the bra, jeans, and underwear I'd left on the floor that morning and took them upstairs, dumping them into the laundry basket I kept at the foot of my futon. I then went back downstairs, picked up the multiple coffee cups and drinking glasses, and took them to the sink for washing.

I worked while trying to consider the conundrum that was this case. In my opinion, the culprit had to be related to Regina's cocaine habit, but I had no evidence. Anyone with a single gray cell in their head could understand the drug dealer's motive with a short explanation, but the DA was insistent about his evidence.

Just as I had begun to develop a half-decent strategy for the evening, a loud crash issued from the other side of my kitchen wall, followed by a cacophony of screaming. My neighbors, the Bakers, had moved in about a year before, and I was just beginning to get to know them in my own special way. That is, I never spoke to them, but I had them pretty much figured out.

Mrs. Baker was a sweet, unassuming lady, likely a first-generation immigrant from Mexico, who never raised her voice and always seemed eager to help. I'd invited her to my self-defense class a couple of times, but she'd always politely refused. Mr. Baker was a certified creep, which was why I asked his wife to come to my self-defense class. He hadn't acted like a total waste of space when they'd first moved in, though. He'd occasionally drink too much and do some yelling and swearing, but things had changed in the last couple of weeks. Apparently, Mr. Baker had been laid off, meaning he was staying at home all day and spending his time unproductively drinking.

I'd heard the yelling, but I hadn't heard the violence—not until that day. The crash had been something heavy being flung across the room, a sound that I was uncomfortably familiar with. This was followed by yelling and feet stomping across the floor, followed by the sound of flesh hitting flesh. Next, there was wailing and the sound of more feet, this time stumbling. A door was opened and slammed shut. I could hear her crying, and for a moment, I couldn't move. Then I heard heavy stomping across the wooden floor and heavy fists banging on the door as he shouted, saying words I don't care to put on paper.

I dropped the coffee cup I was washing in the sink and made my way out of my apartment, across our attached porches, and up to their door. I slammed my open palm against the Bakers' door and listened as the place fell silent. For a moment, nothing happened. The only sound was the blood pulsing in my ears as my heart thundered its fury. You're supposed to protect the people you love, not hit them. That's more than a rule; it's a fact.

"This is your neighbor," I announced. "Mrs. Baker, are you alright? Do I need to call the police?"

No answer.

"Mrs. Baker, if you'd just answer the door, please." I suddenly regretted having never spoken to the woman.

"She's not going to answer," a voice spoke up from behind me. I turned to find a familiar teenage girl sitting at one of the iron tables in the courtyard. It was the same kid with the smoking problem I'd seen before—the kid who also happened to be the Baker's daughter. She fixed her light brown eyes on me as if this whole thing was my fault.

"If you got your key, you could let me in," I told her.

She shook her head. "Not gonna happen. I'm out here for a reason, and I'd like it to stay that way."

For the first time, I looked at the kid—really looked at her. Her skin was darker than either of the Bakers' but tan enough that her race wasn't immediately identifiable. Her heart-shaped face and full lips shaped like a cupid's bow might have made her look younger than her years had it not been for her eyes—which were big, angry, and simultaneously, completely devoid of hope. Those eyes had seen far too much to belong to a kid.

I almost asked her why she wasn't begging me to help her mom, but then I thought back to my home life and realized that I had no idea what was going on with this kid. At the time, I didn't know how right I was. It certainly wasn't her fault her parents were the way they were. Heck, she couldn't be older than fourteen, and with the way she held herself, she already looked smarter than both of them. I felt guilt finagle its way into my soul for stifling my own powers of deduction when it came to my neighbors.

"You might as well go," the kid told me. "Even if she did answer the door, she wouldn't admit anything. She'd just make up some lie and send you on your way."

"I can help," I insisted, but at that point I couldn't have told you which of us I was trying to convince. "I could call—"

"The cops?" she cut me off. "She'd just lie to them, too. It's a sick cycle. There's nothing you can do, so just get gone." At that, the kid stood up and stomped out of the courtyard and onto St. Peter Street. Jeez, she really was smarter than her folks. Smarter than me if I'm honest.

I stood by the door for a moment longer, my pulse still racing and my blood boiling. Every fiber of my being screamed for action, but the kid was right: there was nothing I could do. This wasn't a movie where I could kick down the door and demand that Mr. Baker stop knocking Mrs. Baker around and expect a result other than getting myself arrested. I might not have come from that kind of life, but I had seen it before and knew how it worked.

I can't save everyone.

I went back to my apartment long enough to make sure Louis was sleeping through the nonsense—I swear that ferret could snooze through a hurricane—and grabbed my keys and purse. Then, locking the door behind me, I stomped and slammed my way out of 911 St. Peter Street. Of course, all the stomping and slamming in the world couldn't relieve the tension that'd built up inside of me that afternoon.

I went straight to The Gambler to search for a new way to relieve my tension. It was just my luck that Deuce was working and went on instant alert when I made a beeline toward the bar and ordered my favorite stout from the Boss. Deuce made his way across the room with all the grace of a frickin' swan, taking the tall glass of stout out of my hand in a way that was neither rude nor demeaning and bringing it to his own lips.

"Bonjour, mon amie," he greeted me as he drank my alcohol. "You good? How's yo mama an' them?"

"Deuce," I said through clenched teeth, "give me my beer."

"No can do, ma chérie. You got a rule. You only drink when de case is solved."

"How do you know I haven't solved it yet?"

Deuce placed my now empty glass in front of me and raised a dark, perfectly angled eyebrow. "What's da matter?"

I sighed and ran my fingers through my chunky, coffee-colored hair before moving my thumb and forefinger to my earlobes and massaging. This was how I had learned to process my fiery emotions. It wasn't as effective as alcohol, but it was a lot healthier, and it helped me keep my head clear instead of fogging it up. That way, I'd be ready if anything happened with the case. I would've gone for a run, but I knew Burke could call at any minute with news on Artie the pothead. I kept massaging until, finally, I felt the fight seep out of me.

I looked up into Deuce's concerned eyes and shrugged. Now that I was close to him, I could see that his eyes weren't wholly hazel; they had hints of blue with halos of gold around his irises.

"You really wanna know?" I asked.

He nodded, and I knew he was being honest. I thought about telling him no and going about my business now that I had calmed down, but my pop had taught me that when you found someone willing to let you talk through your garbage, you'd better take advantage because they don't come around often.

"Can I at least get a Coke first?" I asked with a smirk.

Deuce laughed and grabbed a bottle from the fridge under the bar before following me to the booth in the farthest, darkest corner of the room. He handed me the Coke and slid into the booth opposite me. I popped the top on the table and took a long drink. Caffeine can be as useful as alcohol at getting the job done if you have a good imagination.

"My neighbor's a certifiable creep and a complete waste of oxygen," I told him as I finished the first gulp.

"Okay. You want me to kill 'im?" he asked matter-of-factly.

I'm not 100% sure that Deuce was joking, but I laughed like he was. "I don't think so," I told him. "I just wish I could help his wife, you know? And their kid, too, even though she's kind of a jerk."

"Ah." Deuce nodded. "He's that kinda man. You should just let me kill 'im." I couldn't spot a glimmer of humor in his eyes as he spoke, and that should've been my first hint that he was more dangerous than he let on. Did he honestly think killing Mr. Baker would be the simplest thing to do?

"He's the primary breadwinner," I said. "Killing him would just put his family in the poor house. If he could get a job and get off the booze and whatever the hell else he's takin,' it'd be fine, but I can't just sit in my apartment and listen to him knock his wife around, you know? It's not in my nature."

"You say something to 'im? He come after you?" I could tell that idea didn't sit well with my Cajun pool shark, but I was quick to put him at ease.

I shook my head. "I beat on the door, but he didn't answer. I heard his wife crying, but there was literally nothing I could do. I just felt so...helpless."

I sucked down some more of my Coke before slamming it down on the table between us and glaring at it. After a moment, Deuce reached out and slid his hand on top of mine. It felt genuine, not like his usual flirtation, and it scared me how much comfort I found in that touch.

"The fact that you wanted to help, ma chérie, well, that makes you a lot more useful than most of the fools I know." He leaned forward and whispered, "An' if you ever change your mind about the killin' thing, you let me know, aight?"

We both laughed, and I laced my fingers through his. I looked the silly flirt in the eye and I started thinking, which is always a dangerous thing to do around handsome, sweet men with accents. I didn't get to finish my thought as Dice chose that exact moment to make her presence known.

"Ahem." She cleared her throat from a mere foot behind me.

I dropped Deuce's hand out of some vague instinct, and he rolled his eyes. "Don't you got some tables to clean, sista mine?" he asked her.

She sent him a glare that is probably considered a lethal weapon in some countries.

He quickly hopped out of the booth and said, "On the other hand, I think I'll clean those tables for you."

She ignored him as he scampered away from us and told me, "I'm glad you came by. I thought I'd have to get your phone number from my brother."

"Your brother has my phone number?" I asked.

She rolled her eyes. "The fact that you can't remember giving it to him on Mardi Gras is probably why he hasn't called you," she said.

"I don't even remember Mardi Gras," I admitted because it was true.

She ignored my comment and said, "You need to see this." I noticed the phone in her hand and immediately gave her a nod.

She stepped over and straddled the bench beside me, placing the phone on the bar. I leaned to take a look at the screen, which displayed a video, paused on a frame featuring Goldman and some other guys. Judging by their filthy jerseys, I was guessing they had been practicing for a while. Dice pressed play on the video.

At first, the guys looked jovial, shoving each other in that friendly way boys do when they have too much energy.

Suddenly, there was a shout, and another player launched himself at Goldman, screaming obscenities.

Goldman and his attacker didn't struggle for long since the team quickly pulled the other player off their quarterback. The tilt of the camera revealed the attacker to be none other than Jeremy Lackey, and he was so mad he was red.

"Your time's comin', Golden Boy!" he shouted as his teammates pulled him off-screen.

The video ended with the focus on Goldman's face; he looked startled, if not scared, and his lip was bleeding.

When it was finished playing, I picked my jaw up off the ground, shook my head, and asked, "Where did you find this?"

"One of Goldman's fans made a Facebook page," Dice told me, going back to the page on her phone and handing the device to me. "Some anonymous account posted that about an hour ago. The press will be going crazy soon."

I scrolled through some of the posts. Most of them consisted of wishing condolences to Goldman's family. There were a few videos from Goldman's games and several pictures, but the video of the altercation between Goldman and Lackey was the most viewed post by far.

"Look at the comments," Dice instructed.

I did what she said and immediately wished I hadn't. Comment after comment called Lackey out for being a bully before they finally started outright calling him a murderer.

"There's some other chatter online about a 'hazing video' featuring Lackey and Goldman as well," she told me.

After talking to Lackey and gauging his reaction to Goldman's straight-edge philosophy, I really should not have been surprised by the video. I took a deep breath and released it slowly. "All this proves is that they had a complicated relationship," I tried to assure myself. "It doesn't prove murder."

Dice raised a pierced eyebrow.

"Based on the autopsy report, the crime scene photos, and the way the body was hidden—this was a crime of passion," I told her.

"Based on this," she indicated to her phone, "I think Lackey has the capacity to become *very* passionate."

"Throwing a few punches at a football practice isn't the same as murder," I told her.

She studied me in silence for an uncomfortable minute before asking, "Why are you so sure he's *not* the killer?"

Well, that caught me off guard. "I'm not," I admitted. Sure, I didn't want him to be the killer because his father was my client, but there was more to it than that. "I just think that whoever killed Goldman *has* to be connected to what happened to Reggie. It's too much of a coincidence that she overdosed the same night her boyfriend died before anyone knew he was dead."

"So, you think he might be capable of killing Goldman but not Regina Doyle?"

I nodded. "Something like that."

She was quiet for a moment, biting her lip in a way that made me believe she was anxious about something. Whatever she was considering saying was likely something I wouldn't want to hear. "If he is innocent," she said at last, "and they arrest him ... you know it's not your fault, right? It's not like last time."

I felt my body turn cold as my face grew hot. "What the *hell* do you know about last time?" I growled.

She was about to answer when my cellphone rang. I saw who was calling and quickly picked up the call.

It was Burke. Jeremy Lackey had just been arrested for murder.

Chapter 11

_____

I Was Doing Alright

I barged into the police department like a tumbleweed in a spaghetti western. It had taken me under twenty minutes to get from The Gambler on Bourbon Street to NOPD headquarters on Conti Street, where I knew they'd be holding my athlete. According to the GPS on my phone, this is an impossible feat.

As soon as I made it in, I stomped my way over to Burke's desk to make my presence known. He wasn't there.

I looked around until I found the young and green Officer Michael Chandler loitering beside a nearby potted plant. He was tall and lanky with boyish good looks and dimples that made him appear younger than his years. They've promised me that he is legally old enough to be a cop, but I've seen toddlers show more authority. Even dressed in a police uniform and toting a sidearm did not help him appear even marginally intimidating. His blond hair and blue-green puppy-dog eyes didn't help, and I constantly questioned how anyone took him seriously when he was out on the streets. I knew that he would know where Burke was hiding. I also knew that the poor kid was intimidated just enough by me to tell me exactly what I wanted to hear.

"Officer Chandler!" I called, bulldozing my way over to him.

96

He looked up and saw me, his large eyes rounding that much larger at my approach. "P.I. Harlem," he greeted me. "How can I help you?"

"Where is he?"

"W-who?"

"Don't play dumb." I knew he wasn't playing. "Where is Detective Burke?"

"I-I'm not sure. I could find him for you if you want me to."

"I'm right here." I turned at the sound of Burke's voice to see him standing beside his desk. I threw up my hand toward Officer Chandler in a sign of dismissal before storming toward Burke.

"What the heavenly hell, Burke?" I've never been very good at friendly greetings.

Burke lifted his hands in that annoying, placating way that was supposed to make me calm down or some such nonsense. It never worked; it just made me angry. "Just let me explain…"

"Let you explain? You arrested Lackey without calling me?"

Burke stood taller and looked down at me with his intimidating cop face. "I didn't realize I had to run the details of *my* case by you."

Hearing that was like a bucket of cold water to the face. Of course, Burke didn't owe me anything. He was doing me a favor by keeping me updated. I just had a rotten day and was taking it out on him. For the second time that day, I moved my fingers to my earlobes and massaged the frustrations away.

"C'mon, Burke, just tell me what changed." It wasn't an apology, but Burke seemed satisfied by my shift in tone.

Burke plopped down in his chair behind his desk and motioned for me to have a seat. It might have been a power play, but I sat down.

Burke took a breath. "We found the murder weapon in his truck."

I cursed, creatively. "When did you even have time to get a warrant?" I asked.

Burke lowered his gaze and looked me in the eye. "We didn't get a warrant. There was an anonymous tip, and Lackey gave us permission."

I nearly fell out of my chair at that plot twist. On one hand, how could the kid be dumb enough to let police search his car without any kind of warrant? On the other hand...

"You don't think he did it," I mumbled.

Burke shook his head. "I didn't say that, but I gotta wonder: why would a murderer hide the murder weapon in his truck and then allow the police to search it?"

"Think he's being set up?"

"It's possible. If he is, you'd better tell that priest of yours to start prayin', 'cause, based on the evidence, this kid looks pretty damn guilty."

I bit down on the nail of my pinky finger, a habit I'd formed whenever I had a lot to consider. Burke had pointed it out before, but he only commented on it when it became too unnerving. "Can I talk to him?" I asked after a pause.

Burke groaned. "He's in interrogation right now."

"You makin' him sweat before you talk to him?"

"That's how we do it." He stood up, picked his jacket up off the back of his chair, and shrugged it on. "I gotta get a smoke."

In a moment of sheer stupidity, I replied, "I thought you quit."

The look on Burke's face confirmed it was a moment of sheer stupidity before he continued, "You stay right there in that chair. The boss'd get real mad if she found you anywhere near our only suspect. The one who's currently in interrogation room B." He then turned on his heel and trudged out of the NOPD.

Sometimes Burke's a turd; sometimes he's an angel. I was glad that I caught him on one of his angel days.

Before making my way to the interrogation rooms, I noticed Burke's badge sitting on top of his desk, and I couldn't help but think of all the potential uses a NOPD detective badge could have. Sometimes, I'm an angel; most of the time, I'm a turd. I swiped the badge, slipped it into the cross-strapped leather purse I always carry, and headed toward interrogation room B.

Before I could start moving, however, Officer Chandler reappeared by my side, holding out a cup of fresh coffee as if it were an offering to a 16th-century English royal. "I got this for you," he said. "I thought you might need something while you waited on Detective Burke or whatever."

I smiled at him and took the coffee. "Actually, Chandler, I could really use your help with something." Because, honestly, I could use a guard to watch my back and let me know if the captain was going to make an appearance and throw me out of the station, and Chandler was just eager enough for my approval to be that guy.

He smiled so big his face split in half, and I almost felt bad for using him—almost. "Yeah, yeah sure," he said. "Anything you need."

"Do you mind escorting me to interrogation room B, letting me in, and standing guard to let me know if the captain decides to visit?"

His face fell, and for a moment, I thought he was going to turn me down. "I don't know..."

"Look," I interrupted his mumbling, "that guy in there did not murder his best friend. I know it, Burke knows it, and you're a good enough detective that I'm sure you know it, too."

He blushed. "I-I'm not a detective."

"Not yet, you're not." Everyone knew that he'd failed the test multiple times. "I know you will be, though. All of us do. You have what it takes."

His face lit up again, and those puppy eyes looked so happy that I almost grew a conscience. "You really think so?"

"Of course I do," I assured him. "Now, will you help me free an innocent man, or will I have to do this on my own?"

Obviously, the heroic little officer was eager to help. I'm a terrible human, or maybe just a jerk.

"Hey! You're that private investigator the bio-dad hired," Lackey—the human jockstrap—said as soon as I entered the room. "You here to bail me out?"

They probably hadn't even booked the kid yet, and he was itching to get out. "You know," I told him, "most people don't dress up for their mugshots."

Lackey looked down at his button-up shirt, tie, blue blazer, and khakis—the traditional uniform of the college fraternity brother going to a formal.

"Man," he moaned, "I was getting ready for the party tonight when this cop came knocking and asked if he could take a look in my truck. I figured, you know, 'I got nothin' to hide,' so I told him to have at it. Next thing I know, three more cops show up, read me my rights, and then shove me in here. It's bogus. I swear I didn't kill the Golden Boy."

I sat down with a flourish in front of the table he was handcuffed to, plopping my cellphone in front of him and playing the video Dice had shown me. "You've seen this?" I asked.

He watched it, and I watched him. His eyes widened, eyebrows lifting to his hairline as his pupils dilated and his face turned red. He quickly schooled his expression, pushing the phone toward me and plopping back in his chair with a shrug. "So? We got in a fight after practice."

"That a normal occurrence with you two?" I asked.

He tried to keep up the cool act, but his brows furrowed at my question. "Not really," he said.

"Then you remember what the fight was about?" I asked.

He let out a fake laugh and answered, "Nah. We were high on endorphins. It was probably about a missed play, or maybe he made some noise about me subbin' in. Stuff like that happens." He shrugged in an exaggerated way that was way too casual to be taken seriously and said, "It's football."

I stood quickly, slamming my palms on the table between us. "Listen to me, you entitled little troll, two people are *dead*. There is a murder weapon in your vehicle, a video of you *threatening* one of the victims, and you're trying to play Joe Cool. Cut the crap and tell me why the hell I should believe that you aren't a murderer."

Lackey visibly paled and shrank down into his chair, looking more like a scolded tot than the football star he was. Maybe I shouldn't have been so harsh, but the idiot was acting way too casual for someone who'd just been arrested for murder. I needed him to understand the seriousness of the situation.

He stared down at his hands in silence.

"Do you remember why you attacked Eli Goldman in this video?" I asked.

He nodded.

"Care to enlighten me?"

I could barely hear his murmured response, and it shocked me enough that I had to ask him to clarify.

"He cheated on Reggie," he said, loud enough for me to hear but still barely above a whisper. "At least, I thought he did. There was this girl...she showed me some texts...it seemed legit. Turned out, it wasn't."

"How do you know?"

Lackey sighed. "Goldman came to me the day after *that*," he indicated to my phone. "He handed me his phone, I went through the supposed messages, we talked things out, and I apologized." He sat in silence for a moment before looking me in the eye and adding, "I would never kill Gold, and I would definitely never kill Reggie. They were my best friends." To my surprise, tears began rolling down his cheeks.

I said the only thing I could, given the situation. "I believe you. Now, tell me who would want to frame you."

"Well, the murderer, obviously," he told me, rolling his still-leaking eyes.

"Obviously."

He sniffed and wiped his nose with his coat sleeve. "I already told you I don't know who killed him."

"That's where you're wrong, skippy," I said. "You may not be able to give me a name, but rest assured, you know who killed him because whoever killed him was at the party with you the other night."

"There were *hundreds* of people at that party." There was a ring of hopelessness in his voice that might have broken my heart if I'd let it.

"Yeah, but which of them would've had a motive?" I asked.

"I dunno ..."

"*Think*, skippy!" I snapped my fingers in his face. "I may believe you when you say you didn't do it, but there are a ton of cops out there who think otherwise. We don't have much time, so I need you to give me something."

"Like what?"

I took a deep breath. "Who was Reggie's drug dealer?"

"I dunno. She'd never tell me that. I didn't even know for sure she was into that stuff until Gold found out."

Skippy was stupid, telling the truth, and therefore utterly useless. "Did Gold know who her drug dealer was?"

"No. No way. Like I said, she was really private about that stuff. She didn't want Gold to find out about it, so she wasn't about to rat out her dealer."

"But Gold would have ratted him out, wouldn't he?"

Lackey appeared even more confused by the question. "Yeah," he admitted. "I guess, but he didn't know about him."

"But did the drug dealer know about Gold?"

"What?"

I could almost feel the Chihuahua lurking around the building, sniffing me out, and this Q&A was going nowhere fast. I had to get some answer out of him, so I tried again: "How many people knew about Gold's personal war on drugs, the stuff with Stanson, the straight edge thing?"

Lackey's eyebrows shot up to his hairline as it finally dawned on him what I was asking. "Nobody besides the team knew about the Stanson thing, but everyone knew he was straight edge. He talked about it in pretty much all of his interviews. It's not a secret."

Finally, information! "Okay, so I just have one more question—"

First, Officer Chandler entered the room looking like a scared puppy. "P.I. Harlem," he stuttered, "I hate to interrupt, but the captain is on her way over, and I'm sure she'll be here any minute, so—"

The captain stormed into the room, shoving Officer Chandler aside and yelling, "Chase Harlem!" in her grating, bossy voice.

"Captain Millicent Morris," I answered, feigning surprise.

She lowered her perfectly plucked eyebrows, crossed her arms, and stood at her full height, which was significantly taller than mine, even when she wasn't wearing spiked stiletto heels that could be neither functional nor comfortable. "What do you think you're doing in my department?"

"Is *that* where I am?" I asked, looking around the room in over-emphasized astonishment. "I must have gotten turned around."

Her nutbrown skin turned a cherry color. "You have no business here. Get out!"

"Just a minute," I told her, "I have a few more questions for my client."

I didn't think it was possible for steam to actually come out of someone's ears. Honestly, I thought that only happened in old cartoons. I was probably going to catch the raw, brute force of all her anger, and I'm honestly not sure which of us would win that match. Fortunately for both of us, Burke chose that exact moment to come trudging through the door.

"Everything alright?" he asked, feigning ignorance.

The Chihuahua pointed at me and hissed at Burke, "What is *that* doing in my interrogation room?"

"Maybe she took a wrong turn somewhere," Burke told her.

She glared at him. "I know we were close before, but don't you dare think our former partnership will protect you from reprimand. She is *not* a consultant, and she is *not* welcome here."

Burke put his hands up in that placating gesture that always served to piss me off when I was angry and said, "I just thought, with a case as high profile as this one, that we could use all the help we could get. I know you've got your differences, but you've seen her methods work."

"Her methods?" Captain Chihuahua scoffed. "You mean her extensive training in behavioral science? Did you conveniently forget that she was *fired* from the same FBI that thought she was gold?"

I stood abruptly, too angry to stop myself from stepping in her direction.

She quickly put Burke between us, then caught herself and told me, "Get out of my department." Then, turning to Burke without totally turning her back on me, she ordered, "I'll see you in my office first thing tomorrow morning," before storming out of the room.

"Yeesh," Lackey mumbled. "Talk about girl fights."

"Don't say anything without a lawyer, skippy," I told him.

Then I looked at Burke. "You gonna drag me outta here or what?"

Burke stepped back and motioned for me to proceed through the door. "I thought we could just walk out," he said, casually, as if his boss hadn't just reamed him out. "It'd be easier."

As we made our dramatic stroll through the building, the reality of the almost argument I'd had with the Chihuahua, as well as the frustrations I felt about having my interrogation cut off, finally began dawning on me, and I felt the heat of my fiery Harlem temper flaring up inside me. I had a hunch, heck I was 99% sure that I knew exactly who the murderer was, but all the evidence gathered by the police pointed to the kid sitting in the interrogation room—the kid I couldn't talk to —the kid who might be an innocent on his way to life in prison or worse. Louisiana has the death penalty.

As we exited the building, I slammed the door behind me and slammed my fist against the brick wall outside. It was a mistake. The brick was tougher than my flesh and bone. I didn't wince, though. I was too angry. Even when I smashed my fist against a wall a second and third time and felt my skin tear, and my knuckles begin to bleed, I didn't wince. The fourth time I pulled back my fist to land a punch, Burke grabbed my elbow, stopping my fist an inch from the brick.

"You should calm down," he said, gently pulling me around by my elbow so that my back was to the wall. "Gettin' mad won't fix anythin'."

"You get that from an anger management class?"

Burke nodded. "Actually, yeah, I did."

Burke's temper was legendary. I'd never seen it myself, but I'd heard of it. It made the younger guys in his precinct hop whenever he raised his voice. Maybe it's why we get along so well—because we're similar spirits.

I let out a frustrated sigh, draining all the tension I could, and leaned back against the cold brick building. In true Burke fashion, he offered me a cigarette, making me snort with laughter. After my snort, he put the cancer sticks back into his coat pocket and joined me in holding up the wall. I'd have to remember to steal those and toss them later.

"Why's the chihuahua wasting her time on Lackey when it's so obvious he's *not* the drug dealer?" I complained.

"I don't hate your drug dealer theory," Burke told me, "but we need an actual *suspect* with a *name*."

I sighed.

"Maybe that Artie guy?" Burke asked.

"Maybe. He's a better suspect than Lackey, I guess, but there's no evidence that he knew the victims," I shrugged. I thought it would be someone closer to Regina.

"No evidence yet," Burke said.

I sighed again. "I can't let an innocent man go to jail, Bee. Not—not again." He didn't respond to the affectionate nickname. He never did, which is why I'd quit using it so often. "Even if he stinks like a used jockstrap."

"Then don't."

I thought for a moment. As a private investigator, there are certain things that I can get away with that Burke cannot. At least, I can get away with those things if no city-employed detectives find out about it. "Hypothetically, if the drug dealer who sold Reggie the cocaine sold cocaine to someone else, could science prove that it was from the same batch that killed her?"

Burke took a deep breath. He had spent some time in narcotics before being moved to homicide, so I knew he had an answer for me. "Hypothetically, I think so."

"I think I have a plan," I told him after a pause.

"Care to share?"

"Nope. You don't wanna know."

He shrugged. "Do ... what you gotta do, Chase."

He knew what I was planning; I could tell by the tone of his voice. He was hesitant like he wanted to protest but knew he shouldn't. At one point, before he'd really gotten to know me, he might have tried to stop me, but he's learned since then; we both had. We gave each other space to do our jobs because our jobs were more important than our petty differences. Our jobs are more important than feelings.

I started to walk away, but thought better of it and said, "Keep an eye on Lackey, okay? Make sure he doesn't get too... sad."

Burke needed no explanation. He simply nodded and promised he'd have the kid watched.

Before scampering off to my crappy Isuzu, I asked, "Did you have a tox screen run on the coke found at Reggie's?"

My brain took a moment to register the fact that I'd just referred to the dead girl by the nickname her friends had graced her with. I'd been doing that all night. That wasn't good. I was growing attached. Maybe I saw something of myself in the young woman's love for music, or maybe I envied that voice of hers. I pushed that thought aside to focus on Burke's answer.

"It wasn't in the report."

I gave him what I hoped would be a case-altering tip. "Have them run a tox screen."

"Anything in particular we should be looking for?"

"Just have them identify any alternative chemical strands. If we're lucky, you'll find something funny."

"The fact that you think any of that's lucky amazes me."

Chapter 12

Careless

O h yes, I had a plan.

And oh no, Burke would not like it.

I headed back to my apartment, turned the television on to Animal Planet to keep Louis entertained, and got to work. I had a slinky, dark blue romper somewhere in the back of my closet that I never wore—possibly because I think most rompers just look like baby onesies made for grown-ups—but my fashion-savvy former roommate gave it to me, so I figured it would do for a college party. I pulled it out of the closet and hung it on the inside of my bathroom door. I then shed my clothes as quickly as possible—never once facing the mirror—before jumping in the shower. I was hoping the steam would knock out any leftover wrinkles from the romper, as the hot water gave me the energy I needed for the night ahead.

As I washed out the grit and smell of the New Orleans streets from my hair, I thought about my plan. I was not at all confident in my undercover abilities. It had been a *while* since college, and I wasn't exactly known for my partying ways. However, I was not about to fail this client or his big, dumb offspring.

I was raised to be a winner. My Pop taught me that there are two types of people in this world: the type everybody counts on and the type nobody counts on, and I should strive to be the former. I was smart enough to figure out the meaning behind his words—that if nobody can count on me, I don't count at all. So, when I was with the FBI, I had a reputation for never giving up—for catching my suspect, no matter what. That's what made me a successful profiler—at least for a while. A "can-do" attitude can only do so much for you. I'd learned that the hard way when I made the mistake of a lifetime.

I shaved my legs quickly and bathed my body, closing my eyes as I felt the scarred skin on my torso under my fingertips—tracing the pattern even though it made me sick to my stomach. No, I couldn't make another mistake. There would be no more victims this time.

As soon as I was done in the shower, my scarred body safely covered by my blue jumper, I dolled up in the best way I could: makeup, mousse, lotion, jewelry, etcetera. I even pulled one side of my dark, wavy hair back in a bobby pin to keep my long-neglected bangs out of my face.

When I was done, I took a long measuring look in the mirror. I had done my makeup so that my large, green eyes popped in a way that did not look at all bug-like, my lips looked plump without looking duck-like, and my freckles were barely noticeable along with the rest of my insecurities. As far as I could tell, I had achieved the height of "dolled up."

I had just pulled my classy handbag out of the top of my closet and shoved my wallet, lip gloss, and my smallest gun into it, when I heard it again: the sound of male testosterone cranked up on Jim Beam and frustration. There were multiple voices shouting this time, and one sounded awfully young and awfully scared.

I know that I said real life was nothing like the movies—that I couldn't go kicking doors down and making threats. But, hey, I was in a "kicking doors down and making threats" type of mood.

I pointed a finger at Louis, who was still nestled on my bed watching Animal Planet, and said, "You stay put."

Then I grabbed Burke's badge off the nightstand where I'd dumped the entire contents of my traditional leather purse and stomped down the stairs, out the door, and across the porch, my fancy brown wedges adding a lack of authority to my steps as I went. I slammed the side of my fist against the Bakers' door and shouted, "New Orleans P.D., open this door right now!"

For your information, that is not how a cop would do it.

There was a momentary silence on the other side of the door, followed by shuffling feet. Then the door opened just enough for me to see Mrs. Baker's face. Her lip was busted, and her cheek was bruised.

"I need to see your husband," I demanded.

Before she even opened her mouth, I could tell she was going to lie to me. "He's not home." The doors were not chained.

"Bullshit," I said. "Now step aside."

Mrs. Baker had just enough time to shuffle off before I flung the French-style porch doors open with my shoulders, put my left hand on the gun in my handbag, and held up Burke's badge with my right. I immediately spotted Mr. Baker standing a few feet away in front of their living room sofa.

"Howdy neighbor, you see this?" I waved the badge at him. "This is a detective badge, giving me the authority to arrest your ass for domestic violence, and if your sweet wife here decides to cover for you, I can just drag you out on the street and arrest you for public intoxication and disturbing the peace, you got that?"

I noticed the mini-Baker crouched at the top of the stairs, her face barely visible as she bent to watch us adults figure things out. I didn't see any bruises on her, which was good news for Mr. Baker. Normally, I would have been embarrassed about cursing in front of a kid, but I figured that in this place, she'd probably heard worse.

"I asked you a question, Mr. Baker," I insisted.

He looked startled. More than that, there was real fear in his eyes, and I knew it wasn't just fear of the 5'4," dressed-to-party "detective" standing in his apartment doorway. He was afraid of being arrested. I knew how to use his fear to my advantage.

His eyes darted toward his wife.

"Mr. Baker, I'm not a patient woman."

He turned back toward me and mumbled, "I got it. Yeah."

"Good." I lowered the badge slightly. "I could arrest you right now, but as you can see through your bloodshot eyes, I have plans tonight. Therefore, I'm allowing you the chance to leave."

"S'cuse me?" he stammered.

"Get out," I explained, angry enough for my Southern accent to start rearing its head. "You leave tonight. Find a hotel, a shelter, a church, somewhere you can go to cool down and get sober, and I promise not to immediately cart you off to jail. Capisce?"

He understood. He slowly edged past me and made his way out of the apartment, stumbling down the stairs and out the door of our building.

I looked back at his apartment. Mini-Baker had come completely down the stairs. I nodded at her, and she made her way over to her mom, who had started crying again. Mini-Baker put her arm around her, cautiously.

"Are you okay, Mrs. Baker?" I asked.

The sobbing woman nodded and leaned into the girl's one-armed hug.

"I'm going to go now. If he comes back, you need to call someone. Save yourself a hospital trip."

"He's not bad man," she told me through her tears and broken English, but she didn't sound convinced of that herself. "He lost his job. He thinks a man who no work is no man at all, and nobody will hire him, so he drinks. Not his fault."

I might not know much, but I know how to love somebody. I also know that love can make a person blind. That's why I tend to avoid it nowadays. That said, I'd never been in quite the same situation as Mrs. Baker, who stood there looking every bit as addled as Bianca had looked during class the night before. What the hell did I know? I couldn't think of anything to say, so I finally settled on, "It's not your fault," before striding back across the hall to my own apartment.

I can't save everyone, but maybe I'd made a difference for Mrs. Baker.

Five minutes later, I hopped in my car and drove toward the Blue Nile. I had a job to do.

Chapter 13

That Old Black Magic

The Blue Nile is not what one would call "classy." It is, however, a favorite amongst the local college kids, and as a former college kid, I admit that I'd been there before. They had musical variety, as do most venues in New Orleans, and that night, they had a popular DJ. People wanted to dance.

For all its neon lights and promises of purple haze, the bar/nightclub is set up pretty traditionally. When you walk in, there is a bar on the right with every sort of alcoholic beverage you could imagine, and some you've never heard of. On your left are the stairs, one staircase leading up to the balcony that encircles the room and the other leading down to the bathrooms and a lounge. There are a few round tables lined up near the walls since New Orleans cuisine is served all night long, but the giant dance floor takes up most of the space. That night, the popular DJ had set up on the stage on the far wall from the entrance, and since it was already midnight when I got there because parking sucked; everyone was already dancing and twerking and moving to the beat of whatever song he was mixing.

Typically, this was not my scene, but the way my day had gone, I needed a distraction. Turns out sweating, gyrating bodies, and loud music are great diversions. I danced for a while, keeping an eye out for my mark the entire time.

Before I could locate the most obvious suspect in this case, however, I was distracted by a familiar face—the face of Richard Baxter, the most famous man in New Orleans. He was rich, handsome, and one of the most philanthropic philanthropists in the United States, if not the world. Due to the massive investments he'd made after Hurricane Katrina, he also owned the majority of the New Orleans nightlife establishments, including the Blue Nile. I'm going to guess this was why he was here, sitting in the VIP lounge on the upper level, looking over the dance floor like the lion king looking over the pride lands.

He took a sip from his glass and continued looking at the dance floor where I was doing my own embarrassing version of dancing. I have rhythm, but I'm all knees and elbows, so I look more like the Scarecrow from *The Wizard of Oz* than I do Beyoncé.

For a moment, I thought he was looking directly at me. Then he smiled, nodded his head, and lifted his glass in my direction. I lifted my glass of tonic water with a grin and smiled back. Damn, he had a nice smile, and with those ice-blue eyes, it was like he was staring into my soul. He was being friendly, but I was pretty sure he was the devil. Philanthropist or not, nobody with a soul gets as rich as Richard Baxter.

With great reluctance, I turned away from him and began looking for my mark once more. I had to save the day; then, I would flirt with the billionaire.

Finally, after an hour of bad dancing, I saw the suspect at the bar, trying and failing to chat up an attractive young woman. It was Chris Bryce, Regina Doyle's thespian friend.

"I told you," I heard the woman he was harassing shout over the music, "I'm not interested." She was edging away from the bar, but the guy was either too drunk to take a hint or too arrogant—I was hoping for too drunk—and reached out to grab her.

I stepped between them, locking eyes with him. "That's too bad for you," I said, loud enough for the young woman to hear. "He looks damn interesting to me."

The woman escaped with a bit of a huff as Bryce slid his eyes up and down my tight little body. I'm short, I'm fit, and I own it.

"Can I buy you a drink?" he asked me.

"I've already had a few..." I spoke in the ditziest sorority-girl voice I could muster, "but I guess one more won't hurt."

He motioned me closer, and I cozied up next to him. The crowd at the bar didn't give me much of a choice in that matter. "Pick your poison," he told me.

"I'll have a dirty martini with extra olives," I instructed.

He made the order and offered up some random chit-chat while we waited for the bartender to get to my drink. I told him I was a marketing major at Tulane University in New Orleans. He told me he was an engineering major, so we were both liars.

When my martini finally came, I took out an olive and placed it suggestively in my mouth, chewing slowly and swallowing only when I knew he was hooked. "Martinis are so good, but do you know where I could get anything *stronger*?"

"Now, why would I know that?" he asked with a smirk.

"You seem like a strong guy. Strong guys like strong things."

He smiled. "My car's in the back if you care to take a look at my stock."

I cocked an eyebrow. "You got stock?"

"Yeah," he said with a predatory gleam in his dark eyes, "and I'm sure we can find something to your liking."

I started to move away from the bar and head out to the Bourbon Street parking lot, where I knew he'd parked his car.

Ladies, *never* do this. I don't care how hot the guy is or what malarkey he tries to feed you; don't leave the bar with some stranger. This has been a Public Service Announcement.

Before we made it outside, Bryce pulled me toward him, bringing his face right next to mine.

"I haven't had good blow in weeks," I said. "How much?"

He placed the palm of one hand on the nape of my neck and the other firmly on my butt, then leaned forward to the point that our faces were inches apart and whispered, "Blow for blow." Damn commerce.

I leaned in and kissed him while reaching into my handbag to make sure I had my taser. I was so ready to make that creep piss all over himself, but I had every intention of getting those drugs first. If I didn't, it would all have been a wasted night.

That's when I heard it. "P.I. Harlem?" Someone called to me from the other side of the bar.

Crap. Maybe Chris hadn't heard.

Chris hadn't stopped shoving his tongue down my throat, so I was getting hopeful. That's when I felt a hand on my shoulder and turned my head just enough to see Officer Chandler standing there with that goofy grin on his face. "It *is* you, investigator!" he shouted.

"Investigator?" Chris repeated, loosening the grip he'd had on my waist.

"I'm working as a P.I. to pay for school," I told Chris hastily. "I do stuff like prove insurance fraud or stalk cheating spouses. You're not trying to cheat your insurance, are you?" I leaned into him, choosing my words carefully to imply that his cheating on his spouse would not be an issue. He seemed to be falling for the bad girl act, too, but Officer Michael Chandler couldn't catch a hint.

"Don't be so modest, P.I. Harlem," Chandler said. "She's been working on this murder case with our lead detective." Chris's grip loosened, and I felt him begin to shift away from me. "The captain is almost sure she's pegged the murderer, but P.I. Harlem and Detective Burke are skeptical." Chris completely released me, even as I gripped his shirt tighter. "She's actively investigating another suspect. She even said she'd be looking into it to...tonight." Chandler looked from me to Chris, then back again. His idiocy must have finally sunk into his slow-moving brain.

Chris removed my hands and took a full step backward. "You know, you two probably got a lot of catching up to do, so I'm gonna get going."

And just like that, all my hours of shaving and intricate makeup application walked across the dance floor and disappeared with my prime suspect. I turned and glared at Chandler, and the man-child shrank under the look.

"S-sorry," he said. "I guess I owe you a drink?"

"Oh," I said with an irritated laugh, "you *definitely* owe me *several* drinks, but considering I don't drink while on a case, that will have to wait. In fact, you may have this." I picked up the martini Chris had bought me from the counter and handed it to Chandler—it was all I could do not to splash it in his face--and walked away from my wasted evening.

Chapter 14

Good Morning, Heartache

The first thing I thought when I walked in from my night of debauchery was, why is there a kid on my couch? I hadn't been drinking. I hadn't taken any drugs. I had gone without sleep for way longer than eight hours enough times to know that couldn't affect me; therefore, this definitely was not a hallucination. So, why was a kid on my couch?

The fact all my doors were locked when I came in was also a matter of concern. Kid obviously had some mad lock-picking skills.

On closer inspection, I realized this was my noisy neighbor's kid—the one with the big brown puppy eyes who liked smoking out in the courtyard. She was lying stretched out on her back, one foot dangling off the edge and one hand draped across her young face. My Auburn University blanket was draped over most of her young body, and Louis had curled up to nap on her chest—useless ferret couldn't even defend the apartment when I was away.

I meandered a bit closer to the couch, thinking I'd nudge her awake with the toe of my dancing shoe, but the clacking noise the shoes made when I walked woke her instead. She shot up from her reclined position, sending Louis flying to the other end of the couch, where he landed on his feet, chittered angrily at the girl, then skittered over to me and climbed up onto my shoulders as he continued to berate her. The girl sat ramrod straight as her eyes immediately found mine.

I smiled in a way that I hoped was reassuring rather than creepy. "Hey, kid," I drawled. "What's up?"

She didn't respond; just stared at me with her round, surprised eyes.

"You, um, take a wrong turn somewhere?" I asked, trying to sound casual. "Because, well, you're actually in my apartment, not yours. Your place is that way." I pointed in the general direction of her home. Louis chittered at her again, and I was fairly sure that she'd have been offended if she could speak ferret.

That seemed to snap the girl out of it. She quickly stumbled to her feet, grabbing my orange and blue throw blanket that she had been covered up with and trying her best to fold it. "I'm so sorry," she muttered, her skin turning sepia as she blushed. "You weren't here."

"No," I admitted, "I was not here. I got a job with a crazy schedule that leaves me pretty sleep-deprived, which is probably why I'm explaining myself to the person who broke into my home and crashed on my sofa." Louis hissed at her from my shoulder, and I stroked him behind his fuzzy little ears to calm him.

Her blush turned darker as she fumbled with the blanket. "I'm sorry. I—they were fighting, and I—I needed a place to sleep…"

"Wait, the waste of space next door was causing a ruckus again after I'd just warned him?"

"I wasn't the only one to notice you weren't home," she told me, but her tone did not sound accusatory.

"Ah. Gotcha." I pulled Louis down from my shoulders and into my arms, cradling him like the fuzzy little baby he was and running my fingers up and down his back.

There was an awkward silence as the girl finished folding the blanket and laid it across the back of the couch. I noticed she was looking at everything around my apartment except me. Geez, the kid wouldn't even make eye contact.

"Sorry I called your dad a waste of space." I realized that might have been a mistake.

She looked at me then, and if looks could kill, I'd be dead. "He's *not* my dad," she hissed.

"Okay, cool. So, we agree he's a waste."

She nodded, the fire in her eyes dwindling.

After another awkward pause, I continued. "Look, kid, um—"

"It's Reese," she cut me off.

"Huh?"

"My name. It's Reese Kelley."

"Oh." Yeah, I probably should have asked. Heck, the kid had been living next door long enough that I probably should have known her name already. "Well, Reese, it's probably not a good idea for you to crash here. I mean, people get weird about kids having slumber parties with grown-ups. It looks kinda...funny."

"That's why I waited 'til you weren't home," she explained.

"I don't feel like that helps. I mean, what if I'd brought some strange man home?"

She raised her eyebrows in a way that screamed skepticism. "You've literally never done that."

"First time for everything," I said. Getting a little defensive, I turned my back on her and trudged toward the kitchen counter with Louis in my arms. "The point is," I kept my back to her, reaching up and into the cabinet where I kept Louis's food, "you could get me in a lot of trouble." I pulled out the can of ferret food and turned back to the teenager.

"I know," she murmured, and she seemed legitimately sorry. "Something like this could cost you your badge."

"Yeah ... about that," I mumbled, taking Louis over to his cage and depositing him in through the door. "Not my badge. I just used that to freak out your not-dad."

"Isn't that illegal?"

"Yes," I admitted, dumping the ferret food into Louis's bowl and slipping it to him through the bars. "And that's another reason you shouldn't come around. I'm not a good role model."

"You stole a cop's badge just to freak out your neighbor?"

That stumped me so much that I nearly dropped Louis's food bowl before I finally secured it in his cage. "It's more complicated than that," I gave the best explanation I could, even though I knew it was weak as hell. "I'm a private investigator."

"I know. You told me that yesterday."

"Right." I continued, "Anyway, sometimes it's a lot easier to get people to answer questions when you're holding that hideous paperweight known as a New Orleans police badge."

"So, you use it to interrogate people?"

"I plan to, yes. If Burke doesn't realize I borrowed it before I get the chance."

"Borrowed it or swiped it?"

"Semantics." I shrugged. "Again, this is why you should not hang around me. I'm bound to be a bad influence."

She snorted a laugh, and I think it was the first time I'd ever seen her smile. "Well, thanks for trying to put Hank in his place. Most people would've just stayed out of it."

So, the waste of space had a name. I didn't know what to say except, "Your mom shouldn't put up with that."

"She's not my mom," Reese said. "I'm a foster kid."

Oh. Well, that explained a lot, like the fact that she looked and acted *nothing* like the two adults she was living with. Looking at her then, I wondered how I'd missed the signs before. Her clothes were worn, and her jeans were about an inch too short. She didn't seem to own a single thing that was new. Suddenly, I felt really crummy about the type of neighbor I'd been, but even more than that, I felt pissed.

"Where the hell's your social worker?" I asked.

"Look, please don't say anything. The Bakers aren't awesome, but they're not the worst I've had. Besides, I'm fourteen, so I've only got four more years in the system before I'm free. I just started high school, and it doesn't completely suck, so will you please just not say anything?"

I stared at the kid for a moment. What else could I do? She seemed utterly terrified. She also seemed like the type who'd been through hell. I couldn't make things worse for her. At least, I didn't want to.

I let out a sigh before asking, "Has he ever hit you?"

"No."

"What about ... other stuff."

"No! Nothing like that."

"Honest?"

"Honest. He just gets drunk and goes after Rose. When he's sober, he's actually pretty all right, and Rose is great."

"If anything changes, you tell me. Got it? "

"I got it."

I looked her in the eyes, and she kept eye contact. That usually means nothing, but I wanted to trust her.

"Do you want some breakfast or something?" I asked. "I don't know what I have. "

"You got the stuff to make omelets. I can make them for you—for both of us—if you want," Reese offered, and honestly, even without considering it, I knew she had to be a better cook than me.

"Sure, kid."

She immediately got to work, going after ingredients in my cabinets that I didn't even know were there. Clearly, the kid had made herself at home. She made such a noise getting out the pots and pans that Louis, having finished his breakfast, launched himself out of his cage and into my arms, chittering and putting his little paws over his ears.

I was standing there, Louis in my arms, marveling at my strange guest, when I heard a repetitive buzzing indicating someone was at the gate. I went over, pressed the button and gave my customary greeting: "Chase Harlem, Private Investigator."

"Chase!" Burke's voice called from the speaker. Crap. His arrival could only mean one thing. I considered ignoring him, crawling out my apartment window, and making a break for it, but I figured I should be a better example to the juvenile cracking eggs into a frying pan I didn't know I owned.

Therefore, I reluctantly buzzed him through the gate before opening my doors with my biggest smile. "Good morning, Burke! Happy Friday!" I greeted him as he stormed across the courtyard and up to my porch section.

Burke glowered at me and held out his hand. "Give it back, now," he demanded.

I thought about playing dumb, but then he turned up the glower. I deflated and stepped away from the door. "C'mon," I said. "It's on my desk."

Burke followed me into the two-room apartment, shutting the doors behind him. "Of all the dumbass things you could do, Chase," he preached as he followed me over to my tiny office area. "You do know that impersonating a cop is a felony, right? I mean, what the fu—" He stopped talking before the profanity could slip out.

Wondering what on earth could keep Burke from non-stop screaming and cursing, I turned toward him. He was staring at Reese like she was a purple unicorn dancing the hula.

"Chase, what is a child doing in your kitchen?" Burke asked.

"Looks like she's fixing me breakfast," I told him.

Reese looked up from the skillet and waved at Burke. "I'm Reese," she said. "You must be the cop she stole the badge from. Are you here to arrest her?"

Burke let out a short laugh and shook his head. "Wouldn't do me any good," he said. "But it would make my boss happy."

"Charges would never stick," I said, handing him his badge before depositing a marginally less fussy Louis back into his cage and shutting the door. "I know a guy in the D.A.'s office who owes me a favor."

"Do you want an omelet?" Reese asked Burke, sliding a finished one onto a plate. "We have tomatoes, mushrooms, bacon, and cheese."

"We do?" I asked.

Reese snickered and brought me a fork and a plate full of omelets. I took it and plopped down on my couch.

"Sure," Burke said, smothering a laugh at my expense. "No mushrooms in mine, though."

"Sure thing," Reese assured him.

"Thanks, Reese," Burke continued. "Maybe over breakfast, Chase will tell me who killed Eli Goldman."

"Well, if the Chihuahua processed the blow I got for her—Oh wait, I did *not* get that bag of cocaine because of your stupid sidekick."

Burke raised an eyebrow, and it took him only a second to connect the dots. "Chandler?" he asked.

"I had that Bryce kid eating out of my mouth *and* grabbing my booty—"

"Nasty," Burke said, reminding me to keep it G-rated.

I rolled my eyes. "He was itching to sell me some blow," I explained, "when your sidekick showed up and completely blew my cover."

"Chandler is not my 'sidekick,'" Burke said. "He's just the department idiot."

"Of course he is," I groaned.

"You sure Bryce was selling?"

"He told me he was, but there's always a chance he was just being a creep and wanted to get me out to his car." I then turned to Reese and said, "Never follow a guy to his car without a taser."

Reese looked up at me from the omelet she was making. "I don't—um—I don't have a taser?"

"I'll give you mine."

"Chase," Burke grumbled.

"What? Kid needs a taser." I dug into the omelet, relishing my first bite of cheesy goodness. "Shit, this is good!"

"Chase!" Burke reprimanded me.

"What? It was a compliment, and I'm sure she's heard it before."

Reese, for her part, didn't respond. She just continued working on Burke's breakfast.

Burke sat down beside me. "You really think this Bryce kid has something to do with it?"

I tried to ignore him and continue enjoying my omelet, but he shifted closer to me on the couch. He stared at me with his face inches away because he knew I hated that. Finally, his awkward staring became too much. "Look, I have no hard evidence. There's no point in making assumptions without evidence."

"So..." Burke started speaking, and I knew what he was going to say before he could finish the statement, "no profile, then?"

I rolled my eyes. People just weren't letting up on the whole profiling thing, and after the freezer incident, I did not want to think about my former occupation. So, I did the most mature thing I could think of—I turned my back and commenced ignoring him.

Burke sighed in frustration. "You really don't think there is any possible way that Lackey is Gold's killer?"

"I think you were right when you said Lackey'd been given everything," I told him. "Besides, he legitimately cared about Reggie, and whoever killed Gold probably had something to do with Reggie's death, too." I shoved another bite of egg into my mouth and waited for Burke to speak.

He didn't. He simply stared at me.

"You okay?" I asked.

"Just in shock," he explained. "You said I was right about something."

"Oh, ha-ha. You're such a comedian." I made sure to coat my voice in sarcasm.

"Your omelet is ready." Reese shuffled over to the living room area with two plates, handing the one on her left to Burke. He took it gratefully, and since there was nowhere else to sit in my tiny living room, Reese settled for lounging on the fold-out chair next to my couch and dug into her omelet. I wondered if I would have any food left in the kitchen when the kid left, but then I remembered that I hadn't even known about the food I did have and let it go.

Reese looked around my messy apartment. "Is your coffee table made out of concrete blocks and an old door?"

"I'm up-cycling," I told her. "They do it on HGTV all the time."

"You literally just laid a door on top of four concrete blocks," she said, wrinkling her lip.

"I took off the doorknob," I pointed out.

Burke chimed in, "It does look pretty unfinished."

"Makes the place look like a junkyard," Reese noted.

"You know, considering y'all are eating my food, you really shouldn't diss my decor."

"The kid made the food," Burke reminded me.

"Yeah, well, I bought it." I took the last bite of my omelet and chewed slowly, savoring the flavors.

"I could always go undercover for you," Reese volunteered. "I mean, since your cover was blown."

I looked her up and down, considered it for a moment, then shook my head. "That'd never work. You can't pass for a college kid."

"Also, it'd be too dangerous. We'd never put a child at risk just to solve a case," Burke, always the adult in the room, added.

"Also, you look like a fetus," I, always the antagonist in the room, added. "So, it would never work."

Reese argued, "I could pass for nineteen."

"You could pass for twelve," I quipped.

"What Chase is tryin' to say," Burke tried to amend, "is that we appreciate the help, kid, but it just won't work."

"Way to be diplomatic," I mumbled to him. Then I turned my attention to her. "Don't you have somewhere to be?"

She sighed, taking her now empty plate to the sink. I could hear her rinsing it out and placing it in my drainer. "Fine," she called out to me. "I'm going to the park. Let me know if you change your mind." In true teenage fashion, she slammed the door on her way out. Hey, at least she washed her plate and, you know, made me breakfast.

Burke was looking at me with eyebrows lowered, his mouth in a tight line—the Burke judgement stare. I could feel it.

"So," I groused, trying to cut the tension, "do you wanna go interview pothead Artie from The Willow? You know, the guy Corbin said was sketchy?"

Burke finished his omelet with one last, huge bite. "He didn't say Artie was 'sketchy.' He said he smoked pot."

"It's a gateway drug. He could be our drug dealer, and therefore, he could be our killer." I didn't actually believe the nonsense coming out of my mouth. After all, I was pretty sure I had my suspect, but I had to keep my options open. If I didn't explore every option and tie up every loose end, the wrong person might end up behind bars, which is the one thing I was hired to prevent.

Burke rolled his eyes. "Chase, the powers that be want this case closed," he told me gently. "I had my meeting with Captain Morris this morning. She's determined that Lackey is our guy."

I slapped my palms over my eyes and groaned.

Burke continued, "*And* since you so helpfully reminded Lackey not to talk without a lawyer, he ain't talkin', and neither Morris nor the DA want you anywhere near this case."

I lowered my hands from my face and asked, "Does this mean I'm not allowed to ride along?"

"You were never technically allowed to ride along; I just have a tendency to do what I want."

Honestly, I couldn't tell if Burke was sincerely trying to break off our unofficial partnership or not, and I was too scared to ask for clarification, so I just gave him the saddest, most dejected look I could manage.

He stood up from the couch, clearing his throat and glancing at his watch. "I'd planned to talk to Artie today, actually," he told me. "Right now looks like a good time for me. Your wheels work, right?"

He was extending an olive branch, and I should have just taken him up on it. However, I'd gone far too long without sleep, so I asked, "Can you give me about three hours? I haven't slept." Now that my stomach was full, my eyes were getting heavy, and I seriously contemplated falling asleep on my lumpy couch.

He laughed at my pain, then checked his watch. "It's just now 5:20 a.m., so I'll head over to Artie's apartment around noon. That should give you enough time to wash the bar stench off and make yourself up like an adult."

"I am an adult."

"Sure you are."

Burke dropped his plate into the sink before making his exit, locking the door behind him with the key I didn't remember giving him. I forced myself to get off the couch and put my own plate in the sink. Insomnia was not going to get in my way this time. I stumbled upstairs to my bedroom, kicking my stupid dancing shoes off as I went, and flopped face-first onto the mattress. I don't even remember my head landing on the pillow, but I'm pretty sure that's what happened.

Chapter 15

Smooth Criminal

I woke up gasping for air, my chest so tight that I could feel my heart crashing into my ribs like it'd break free at any moment. The scars littering my torso felt like they were on fire, and I took a deep breath and held it. The sun shone through my bedroom window, and Louis worriedly chittered at me from his spot on my pillow, both instant reminders that I was not trapped in a frozen box of darkness and death while an innocent man hung dead in a prison cell, even if my dreams were trying to convince me otherwise. I let out my breath as slowly as possible.

After nearly an hour of breathing exercises and cuddling a clingy ferret, I was finally calm enough to drag myself out of bed. I took a shower so hot that my skin turned pink, before getting dressed and ready to drive to the address Burke had texted me.

However, before I had to leave to meet Burke, I noticed that an important client had called me a few times. I dropped down on my couch before calling Father Nolan back. He answered on the first ring.

"P.I. Harlem?" I could hear the strain in his voice.

"Sorry I missed your call, Father. I had a late night," I explained.

"I guess you've heard the news?"

"Yes," I said. "I know that the police arrested your son, and I'm sorry I didn't call to inform you myself. I was chasing a lead that I had hoped would clear him."

I could hear Father Nolan sigh over the phone, and it really bothered me that I couldn't get a read on his reaction. "P.I. Harlem," he said, "please be honest with me. How bad is it?"

"I wouldn't lie to a client, sir," I assured him. "It's bad. The police found the murder weapon in his truck and there's some incriminating footage online."

"I've seen that, yes." I heard what could have been a sigh or a sob from his end of the phone, and I found myself completely unable to fathom what I should say to a father whose son was being framed for murder. After an awkward pause, he asked, "Do you think it's possible that my son did this?"

"Father, if I thought your son was a murderer, I'd have already dropped the case. That's the great thing about being my own boss."

Father Nolan let out a watery laugh, and I hoped it meant that I'd said the right thing.

"I hope you're right," he said.

"Keep the faith, Father," I reminded him. "It'll all work out."

"Thank you."

"Now, I'm about to drive out to meet a detective and hopefully track down another suspect," I told him. "I'll do my best to keep you posted."

I hung up the phone and went to meet Burke.

Of course, Burke made it to Artie's apartment complex at the exact time he had planned, because punctuality is important to men like Burke. I admit that I will occasionally drag my feet when meeting up with him just to get on his nerves, but considering he was risking his good standing with his boss, if not his job, just so I could do the interview with him, I honestly tried to get there on time. Also, after my nightmare, I was too tired to be intentionally antagonistic. Seriously, I was only three minutes late, but I could tell he was pissed about it when I drove up to the Oak Street address he'd sent me, because he was standing outside his car smoking a cigarette.

I got out of my Isuzu and ambled over to him, leaning on the car beside him and trying not to gag at the mere smell of cigarette smoke.

"Hi there," I greeted him, resisting the urge to steal the cigarette and stamp it out like a true friend. "Ready for an adventure?"

Burke released a puff of smoke between his lips before informing me, "You're late."

"I had to make a pit stop to the little detective's room, if you know what I mean."

"You take an extra spin around the block to leave me waiting? Pass by to see me waiting in my car?"

Usually, that is exactly what I would have done, and he would have been absolutely right. That's why we work so well together: we're both such good sleuths. "I have no idea what you're talking about. That sounds stalkerish, and I only stalk people when I'm getting paid to stalk people." I pulled out my phone and started sifting through social media, only for Burke to reach over, grab my phone, and stuff it into his pocket. "Rude," I accused him.

He ignored me. Burke was notorious for giving me the silent treatment whenever I frustrated him, and I knew I had it coming after the whole badge-stealing incident. It made me wonder why I did it, but then I remembered it was fun to see exactly how much I could get away with.

After approximately four minutes of silence and disgusting gray smoke, he asked, "You get any sleep?"

My minimalist makeup routine must have failed me because he had clearly spotted the dark circles under my eyes. Making a mental note to buy some concealer the next time I went shopping, I told him, "I'll sleep when I'm dead."

Even though I didn't say it, Burke knew exactly what was going on, and bless him, he changed the subject. "How's your kid?" he asked.

"My kid? You mean Reese?" I asked, but the answer was obvious. "She's cool, I guess. I mean, as cool as a kid who breaks into my apartment and makes me breakfast can be."

Burke smirked. "She's letting herself get attached."

"Excuse me?"

"Foster kids usually put up a lot of walls. You've heard the old saying that you can't always get what you want, haven't you? Well, kids like Reese get used to *never* getting what they want, so they don't form attachments."

That's right, folks. Matt Burke just slammed down some psycho-analysis on me about my next-door neighbor but pay attention because that was not the most surprising part of his little speech.

"How did you know she's a foster kid?" I was almost afraid to ask.

He raised an eyebrow and nearly grinned. "Did I catch on to something the amazing Chase Harlem missed?" He laughed with one annoying little "ha."

I rolled my eyes and may have even pouted a little—just a little.

"It's fine, Chase," he assured me. "When it comes to foster kids, sometimes it takes one to know one."

"You were a foster kid?" This day was already full of surprises.

Burke shrugged. "Not for long. It was right after my ma died. The state was having trouble tracking down my uncle, so I had to live with a foster family for a couple of weeks."

What Burke didn't mention was that the state had to look for his uncle because his deadbeat dad refused to raise him. When I said that Burke is *like* one of those noir detectives with a dark past, I meant that Burke is a noir detective with a dark past—possibly the darkest. My childhood might have had moments of pure suck, but Burke's childhood made mine look like pure *heaven*. What's worse, I have a feeling that I don't know half of it.

I was quiet, letting my mind drift back to that moment with Reese Kelley when I suggested telling her social worker about Hank. She was terrified. She was living by the idea that the monster you know is better than the monster you don't. I was finally beginning to understand her fear—at least on a logical level.

Stamping out his cigarette, Burke said, "Don't let that kid down, Chase. When she pushes you away, don't leave."

"I'm not anything to her."

Burke shook his head. "Maybe not now, but you could be."

I thought about that statement.

At least, I would have had the next words out of Burke's mouth not been a commentary on my Converse and comfortable clothes. "By the way," he said, "what happened to that outfit you wore earlier? You know, the baby onesie."

"Um, it's called a romper, and it did not match my Chucks as well as I would have liked."

Burke chuckled.

We walked to the apartment complex across the street from where we'd parked. Calling it "run-down" would be a massive understatement. It was downright unsettling. An edifice of cracked stucco standing at two stories with nearly every other window broken. There was what looked like mold on the walls, and the rain gutters were falling off. We walked up the rickety iron steps to room 203, where Pothead Artie lived. I was trying to cover my nose and ignore the stench of rotten food, old garbage, backed-up sewage, and—you guessed it—marijuana. Burke, of course, walked right up to the door as if it were any other apartment and knocked loudly.

We stood there for a good five minutes before the door finally swung open. "Arthur Lillard," Burke addressed the obviously baked dude at the door and showed him his badge, "we have a few questions for you."

Pothead Artie took one look at the badge before slamming the door shut in our faces. We could hear him shouting to someone else in the apartment.

I pulled the pint-sized handgun out of my ankle holster and looked at Burke. "That probable cause for you to enter?"

"Seems probable to me." Burke drew his own sidearm. "You comin'?"

"I'll go 'round the back. You know, where he's probably escaping out a window or something right now." I scampered off just as Burke kicked in the front door. I heard it splinter into toothpicks behind me.

I jumped down the rusted iron stairs and ducked down and through a cramped open-air corridor between two apartments. Sure enough, Artie was climbing out the window and onto a large oak tree branch nearby. He hadn't spotted me running toward him, so I skidded to a halt and hid, leaning back against the nasty stucco wall of the apartment complex, careful to avoid the chewed bubblegum serving as wall art, to wait for him to drop down.

As soon as his feet hit the dirt, I aimed my gun and cleared my throat. Artie turned around, panicked, and fell on his butt in some mixed-up effort to get away from me. On the bright side, he held his hands up in the air, palms facing me.

"D-don't shoot, lady," he stammered.

Lady? I've been called many things in my life, but rarely "lady." This guy was clearly an idiot.

"Lie flat on the ground and put your hands behind your back," I told him.

Despite the gun in my hand, he did not obey my orders. He hopped up from the ground and took off—scuttling across the street and between two shotgun houses, one blue and one gray. I let out a sigh before chasing after him, taking what would have been a much longer route around the gray house had I not been a much faster runner. I caught a glimpse of Artie opening a gate into the backyard of the blue house, so I picked up speed. I jumped over another backyard fence, planning to cut him off. However, I then saw a trampoline that looked way more fun.

I spotted Artie running toward the back of an adjacent backyard—too busy running to notice me bouncing on a trampoline—and aimed my body toward him before taking a running leap. I used the momentum from the trampoline to launch myself over the fence and right on top of Artie, slamming into him with a satisfying *thump*.

He groaned under my weight, and I quickly cuffed him with the spare handcuffs I'd procured—stolen—from Burke months before.

"On your feet," I ordered, leading him by the elbow back to the apartment complex.

"Hey, Burke!" I shouted up to the open door of room 203.

Burke stepped out of the apartment, shoving another cuffed man out in front of him. Burke looked perturbed, and I had the sinking suspicion that this entire afternoon would do nothing to help us find the murderer and a lot to make Burke fill out extra paperwork.

"Got the guy," I told him.

"He ain't our guy!" Burke yelled, "But he does have more weed growing in here than the entire state of Colorado."

"Hey now, I'm a businessman," Artie said to me.

"And from the smell of him, he's been sampling his own product," I informed Burke, turning my nose up.

"Let's get these boys in the car, and I'll book it."

I did what he asked before getting back into my Isuzu and banging my head against the steering wheel. It was obvious that we'd hit a dead end. Even though Artie was technically a drug dealer, he wasn't selling the hard drugs Reggie had been buying. Also, he wasn't trying to hide what his "legitimate business" actually was, so he would have no motive to kill Goldman and keep it quiet.

Chris Bryce, on the other hand, had a scholarship to defend and a dream of making costumes on Broadway, at least according to his Facebook profile, so as far as I was concerned, he was still the prime suspect. Of course, I had no evidence that it was Chris, making Lackey look super-guilty, and while Burke might give me the benefit of the doubt, it was his job to follow the evidence.

I was back to square one, and man did it suck.

Chapter 16

I Cried for You

I waited at Burke's desk for him to book Artie. As much as I couldn't stand his boss, I couldn't stand the smell of the parking garage more. Besides, maybe if I were nice enough, he'd take me to talk to Bryce again. I had the feeling if we just leaned on the guy enough, he'd break. By the time he finished doing the boring part of police work, I was leaning back in his chair with my feet on the desk, polishing off a cup of coffee.

"Get outta my chair," he growled.

"I made you coffee," I said, holding the cup up to him and pointedly not moving. "You took too long, though, so I drank it."

He raised an eyebrow, and I sensed my coming doom. I scooted out of the chair just as my phone started ringing. Fishing it out of my pocket, I was surprised to find Bianca's name on the screen. I answered too quickly, turning my back to Burke. "This is Chase."

I could hear Bianca hiccupping on the line, breaths short, fast, and scared.

"Bianca, can you hear me?"

"Ch-Chase?" Her voice cracked like a branch in the wilderness, echoing its importance through the trees.

I kept my voice as low and level as I could. "What's wrong, Bianca? What do you need?"

"You were *right*." Bianca sobbed.

"Where are you right now? I'll come get you."

"I'm so scared."

"Is Tarant still in the apartment?"

"Y-yes ... I'm in the bathroom."

"I'm on my way." I grabbed my jacket and started toward the door, Burke right behind me. I wasn't sure how much he'd heard, but his wife had been with me the first time I'd moved Bianca out of Tarant's apartment.

"Please hurry."

"Can you stay on the phone with me?"

"I don't know—"

I heard a male voice call out from somewhere in the background. "What was that?"

"He wants me out of the bathroom." Her voice was shaking more now, like she was the New Orleans levees holding back a wall of tears. "Says he gotta use it."

We'd made it into the parking garage, and Burke was motioning me toward his car. No way I was riding with him. I got into my Isuzu, knowing he'd follow.

"Try to keep the phone on and get out of the apartment while he's in the restroom. I'm in my car."

I pulled out of the parking garage and headed toward her apartment complex. It was on Pine Street, which was not too far from the precinct, but traffic was never my friend. I heard shuffling followed by a muted shout on the phone. "Bianca?"

"Hold on." There was more shuffling, and the line went dead. I borrowed one of Burke's swear words and stepped on the accelerator, even if it meant leaving Burke in my dust.

I somehow made it to Bianca's apartment building in record time, without running over a single cyclist or tourist. Bianca was standing out on the grass in front of the building. I pulled onto the sidewalk in front of the run-down brick structure and stepped out of my vehicle. As I did, a tall, lanky man I recognized from my one encounter with Tarant came out from the door behind Bianca.

"The hell you doin'?!" he screamed at her. "Get in here!"

Bianca, just a few feet away from him in the grass, stumbled further away, and I took the opportunity to run the short distance between us and plant myself between Bianca and Tarant.

"Bianca, let's go," I said, putting my hand on her shoulder but keeping my eyes on Tarant.

His dark skin grew three shades deeper at my intrusion, and he screamed, "What's *this* bitch doin' here?!"

"Watch your mouth," I told him. "We ain't on your property, and you better behave."

Tarant stomped out his door and down the two brick stairs, crossing the yard to me, screaming obscenities the entire time. I should have been scared, but honestly, I was itchin' for a fight. I took my hand off Bianca's shoulder and turned to face Tarant just as he grabbed me by the arm and screamed insults in my face. His grip was tight, and his face was purple.

When he stopped screaming to breathe, I said, "You need to get your hand off me."

"You don't come here and tell me what to do!" He used more colorful language.

"Again, we're not on your property, and you're hurting my arm."

"Please, Tarant!" Bianca shouted from behind me.

Tarant's grip only tightened on my right arm, and he shook me, which I took offense to. My mind focused on Tarant, this mini-monster who thought his height and strength put him in charge and that beating a woman was okay.

Somewhere in the background, Burke pulled up in his SUV. I heard him shout out a warning.

"This is your last warning, Tarant." My voice was eerily calm.

He called me a bitch.

I jabbed the flat of my palm into his throat, and his grip loosened. I took advantage of that by grabbing his thumb, now loose around my arm, bending it toward him, and taking one step around him. He cried out as I twisted his arm behind his back and kicked him in the back of the knee. In an instant, he was stomach-first on the ground, and I had my knee in his lower back, his arm twisted. I could tell he was screaming, but all I could hear was the blood rushing in my ears. With just a slight shift to my left, I could pop his left shoulder out of its joint. It'd be hard for him to hit Bianca with his arm in a sling. I applied pressure, but instead of the pop I was expecting to feel, there was a hand on my shoulder. Out of instinct, I grabbed his wrist with my free hand.

"Don't do this, Chase. You fight monsters. Don't become one." His words made me angrier because I knew what he was talking about. He was telling me not to be like *her*.

But then I looked up and saw Bianca cowering behind him. She wasn't scared of Tarant anymore. She was scared of me.

She might as well have thrown a bucket of ice water over my head. I released Tarant and stepped away, the sound coming back at once. Bianca was murmuring, "Please don't, please don't," while Tarant wept.

I faced Burke, and he hesitantly put his hands on my shoulders. "You good."

"You gonna arrest me?" I asked him.

"Me and half the neighborhood saw him grab you; we heard you ask him to let you go. What you did was self-defense."

I nodded and turned to Bianca. She was still standing, frozen where I'd left her. "You ready to go?"

"Sh-should I take him to the hospital?"

Tarant was still lying on the ground, whimpering.

"I didn't break anything. He just needs some ice."

Bianca nodded, but her eyes wouldn't meet mine, and my heart shuttered.

"You wanna grab your stuff?" I asked, feeling like a wall had grown up between us.

Bianca shook her head and crossed her arms over her chest. "I think I'll call my sister."

All I could say was, "Okay," as I turned and walked to my Isuzu, Burke right behind me.

I got into the car without saying a word to him, shoving my key into the ignition. Burke grabbed the door before I could close it in his face and said, "I'll have Maria give her a call. Make sure she gets somewhere safe."

"Thanks," I mumbled.

"Remember, you can't save—"

"I know, I can't save everyone."

Burke grunted. "I was going to say, you can't save someone who don't want to be saved."

I nodded. "Thanks for not letting me ... you know."

"You're better than you think you are, Chase," Burke said, closing my car door. I drove away without another word.

Chapter 17

You're My Thrill

"Hi," I greeted the teenage intruder as I entered my apartment. I had fully intended to go in, grab my running clothes, and jog out all the emotions I was feeling after that encounter with Bianca. That plan didn't work out because Reese Kelley was standing at my stove making a grilled cheese sandwich, Louis lounging listlessly across her shoulders.

"You're back."

"I am," Reese said. "You want a sandwich?"

"Since that's my bread and cheese," I grumbled, "yes, I think I would like a sandwich."

She slid the finished sandwich out of the skillet and onto one of my plates, then grabbed another slice of bread and started buttering it. "You can have that one," she invited me to eat my own food.

"Sure." I picked up the plate and took a small nibble. It was hot, but it was good. Also, she'd used my pepper-jack cheese. "Pepper Jack's a good choice."

"It's how my dad made them," she said, plopping a spoonful of Country Crock into the skillet.

I tore off a small piece of my sandwich and fed it to the ferret, who was still sitting on Reese's shoulder. "You've really made yourself at home here," I said.

"You said I could come over. Do I need to leave?" I considered kicking the kid out, but then I remembered my previous conversation with Burke.

I shook my head. "You're good. Just don't break my lock."

She grinned, putting two slices of my pepper jack cheese between the two slices of bread, and throwing the sandwich into the skillet of melted Country Crock. "I'm too good for that. How'd your interview go?"

I threw my leather purse onto the coffee table before plopping down on the sofa. "Pothead Artie didn't do it," I announced with a sigh. "Trip was a total waste—even if jumping on the trampoline was nostalgic."

"At least you got to spend some time with your boyfriend," she said over the sizzling of the skillet.

"Burke's not my boyfriend," I informed her, trying not to gag at the implication. "He's more like my zany cousin who stops by when he smells food ... or when I, you know, steal his stuff."

"He's a pretty hot cousin for an old guy."

"He is old." He's as old as my older brother, who is ancient at 34. "He's also happily married to a saint of a woman."

"Gotcha," she mumbled, "no hitting on the old guy."

I kept eating, and for a moment, the only noise in my apartment was the sound of margarine and bread sizzling in the skillet.

"So, are you back to thinking that Chris guy did it?" she asked, putting her sandwich on the plate, turning off the stove, and shuffling across the brick floor before sitting down in the fold-out chair nearby. She relinquished a small corner of her sandwich to the ferret on her shoulders before taking a bite herself. I could feel her curious gaze on me.

"How did you...?" I stopped eating and stared at the kid before looking across the room toward my office area. My laptop was sitting open on my desk. I couldn't see the screen from my spot on the couch, but I was pretty sure I had left my web browser open to Chris Bryce's social media. "If you're going to snoop, you should be sneakier."

"It's not snooping when you leave your laptop open for the world to see."

"Not the world," I countered, "just my apartment, which you now seem to be a part of. So, how much snooping did you actually do?"

"I plead the Fifth."

Again, I felt my temper niggling at the back of my neck, but truthfully, I could use an unbiased third party to bounce ideas off of on occasion. I didn't mind too much, and the ferret seemed to trust the kid, so I just shrugged and slouched back on the couch. It wasn't like she was using my computer to hack the Pentagon or anything, and the kid probably didn't have a laptop of her own. "Can't prove anything on Chris," I admitted as I finished my sandwich and tossed my empty plate onto the coffee table in front of me.

"Why can't they just search his apartment?"

"They've gotta have probable cause to get a warrant. Judges are pretty strict about that," I told her.

"Didn't he offer to sell you drugs?"

"I'm not a cop, and Chandler didn't hear anything because he's useless," I told her.

"Couldn't they get a warrant based on your testimony?"

With the Chihuahua in charge? No way. Of course, I wasn't going to tell this teenager about my senseless grudge match with a legal authority figure, so I simply informed her, "It wouldn't matter anyway. With Chandler giving me away at the party last night, there's no way Chris wouldn't have cleared out any evidence by now."

I glanced over at Reese, who was once again sharing a bite of her sandwich with Louis and noted the DVD rack on the wall behind her. "Did you alphabetize my movies?"

"Yeah," she admitted to it as if it were no big deal. "I got bored."

"Don't most teenagers check social media when bored?"

"I can't have any social media accounts." She took a bite of her sandwich, then continued with her mouth still full, "It's part of my foster child status."

"That sucks."

"It's not the worst, but yeah, it sucks." She shrugged before politely returning to the original subject. "So, do you think he's moved the evidence? Where would he move it? Does he got a girlfriend? It's probably the girlfriend."

"Nice try, kid, but you watch too much TV, and in case I haven't made this clear, this case is none of your business, but thanks for playin' and fixing lunch."

"Excuse me, I watch a lot of *true* crime TV and documentaries. The romantic partner is almost always involved in some way."

"That might be a pretty factual statistic, but I don't think it applies here." Man, this kid was kinda smart, and she might be onto something with the whole girlfriend hunch. But I needed more than a theory to go disturbing Burke from his paperwork. I pondered over it in silence for a moment, letting the kid finish her sandwich.

After she was done, she took my plate and walked the absurdly short distance to the sink. She had just started cleaning when she said, "I wanted to thank you for—you know—sending that big guy to intimidate Hank."

I sat upright on the couch and stared at her. "What's that?"

"The guy who came by the apartment earlier with the black hair and Cajun accent—you sent him, right? When you realized Hank was back?"

Okay, so apparently Hank had not stayed away as I warned him to do—I knew that already—and—news flash—Deuce Marlboro had discovered where I lived and decided to handle my little neighbor's dilemma. Now that I thought about it, I did have a vague memory of drinking one too many Jell-O shots last Mardi Gras and having to be escorted home by an only marginally less drunk Deuce. Had he slept on the couch that night? I know I spent the night on the bathroom floor, so maybe he'd slept on the bed. Then again, that would go against his Southern-boy manners.

Anyway, I now had several questions for Mr. Marlboro, but first, "Not that I know what you're talking about, but what exactly did this Cajun man say to Hank?"

Reese laughed and grabbed a couple of Cokes out of the fridge, tossing one to me. She popped open the Coke she'd kept for herself and took a sip between giggles. Then she answered, "He didn't really *say* that much. He just barged into the apartment, said that he was *not* a cop but was there to take out the garbage—like, it was so cool! Then he said that Hank had ninety seconds to get his stuff, hand his wife his key, and get out. Hank did what he said. Before he left, the dude told Rose that Hank could come home when he'd learned to behave himself. It was the coolest thing I've ever seen."

I popped open my Coke and reminded her, "It was pretty cool when I came in and kicked him out."

"Yeah, but this dude was *intimidating*."

"I'm intimidating."

"You're barely over five feet tall."

"I am 5'4", *and* I was wearing heels!" I was borderline offended. Louis must have picked up on that fact because he hopped down from Reese's shoulder and raced across the living room area, landing in my lap with a soft plop.

"But this guy was tall and totally ripped," Reese continued.

"I've got some muscle."

"He had a scar over his right eyebrow that looked like it came from a serious fight, and I think he had prison tattoos on his neck and arms." She described him as if he were some movie star.

"The scar could have been from getting drunk and cracking his head on a table," I told her, but I knew where the scar had come from. Her story was much closer to the truth. However, her tattoo theory was totally wrong. In fact, he would have been pretty upset if he knew that someone thought the super-expensive tattoos he'd bought from some relatively famous tattoo artist, looked like prison tattoos. "And don't ever mention his tattoos," I warned her and proceeded to give Louis a belly rub for his loyalty.

Reese smiled. "So, you *do* know him?"

I choked on the Coke just a little bit. I didn't care if she knew about my connection with Deuce, but I'm a naturally secretive person. Plus, I had no real desire to let the teenager who kept breaking into my apartment know too much about my life. Even if—especially if—it was obvious that she needed a positive female role model in *her* life. As I've said before, I'm not a good role model. If you don't believe me, please note the fact that I live in a run-down, dirty apartment, surviving off pizza and junk food. Also, my friends are a homicide detective and a few sketchy folks who work at a New Orleans bar. I've killed every houseplant I've ever owned, including a cactus, and the only reason I'd managed to keep the ferret alive for the whole three weeks he'd been with me was because he also lived off pizza and junk food.

I cleared my throat and proceeded to ignore her question in the calmest manner I could muster.

"So, is *he* your boyfriend?" she asked.

I spewed my Coke all over my nice coffee table as well as the ferret in my lap. Louis hissed at me as he scrambled up the stairs to hide under my piano and probably piss on my floor in retribution. "No," I answered, hopping up to get napkins from the kitchen. "Not that that's any of your business."

"Hey, you like the bad-boy type. That's nothing to be embarrassed about."

"You sound like a thirty-year-old," I said as I re-entered the living room and wiped up my Coke spill.

"He's hot," she added, ignoring my comment.

"Now you sound like a teenager." I returned to the couch and kicked my feet up on the coffee table. "Anyway, he's just a friend, and I didn't send him."

"Whatever," she said with a shrug. "He got rid of Hank, so he's cool in my book. You can continue secretly dating him."

"I'm glad I have your permission," I grumbled, standing up from my lumpy sofa. "Now, if you don't mind, I think I'll go for a run to clear the fog in my brain." Chasing Artie through multiple backyards had not been enough exercise to deal with this kid.

"And to stop by and see your boyfriend?"

I ignored that question, bounding up the stairs to my bedroom. I quickly changed from my work clothes into my running gear, strapped on my gun, and grabbed my mace. I also managed to lure Louis out from under my bed with whispered promises of beignets. I walked back out to find Reese organizing the canned foods in my cabinets.

"You know, you could watch a movie or something," I told her, placing Louis back into his cage, even though I knew he'd break out within minutes.

"Maybe later. Your place is a mess."

"Thanks. Lock the door when you leave." With that heartfelt goodbye, I walked out.

I did go for a run, but I didn't go to the graveyard. I ran around the block from my apartment to try to calm myself down, but the more I thought about the fact that Deuce Marlboro had tried to take care of my problems without my consent, the more heated I got. What's worse was that those thoughts were destroying my rhythm. I ran around the block once more before crossing the street and heading toward the bar. My back was sweating, and I was feeling pretty disgusting under the Louisiana heat, even in November. The red rage I was entering was not helping any of that, and it was all that stinkin' gambler's fault.

"Deuce Marlboro!" I shouted as I walked into the nearly empty bar. It was almost 3:00 p.m. on a Friday, so people hadn't hit the bars quite yet.

Deuce jumped up from behind the bar and gave me his devil-may-care smirk that would make a weaker woman melt. The white tank top he wore left little to the imagination as he stood wiping shot glasses with a white dish towel.

"Ma chérie," he said, "You don't know how long I been waitin' to hear you shout my name like that." His tone was suggestive, and I couldn't help but roll my eyes.

"Not what I'm here for, but we might revisit it later," I told him. "We need to talk about your habit of threatening my neighbors."

Deuce's eyes widened marginally, and he slung the towel over his muscular shoulder. I strode up to the bar and plopped down on the stool in front of him.

"Care to explain your actions, Mr. Marlboro?"

He leaned forward, placing his elbows on the counter between us and bringing his face close to mine. "You got no idea how long I been waitin' to hear you call me that, too. You sound so... *strict*." He nearly purred the last word, and I have to admit that I had no idea that a man purring could ever be considered sexy. I was wrong.

My anger was beginning to fade slightly, and I'm embarrassed to say that I nearly giggled. However, I managed to keep the giggle from bubbling up and regained my composure. "First of all, you followed me home when I was drunk, and then you retraced your steps and threatened the neighbors. Why?"

"I wanted to help my girl."

When had I become his girl? "How very chivalrous. I can fight my own battles." My mind flashes back to the actual fight I'd been in that day, and I buried it fast.

"Yes. It's what I like 'bout you, chère."

"And for your information, I'd already dealt with my little Hank issue."

"Hank?"

"That's my neighbor's name."

Deuce raised an eyebrow. "An' how'd you deal with Hank, Ma chérie? Tell me you used that strict tone, Ange."

"Actually, I used Detective Burke's badge and told him I was a cop who would arrest him if he didn't stop disturbing the peace. Then I kicked him out of his apartment so he could sober up."

Deuce blinked once before letting out a loud laugh. "Mon ange! You impersonated a po-po. I thought you was a good girl, chère."

"Surprisingly, he's more intimidated by you than he is by a cop version of me."

"Aww," Deuce moaned. He was mocking me. "We all got our strengths, an' you are too much a bebelle to be intimidating."

"Look, I never would have told you about my neighbor if I'd thought you were going to go all vigilante. I can handle my own problems." Another flash of Bianca's terrified face would not make me question this mantra.

"You always do, chère. It's why I jumped at the chance to help you. I'm sorry if I crossed a line." His greenish eyes dropped slightly, and he reminded me of a puppy that'd been chastised—a six-foot-tall puppy with 200 pounds of pure muscle, but you get the point. He looked sorry.

"You're one manipulative con," I told him. "Buy me a beer, and I'll consider you forgiven."

"You solved your case?"

And there I'd been thinking I'd bust him. "A cup of gumbo, then," I demanded.

Deuce smiled and shuffled off to get me a fresh cup from the kitchen. His jeans were clearly from the thrift store, but the way they fit his butt made me wonder if they'd been tailor-made for him.

I felt another presence enter the room, and I turned to see Dice Marlboro sitting on the stool beside me, studying me as I ogled her brother. I gave her a look that said, "May I help you?" because I wouldn't dare say that out loud. Dice is nearly as intimidating as her brother.

"What are your intentions with my brother?" she asked.

"Excuse me?"

"You heard me."

I tried to laugh and shrug her off, but she clearly wasn't letting up. "Dice, we flirt and carry on, but you can't really believe he's interested in me."

"You're all he's interested in."

"Malarkey."

Dice gave me a look that said, "Not malarkey." I felt my insides do a little flip. Surely, they were playing me. Deuce wasn't the type to settle for one woman. He wasn't looking for a relationship, at least not with a private investigator who caught criminals for a living. Right?

"Seriously, Chase? The guy's never been able to turn away a damsel in distress."

"I am *far* from a damsel in distress." I was, in fact, an offended damsel who was *not* distressed.

"I know that. Do you know how long he's been waiting to hop in and help you? It's freakin' annoying how you've gotta do everything on your own."

"Then why would he like me if he likes ladies in distress?"

She rolled her eyes as if the answer was obvious. "He *likes* to help distressed damsels, but he *respects* women who can hold their own."

"Then why hasn't he made a move?"

Dice raised an eyebrow. "I think he just did."

Before I could ask her what on earth she meant by that cryptic gem, Deuce re-entered from the kitchen behind the bar with my cup of gumbo in his hands, and his sister scampered away so quickly that I would have thought her an apparition had I not known better.

"Your grub, ma chérie," he announced with a flourish and put the cup of homemade gumbo in front of me.

I eagerly took the spoon, mixed the rice and gumbo, and took a bite. The Gambler has *great* gumbo, which is a must-have at any New Orleans dining establishment. I let the spicy goodness linger as I chewed the crawfish and smelled the mixed-in basil leaves.

"This is perfect," I intoned.

"So, I'm forgiven?"

"I'll let you threaten everyone who annoys me if I can get a cup of your boss's gumbo every time you do it."

He smiled. "Sounds good to me, ma chérie."

"You might run out of gumbo. There are a lot of people who annoy me. Like, just the other day, I saw a kid stick his gum under the bench at the trolley stop."

Deuce feigned shock with a sharp intake of breath. "I will find the couyon and avenge the sensitivities of my favorite girl."

"I would appreciate that." I ate a few more bites of my gumbo as Deuce got back to work at the bar. He was in the middle of cleaning the taps and would soon start wiping down the bar again. We went on in amicable silence, him working and me watching him work. I was comfortable, and I had to admit that I enjoyed the view almost as much as I enjoyed the food.

As I watched him, I considered what his sister had said. He was everything I could ever want in a man: handsome, strong, loyal, and willing to make me a cup of gumbo whenever I asked for it. However, there's a pretty good reason I don't actively seek romantic entanglements. I'm no good at commitments, and as I sat staring at Deuce's tight, muscled gluteus maximus, I knew at that moment that a relationship with him would be just that—a commitment. Harmless flirting was one thing, but anything more would put my good buddy's heart at risk. He didn't deserve that, and I would never be deserving of a man like him.

So, I did the only thing I could think of doing in that moment. While Deuce was cleaning the taps and the early bar crowd was filing in, I left about one-third of my gumbo unfinished and walked out without saying a word. I knew I'd come back later, but it would be at a time when I was more in control of my emotions, when I didn't have Dice's voice going through my head telling me I'd had an actual effect on her brother, and when I didn't have an abundance of something that might be feelings burrowing around inside of me.

Chapter 18

Ain't Nobody's Business If I Do

As soon as I got out the door, I knew I needed a distraction from whatever the heck was going on with Deuce, so I called Burke on his cell phone. It was Friday afternoon, and the town was beginning to get busy, but Burke was always working. Even so, he answered the phone with a grumble, saying, "It's Friday, Harlem, and I need happy hour. You better have a damn good reason for calling me."

"Hello to you, too, Mr. Grumpy Pants," I greeted him. "Maybe I was calling to offer to buy you a drink."

"You don't drink when you're on a case."

How does everyone know that? "Fine. I called you about work," I admitted. "We need to check out Chris Bryce's girlfriend."

"Candace Moon? She was the one who found the Doyle girl's body."

"Yes, *and* she's dating a drug dealer who would have a motive to kill Goldman."

"An *alleged* drug dealer," Burke helpfully reminded me.

"He offered cocaine to me, Burke! He did! Your detective was the one who messed stuff up."

Burke sighed, and I could sense the resignation. I had won. "Why should we interview Miss Moon?"

"Because if anyone knows whether or not Chris did it, it's his girlfriend," I answered his stupid question. "I mean, have you seen her Instagram? It's literally all pictures of him."

"So?"

Geez, the guy was going to make me beg. "Please just get me an interview with the chickadee. I swear it won't be a wild goose chase like the Artie situation."

Burke grumbled, and I could hear sports playing on his TV in the background. "Let me make a few calls. Then we'll meet at Tulane tomorrow—"

"Tomorrow?" I whined.

"It's nearly 3:00 p.m., Chase. We wouldn't get to Tulane until about 4:00, and no college kid would be in their dorm room at 4:00 on a Friday. I'll pick you up at 8:00 tomorrow morning."

Any other day, when I hadn't overstayed my welcome at my favorite bar, I probably would've agreed with him, but I needed a distraction, something to get my mind off a few hypothetical feelings I needed to ignore. So, I argued, "Dude, you clearly didn't have the same college experience I did. Only the old folks try to hit the bars for happy hour. The kids don't hit the streets until 9:00. If we leave now, we can still catch her, and you can punch in some overtime."

Burke grumbled something that sounded a lot like, "That ain't how overtime works," and I knew I'd won him over to my side.

"I'll meet you in front of Warren Residence Hall at 4:00," I told him.

Right before I hung up, he demanded, "Be on time!" Ten minutes later, I decided it would be best not to make him wait for me, so I hopped in my Isuzu and headed toward the college.

If you thought that Burke and I would venture to yet another hotel room, which would sound super-steamy in any other context, then you'd forgotten that Candace, aka "Candy" Moon, was also a musical theatre major at Tulane University with a decent-sized dorm room on campus.

Candy opened the door to Burke's loud knock with a cordial smile. She was a pretty girl, slightly taller than me, with shoulder-length dark hair, dark eyes, and a thin line of freckles across her pale nose. She could probably be absolutely gorgeous when she wanted, and I got the feeling that she had a massive amount of talent hidden in her lithe frame. Wearing cotton shorts with Tulane written in little boxes all over them and a white tank top, she looked like she'd spent most of her Friday afternoon studying. When Burke flashed her his badge, she didn't even flinch. However, her whole demeanor changed when she laid her eyes on me. Her eyes turned more of a steel color, and her face darkened to a cherry-like hue. I think her teeth also elongated and became pointy. Basically, she looked like a very angry dachshund.

"You!" she snarled before launching herself toward me. I take it back; she looked way more like a lynx than a dachshund, with her nails extended, ready to claw my eyes out. Fortunately, I had the wherewithal to step aside and put Burke between us.

"Miss Moon," Burke stammered, apparently as shocked as I was by the sudden display of violence, "I think you might be confused. This is my consultant, Investigator Chase Harlem."

"You're that little whore who threw herself at Christopher!" she hissed. "Your slut show is all over Snapchat."

Damn modern technology. Also, I don't think a "slut show" is a real thing, but I'm too afraid to look it up and find out.

"I think there's been a misunderstanding," I tried to evade.

"Oh no there's not! I know a *slut* when I see one." Well, that was just uncalled for in my opinion—not to mention rude. "Christopher told me how you threw yourself at him. You were so obviously desperate that he felt bad for you."

She launched herself at me again, but Burke stepped between us, holding his badge out and in her face like it was an actual shield. I could tell he was getting tired of it, but it'd been so long since I'd had a good girl fight that I couldn't resist throwing a little shade.

"Oh really?" I said. "Did your cheating boyfriend tell you that?"

She gasped, raising herself to her full height, and said, "Christopher could never cheat on me. We're in an *open* relationship."

"Then why are you coming after me with your claws out?" I asked.

"You nearly got him arrested."

Say what? How does hitting on him at the bar and asking for some drugs count as almost getting him arrested? It's not like Chandler was there to arrest him for me. That would be ridiculous. What lie had Chris Bryce thought up to get this girl off his back?

"Not how I remember it," I told her. I really didn't have time to delve into her open relationship problems, so I reminded myself of why I was there and tried to continue in a professional manner. This was unsurprisingly difficult, considering the girl had just called me a slut. "Now," I continued calmly, "you wanna let us come in and ask you some questions, or do you want to continue to cause a spectacle?"

She deflated and seemed to come to her senses, looking around as if she expected an audience. We were the only people in the hall. Most of the young women had probably headed home for the weekend, or they'd headed over to some sorority house to get ready for a night out on the town.

"Come in," she said, almost meekly.

She led us into her small dorm room, where two twin-sized beds sat with a large sofa and seating area between them. At the foot of the beds were two matching desks. Despite the matching furniture, the two sides of the room couldn't have been more different. One side was decorated in complementary pinks, greens, and browns. The comforter and bed set matched and were perfectly aligned, not a stitch out of place. The posters on the wall were of inspirational quotes and phrases, and the books were all lined neatly across the shelf on the top of the desk.

On the other side of the room was nothing. No sheets, no pillows, no books, no posters, no laptop—just bare, ivory-painted walls, an empty bed frame, an empty desk, and more emptiness. Of course. Regina Doyle had been her roommate. Her parents must have come and cleaned out her things already.

As we entered, Candace took the bed that was obviously hers, and I let Burke take her desk chair. It didn't seem right to sit leisurely in a place where someone had died, so I stood awkwardly by the closet just left of the entryway.

"She was alone," I muttered, looking at Doyle's empty desk.

Burke gave me a quick, steely-eyed glare, and I knew I'd probably messed up.

Candace followed my gaze, and it was as if a dark cloud stalled right over her head. She shifted, and for a moment, I honestly thought she'd start screaming at me again. But all the fight must have seeped out of her as she nodded slowly. "We dropped her off here, and I went to Christopher's," she explained. "Had I known—but Eli had taken her drugs, so I didn't think..." Her voice was weak, shaky. She seemed legitimately upset, and I had to remind myself that she was an actress in training.

"Did you know about her drug use before?" Burke asked.

Candace shrugged. "I had my suspicions. I mean, I knew she smoked weed and stuff, but the fact that she did hard drugs—well, that surprised me."

"Do you have any idea where she got them?" I asked. Of course, she knew. Chris sold them to her, didn't he? That was the only thing that made sense. What I really wanted to know was whether or not she'd lie for him. How willing was she to defend her not-boyfriend?

She glared at me. "*No.* I don't." Apparently, she was supremely willing to defend him. Interesting.

"Tell me about that night," Burke said, shooting me another warning glance. He had caught the lie as well, but instead of calling her on it, he wanted to see if he could catch her in any other lies.

"Well," Candace hesitated, "you already know what happened."

"I want to hear it from your perspective," Burke said.

"I don't know what else I could contribute."

Burke held up a placating hand. "Look, Miss Moon, two good kids were killed a couple of nights ago. Those kids were your friends, and they deserve justice. Maybe you don't know anything, but your testimony could still help us find justice for them and peace for their families." Oh, he was guilt-tripping hard. It wasn't a tactic I would have used, but that was probably because I was still salty about being called a slut.

Candace nodded nervously, taking a deep breath. "It was Reggie's idea. To go out, I mean. She wanted her Tulane friends to meet her LSU boyfriend, and she had a way of getting what she wanted. Not that I'm complaining; it was one of her more... *engaging* qualities. It was what made her a leading lady. Anyway, it took some planning, but when we realized that LSU would have a bye week right around Halloween, Eli, Jeremy, and Tanya planned to come here. I mean, what better place to spend Halloween than New Orleans, right? It was no coincidence that the Willow was having a masquerade on *that* particular weekend. Reggie never could resist a costume party, and once Jeremy and Eli painted their faces, we knew nobody at the party would start asking for autographs.

"They really do that around here, you know?" she continued. "Like, people ask college jocks for their autographs like they're actual NFL football players." If her lack of a southern accent weren't enough to go on, that last statement would have solidified the fact that Candace was from somewhere up north. In the southern states, football rules, and the men who play football are gods.

I was still listening to her, but I was also looking around the room as surreptitiously as possible. While she was talking about costumes, a black piece of fabric sticking out from the closet caught my eye. I went over and picked it up, revealing a black catsuit. It smelled like sweat and death.

"Was this your costume?" I asked.

She thrust herself off the bed as quickly as possible and removed the garment from my hand. "Sorry about the mess," she said, sliding open her closet door just enough to take out a hanger and put the catsuit on it. As she closed the door again, a familiar purple suit caught my eye. I started to say something, but Burke gave me one of his "I'm the boss, and you're only here with my blessing" looks to silence me.

"So, was Reggie the one to pick the costumes?" Burke asked.

"Actually, that was Christopher," Candace explained. "That's what he does. He makes costumes for the theatre. He's really good at it, too."

"And you and Reggie, you were both actresses?" Burke asked.

Candace nodded. "But she was the best, at least when it came to musicals. She had this powerful voice that was so full of emotion—nobody could compete with that."

"Yeah," I agreed before I could stop myself. She gave me a quizzical look, so I explained, "Lackey showed me a video. She was really talented."

I couldn't read the expression on her face, but I wasn't sure I liked it. I could tell she was uncomfortable, and it was making me uncomfortable. "Did he—" she started to speak but stopped herself. "Do you think he did it? Killed Goldman, I mean."

"We're not at liberty to discuss the case, ma'am," Burke told her.

"Of course." She nodded. Biting her bottom lip, she glanced over at what had been Reggie's bed. "I thought they were friends," she mumbled. Then, as if coming out of a trance, she added quickly, "I guess you can never really know a person."

"What do you mean?" I asked, despite the look Burke was sending me.

She seemed to be knocked off balance by the question, which was exactly what I wanted. "I-it's just," she stammered, "Goldman and Lackey were supposed to be best friends. That's why Lackey introduced Goldman and Reggie, you know? He wanted his best friend from high school and his best friend from college to be together. He was always bragging about playing matchmaker. It made Christopher sick."

"Why would it bother him?" Burke asked the question this time.

She let out an awkward laugh and glanced up at the ceiling before answering. "Lackey can be kind of obnoxious, especially when he's right about something."

Burke asked a few more questions, but I'd heard all I needed to hear. I had a pretty good idea about what kind of guy Chris Bryce was before

I'd walked into that dorm room, and what Candace Moon had said had only cemented my theories. After a while, Candace made some excuses, and Burke and I made our exit. I'm sure she called Chris Brycc as soon as the door closed behind us.

"She did it," I said as soon as we left the building. "She's the murderer."

"You're just saying that because she called you a slut," Burke told me, reaching into his coat pocket and pulling out a cigarette. He put it between his lips before digging around his pockets for his lighter. He wouldn't find it.

"Maybe so," I admitted. "But since we can't arrest her for calling me a slut, I vote we arrest her for murder. It's only just."

Burke had stopped walking and was now searching all the pockets in his ridiculous long coat as frantically as a cool noir detective could. I stopped and watched him because it was fun and because walking away would have been rude. Finally, he froze and slowly raised his eyes to meet mine.

"Chase, you stole my lighter." Of course, it wasn't a question. He is a detective.

I smiled. "Smoking kills."

"So do firearms."

"Not when you're pulling the trigger," I reminded him. "I've seen your aim."

"That was my lucky lighter, Chase!"

"You got it for fifty cents at a gas station."

"Yeah, but it was red," he deadpanned. "I like red."

I laughed. The excuses he used to maintain his nasty habit were absolutely ludicrous. "I'll get you a red pocketknife. It will be just as pretty and twice as useful."

"Unless we need to build a fire."

I rolled my eyes. "Why on earth would we need to build a fire?"

"Emergency camping trip."

"You don't camp."

"I might decide to camp. What if my friends invite me on a camping trip?"

"What friends?" I quipped. "I'm your only friend, Burke, and I don't camp."

Something from across the parking lot caught my attention. Chris Bryce was getting out of his car—a silver SUV—so popular in make and model that there were three identical ones in the same parking lot. Watching him get out and hoof it toward campus gave me an idea.

"Hey Burke, you go on back. I want to do some exploring."

Burke raised an eyebrow but decided not to question my wanting to hang out on a college campus at 5:00 p.m. He had to make it to happy hour, after all.

Chapter 19

I'm Following You

Chris Bryce had a late class starting at 5:30 p.m. in the Telecommunications building. I know because I followed him there—all the way to the classroom door. Once he was settled and I was sure he hadn't seen me, I went to grab a coffee from the PJ's in the Goldring/Woldenberg Business Complex, before returning to the Telecommunications building to sit and wait for Bryce's class to finish up. There was a bench down the hall from his classroom, dedicated by some alumni or another, and I got as comfortable as I could while I waited.

The class was nearly three hours long, and by the end of it, I was really wishing I'd brought a book or a crossword or something to pass the time, but you can't plan for spontaneity. Finally, sometime after 8:00, Bryce and a couple of his friends came out of the classroom. I pretended to be looking at something on my phone as he passed, then waited until he'd stepped out the door to get up and follow him.

The way I saw it, if Bryce really was a drug dealer, all I had to do was follow him until I caught him dealing. Simple. The fact that it was now dark outside, and I was following him through a poorly lit campus—across the Monroe Quad, past the McAlister Auditorium, and into the LBC food court—should have made it easy for me to go unnoticed. However, once I settled down at a small round table near the door, I realized that my cover'd been blown.

Chris Bryce walked up and sat down at the table across from me, tossing me a wrapped sandwich with a "Pickles" label on it. He sat his own basket of chicken stir-fry in front of him and looked up at me. "You've been following me since before class. I figured you could use some calories." He smiled that bright, dimpled smile, and I nearly laughed at his confidence. This guy had so much charm it was leaking from his perfect dark gray eyes.

I reached for the wrapped sandwich. "What is it?"

He laughed. "Don't worry. It's not poisoned. It's a turkey and avocado BLT. Figured I couldn't go wrong with turkey. Everyone likes turkey."

"What if I'm a vegetarian?"

He shrugged. "You look like a carnivore to me."

He was right. I unwrapped the sandwich and took a bite. If it was poisoned, it'd be worth the inconvenience—I was hungry.

"Candace said you came by her dorm with that detective earlier. Why're you following me now?" Bryce asked.

I was on delicate ground here, so I decided to tread softly. "I think you killed Goldman," I told him over a mouthful of sandwich.

Bryce nearly choked on his stir-fry. "W-why would you think that?"

"You were in love with Reggie," I said, being honest about what I thought was *part* of his motive.

"Everyone was in love with Reggie," he said. "Doesn't mean we were planning to kill her boyfriend."

"Yeah, sure." I took another bite of my sandwich. Bryce wasn't the type of guy who could handle too much silence.

"Besides, the cops already have a suspect," he said. "They think that Lackey guy did it. He's the one who introduced them. You should be talking to him."

I continued to eat my sandwich in silence.

"I mean, it was obviously him. He was always fighting with Goldman; even his teammates said so."

To have come from a college food court, my sandwich was actually really good.

"Have you even talked to him? I mean, the police found the murder weapon under the passenger's seat of his truck, you know."

I swallowed my bite of sandwich, wiped my mouth, and said, "Interesting you know about the murder weapon since the cops haven't released that information."

Bryce's caramel skin turned a pale yellow. "That's just—just something I heard one of the theatre kids saying. You know drama kids love drama."

"Really, which kid? I'm sure my best friend, who happens to be the detective over the case, would be very interested in knowing that kid's name."

"It's just a rumor, okay," Bryce squawked. He was visibly sweating.

"That's a lot of valid information to be 'just a rumor.'"

Bryce sputtered for a moment before saying, "Look, I had nothing to do with that jock's death. I wasn't even at the party when he died, and I have a ton of people who can verify that. I'm not a suspect, so stop following me. It's creepy."

I shrugged. "It's a free country."

"It's stalking."

"I'm a PI. I have a license to stalk people."

Bryce slammed his hands on the round table and shouted, "Leave me alone, or you'll regret it!"

"You gonna make me regret it, Bryce?" I asked. "The way you made Goldman regret dating Reggie?"

He blanched at that. "No. I'll just—I'll call campus security, okay? You have no right to be on this campus, and they'll make you leave."

He had a point there. "Fine. I'll finish my sandwich and go."

Bryce shook his head, standing abruptly from his chair with his tray in his hands before turning around and stomping away from the table.

"Hey Bryce," I shouted at his back, "how does it feel knowing the last thing Reggie said to you before she overdosed was 'I don't think we can see each other anymore'?!"

Bryce froze. Even from ten feet away, I could see his ears turn red. I'd struck a chord and found out who that 407 number belonged to before the team at the NOPD did.

"Stop following me," Bryce warned again before stomping the rest of the way out of the food court.

The night had grown darker by the time I finished my sandwich and left the food court. The full moon had come and gone, leaving only a faint sliver to light the autumn darkness. I managed to find a parking place in the lot outside the residential college, which meant I had to cross the Berger Family Lawn to get there. It wasn't a long walk, per se, but I figured I could use the time to call Burke.

"What?" he answered on the first ring.

"Hi, buddy! Guess what?"

"No."

"You're no fun. I figured out who that 407 number belongs to."

Burke was quiet for a moment before letting out a sigh and muttering, "Who?"

"Chris Bryce. Regina's theatre friend."

"Chase, where are you right now?"

"Oh, you know, just making my way across campus."

"And you've been following this kid since I left you on campus at 5:00?"

"Affirmative."

Burke moaned. "Chase, you can't just—it's not right to—He's not even a suspect!"

"Well, he should be because he's very suspicious."

I had made it across the lawn and was crossing the parking lot when the roar of an engine sounded off somewhere to my right and I turned just in time to see two blindingly white headlights flash on. Wheels squealed, and gravel crunched as the headlights quickly grew larger.

I stepped out of the way just in time for an SUV's mirror to strike my right shoulder and throw me onto the hard pavement, the momentum sending my body careening across the parking lot. Gravel dug into my bare left shoulder and tore at my Grace Potter T-shirt. I was running on pure adrenaline when, after my painful slide, I scrambled and rolled away from the SUV and back onto the soft lawn. The brake lights of the offending vehicle flickered only for a moment before the car took off again. I couldn't get a clear picture of it in the darkness, but it looked like it might have been silver.

My ears were ringing, either from the impact or from adrenaline, I'm not sure. Over the sound of ringing, I heard a nasally female voice cry out, "Oh my god, are you okay?"

Footsteps crunched over the gravel coming closer to me, but I couldn't take my eyes off the retreating taillights in the distance.

Suddenly, a light was shining in my face, and I turned to see a shadowy figure crouched in the grass beside me, holding the offending light with one hand and offering me my cellphone with the other. I couldn't move—couldn't make myself reach for it. Someone had just tried to kill me.

"Are you okay?" the shadowy figure asked. "Do I need to call 911? What's your na—" The flashlight dipped to my torso, and the friendly shadow stopped talking. My eyes followed the light down, and I soon realized the reason for the sudden silence. Like most of my left shoulder and arm, my Grace Potter T-shirt had been torn by the gravel. A jagged tear went from the bottom hem up to my breasts, leaving my entire abdomen exposed to the night air. There was fresh blood from the road rash, but worse were the grizzly scars—on full display to this stranger with a cellphone flashlight.

My breath hitched, and my stomach churned at my vulnerability. My formerly frozen body leaped into action as I pulled my shirt closed with unnecessary force and scooted away on my butt from my would-be good Samaritan. "Don't touch me," I heard myself hiss. I was struggling for air, my breaths coming shorter and faster, and my chest entirely too tight to let the air reach my lungs.

"Just let me call someone for you."

"Get away," I warned the stranger. "Leave me alone."

"Okay-okay. Here's your phone." The stranger tossed the phone the short distance between us. It landed softly in the grass. "How can I help you? You seem really hurt."

"Don't-don't look," I pleaded, hardly knowing what I was saying. "Just-just-get-*away*!"

"Okay, I'm gonna leave, but you should seriously call somebody." The stranger stood up and walked slowly away, as if she were unsure whether it was the right thing to do.

Finally alone, with nobody to see my scars, I took a deep breath, held it, and then released it slowly. I looked around me and rattled off five things I could see. "Trees, moon, cars, parking lot lights, buildings." Then, four things I could hear. "Traffic, music from the dorms, crickets, an owl." Then, three things I could feel. "Cool air, grass," I reached out and grabbed my phone, "phone." My breathing was finally normalizing.

I looked down at the cracked phone screen. The good news was that the phone still worked. The bad news was that my call with Burke was still live. I put the phone to my ear and said, "Hey, buddy, you still there?"

Burke let out a string of expletives that would've made my pop, an ex-combat officer, blush.

"It's fine. I'm fine," I assured him, but I could tell my voice was shaking. The adrenaline was draining fast, leaving me empty, cold, and in pain.

"None of that sounded *fine*, Chase," Burke said. "What the hell happened?"

"I got—I was hit by a car."

"*What?*"

"It just, it just bumped me, really."

Burke swore. "You hurt?"

175

"Not really." I had no idea. "Just some scrapes. My shirt—when I fell, I tore my shirt. You can see my..."

Burke seemed to understand and sighed as he tried to reign in his temper. "Do you need me to come get you?"

"No," I answered quickly. "I'm good. I'll drive myself home."

I could tell Burke was debating arguing with me, and I knew damn well that I should tell him my suspicions: that the incident was no accident. But I was tired and shaking, and I needed a drink.

"Fine," Burke said at last. "Go home. Shoot me a text when you get there so I know you're alive. We'll talk about the case again tomorrow."

Chapter 20

Just One of Those Things

I did not go straight home. I'm not 100% sure what I did. Shock will do that to a person. If you're ever in a car wreck or another life-or-death situation—it's like your conscious mind takes a vacation somewhere in the back of your skull, and your body takes care of all the basic mechanical stuff.

By the time I made it back to my apartment, it was nearly 11:00 p.m. I had an open bottle of Sazerac Rye in my right hand and was holding my bloody shirt together with my left. Any other night, I would've made it to my apartment without interruption, but as luck would have it, Rose and Reese were standing with none other than Deuce Marlboro when I stumbled through the gate and into the courtyard. Simultaneously, they turned their eyes toward me. The looks of horror on their faces made me laugh.

"Evenin' folks," I greeted.

I'm pretty sure Rose swore in Spanish just as Reese asked, "Is that *blood?*"

"Don't worry about it. It's all mine," I assured her.

She did not look well assured.

"What happened, chère?" Deuce asked.

Standing still and talking was making me dizzy, so I put my bottle on the table and held myself up as best I could. "I got hit by a car."

A lot happened at once then: Reese swore, Rose slapped Reese on the shoulder, Deuce asked Rose for a first aid kit, Reese went to get the first aid kit, and I stared blankly as Deuce walked across the courtyard toward me.

"C'mon, chère, let's get you cleaned up."

The charming Deuce Marlboro somehow got me into my apartment, up the stairs, and into my bathroom, all while surreptitiously stealing my bottle of Sazerac.

"Where's my whisky?" I asked as he sat me down on the edge of my bathtub, sitting himself on the toilet before he began examining my left arm. He didn't answer my question, so I pulled my arm behind my back and asked again, "Where's my whisky?"

"It's downstairs," he said. "Is the last thing you should be drinking with this blood loss."

"I didn't realize you were a doctor as well as a bartender."

"Gimme your arm," Deuce said in a stern voice I'd never heard him use before. I'm not usually one to obey anyone, but something in his tone made me do as commanded.

"I'm fine," I slurred.

"You got gravel lodged under yo' skin," he told me.

"It'll buff out."

"That ain't how it works an' you know it." His eyes lowered to my torn shirt, which I was holding together with my right hand. "Take your shirt off."

I froze, my right hand tightening and twisting in the tattered remains of my shirt. "No."

"Chère, I'm serious. I ain't gonna do nothin' to you; I just need to check your road rash."

Using both hands, I pulled my shirt closed tighter and said, "I can clean it myself."

"In your condition? I doubt it." Then, more gently, he added, "Chère, I know you been hurt by men before—you got a lot to be scared of, but I ain't never gonna hurt you."

I'll let you in on a little secret: whisky never actually makes things better. One minute you think it's dulling the pain and the next it's whispering awful ideas into your brain. I thought of all the times Deuce had been kind to me—the times he'd asked permission to hold my hand or shielded me from perverts at the bar—and suddenly, I couldn't see the love in those moments; all I could see was pity. Deuce thought I was some poor, broken girl who'd let some boy get too close, and he pitied me for it. I felt the bile boil in my stomach, but instead of throwing up, I ripped open my shirt.

Deuce leaped up from the toilet at the sight. I couldn't look him in the eye. Instead, I looked past him at the long mirror hanging on the bathroom door, my reflection revealing the terrible scars on my torso spelling out the word "victim." Deuce turned, either trying to look away or trying to find out what I was looking at. He saw the word. I could tell by his expression.

"Do you think a *man* gave me this?" I hissed.

Deuce's mouth moved, but no sound came out. I still couldn't look him in the eye—not now that he knew what I was—so I simply said, "Get out."

He did.

Chapter 21

Do I Love You

It took me nearly an hour to get myself cleaned up. Mostly because I couldn't stop sobbing long enough to actually stand up. I simply sat in the tub with the shower cranked as hot as it could go, as my salty tears mixed with the steaming water of the bath.

When I was finally ready to step out of my bathroom, I had managed to remove most of the gravel from my left arm. I could still feel a couple of tiny rocks digging into my shoulder, so I decided I needed some tweezers and some more whisky. After throwing on a tank top and some shorts and grabbing said tweezers, I went downstairs to find Deuce sitting at my tiny kitchen table with my ferret in his lap. The bottle of Sazerac and a very large first aid kit sat on the table in front of him.

"Hey, chère," he called, scratching Louis behind his ears.

"You're still here?"

"Just getting to know this guy," Deuce said. He stood up, Louis in his arms, and sauntered over to the ferret cage. Deuce poured the ferret food into the bowl before depositing Louis into the cage and returning to the kitchen.

"I thought you left," I said, hating the way my voice sounded weak and full of sand.

"I will if you want me to." The way he said it reminded me of a sad puppy being left out in the cold.

"Actually, I could use your help." I held up the tweezers.

Deuce offered me the chair he'd been sitting in with Louis. "I'll do my best."

As soon as I was seated, Deuce got to work, kneeling beside me, using a cellphone flashlight to get a better look at my road rash as he dug around with the tweezers. "You sure you got this good an' cleaned?" he asked me.

"I scrubbed off chunks of skin with soap, and it hurt like hell." I felt a particularly hard dig of the tweezers and let out an involuntary hiss.

"Sorry."

To get my mind off my pain, I asked, "What were you doing here, anyway?"

Deuce blushed, and that made me even more curious. "I was talkin' to Rose an' Reese about Hank. I got him set up at one of the nicer shelters, he went to his first AA meetin' last night, an' he starts work on Monday."

"You got him a job?"

Deuce dug farther into my arm with the tweezers, and I'm not sure if it was intentional or not. "Is no big thing. Someone owed Boss a favor, so he called it in."

"Why? Why would you do that?"

He shrugged. "Didn't make much sense to just chase him off. He weren't the problem—not really. He was strikin' out like a whooped pup 'cause he'd been whooped."

"I would've just whooped him again." What I'd done to Tarant was evidence enough of that.

"Nah. If you could've seen the way to help, you woulda. It's what I like about you." He winked at me as he said that last part. Then he dug the tweezers into my shoulder, squeezed, and yanked out a rock the size of my pinkie nail. It felt like I'd been shocked by electricity.

I cursed as fresh blood trickled down my arm.

Deuce opened the first aid kit, grabbed a cotton ball, poured some peroxide on it, and dabbed at my arm until the blood was gone. He then pulled out fresh gauze and asked, "You mind if I wrap this up?"

I nodded, still in too much pain to speak. As Deuce worked, I thought over the fact that the man had not only taken his time to help Hank, but that he'd also convinced his boss to help out. It was almost too much for me. How could a man be willing to do that for a complete stranger? Me, I do stuff to help others because that's what I'm *supposed* to do, and more often than not, that's what I'm *paid* to do. But Deuce does stuff that I wouldn't even think of because...

"Why?" I asked again. "Why help some stranger?"

Deuce shrugged one muscled shoulder and really seemed to think about it for a moment as he finished taping some gauze over the worst part of my road rash and began pulling out the Band-Aids for the smaller wounds. Finally, he offered what I suppose passed as an answer. "If I didn't do it, who would? Most folks, even good folks, just condemn the man for beatin' his wife, an' maybe they right to do it. But me, I like to think that e'rybody can be helped if they want it bad 'nough. Turns out, he wanted it purty bad."

"That might be the noblest thing I ever heard." I still can't believe I admitted that out loud.

Deuce smiled again, adding a Band-Aid to a particularly torn part of my palm and kissing it gently. "Funny what a feller'd do to get the girl, ma chérie."

I pulled my hand away as if I'd been burned. "Don't do that."

His hazel eyes looked up at me, big as two Moon Pies, and I knew I'd hurt him.

"You've seen what I am now," I told him. "It's time we stopped pretending I could be anything else."

"Chère—"

"Don't call me that. You've seen what I am."

Deuce stood from his kneeling position and walked to the other side of the table, taking the extra chair and looking me in the eyes. "What happened to you?"

Had it been anyone else on any other night, I'd have told him to screw off. Instead, I reached for my bottle of Sazerac. Deuce moved like he was about to stop me, but I pulled the Sazerac to my chest and said, "I can't tell you without this." I then took a long swallow before setting it down on the table and looking at Deuce. He stared right back, steady and strong—nothing like me.

"You know I worked for the FBI?" I asked.

He nodded.

"You know they fired me?"

He shook his head.

"Well, they did, and they had every right to do it. I was an alcoholic who couldn't keep my personal life together, not to mention my work life. They fired me, and nobody could blame them." I took another swig of whiskey. "But before I became a damned drunk, I was one of Quantico's most promising profilers. I was *good*. Like, I was one of the best in my class—supposedly remarkable. My career was on *fire*, Deuce. I was only two years in, and people were requesting me." I laughed at how proud that fact used to make me—back when I was too young and stupid to realize that I shouldn't have been proud. I should have been scared.

"Don't let the headlines fool you: most people in that line of work can go their whole careers without encountering any noteworthy crime. For most agents, serial killers are just fiction. I was *special*." The words were bitter, even to my own ears, but I took another drink and kept talking. "In Georgia, someone was kidnapping and killing young guys. Police would find their bodies naked, mutilated, and castrated in the mountains near Athens—words like 'pedophile' and 'creep' forcibly tattooed onto their torsos or foreheads." I took a deep breath to slow my heart rate.

"I think I heard about this one," Deuce said. "Wasn't the killer called the Artist?"

I nodded. Of course, he'd heard of it. Everyone had. A serial killer targeting men? That was gold to reporters, who were obligated to give the killer a cool nickname. "It was a huge case, and the FBI wanted *me* to profile the killer." I laughed at my naiveté, my arrogance, my *stupidity*. "So, I did exactly that. I pored over case files, crime scene photos, and reports. I followed all the clues, applied all the rules, and I came up with what everyone thought was a *brilliant* profile. It was detailed; it was exact; it was *mostly* right... but I missed something."

I took a long drink from my whisky, counting on the liquid courage to complete my tale. When I felt my nerves were ready, I continued, "The agents and cops used my profile to snag a suspect. He was young, awkward, a social pariah, and he fit the profile." I felt my throat tighten, and my eyes begin to burn. I had to choke back a sob before I continued,

"After one night in lockup, this awkward kid killed himself. They found him hanging right before his brother got back into town with bail money and an air-tight alibi."

"That ain't yo 'fault," Deuce lied.

I waved him off. It wasn't an argument I was willing to have—drunk or sober.

"Right around that time, I wasn't exactly being cautious about my safety," I admitted. "I figured that the killer was focused on guys, so I would be safe. I was arrogant and stupid, just like I was tonight before that car hit me. I got cocky, and I nearly got killed—again."

Deuce started to interrupt, no doubt to ask about my most recent near-death experience, but I waved him off. It was time to tell my story.

"Right after getting the call about that poor kid's suicide, the *real* Artist came for me. Abigail Dunlap—the world's most infamous female serial killer—took me to her warehouse and tied me down." I stared at a hole in my thrift store rug. "She didn't have her tattoo gun with her. She had planted it on the guy the police had arrested based on *my* profile, so instead, she used a dull pocketknife to carve the word 'victim' into my torso. The whole time, she was telling me how much we had in common—how *impressed* she was with me. She told me we were the same, and she'd prove it."

I felt a tear roll down my cheek and let out a startled laugh. Abigail had killed men who'd hurt women. After what I'd done to Tarant that day, maybe we were more alike than I'd ever admit. "I thought she was carving 'murderer' or even 'monster.' Instead, she carved the word 'victim'—making sure it was backwards, so I could see it in the mirror every day. She then locked me in a freezer with one of her castrated corpses. I thought she'd left me to die. Instead, she got herself caught and let the cops know exactly where they'd find me."

I took a sip of my whisky and wiped tears from my cheeks. "I should have died that day—they would've called me a hero. Now, I will never be anything other than a victim. I forgot about that for a minute. For just a moment tonight I was that naive little agent again, trying to catch a bad guy. Then I was knocked silly by a mid-sized SUV, and it reminded me that I will *never* be anything other than what *The Artist* made me."

Deuce reached for me across the table, and I stood and stepped away like a cat struck by water. "Don't you get it?!" I shouted. "I can't be your chèrie, I can't be the profiler Burke needs, I can't be whatever it is that kid needs me to be. I am *only* what the Artist made me."

Deuce slowly stood from his chair. "If that's how you feel, chèrie, *I* can't change yo mind. You're the only one who can choose who you can be."

He slowly walked toward the door. Placing his hand on the doorknob, he said, "Fo' the record, you been more than a *victim* to me and a lot of people for a long time. If you'd stop feelin' sorry for yourself, maybe you'd see that."

Chapter 22

I Say Grace

Once Deuce left, I pulled out my cellphone and texted Burke two simple words: I quit. It was after midnight, and I was sure he wouldn't get it until the next day.

After that, I either drank or cried myself to sleep. Whatever I did, it didn't keep the nightmares away.

Too soon after I'd fallen asleep, I felt it—the cold seeping in through the walls, through my clothes, right into my soul—and I couldn't move. Then, I smelled it, the acrid, coppery smell of fresh blood filling my nostrils and making me sick to my stomach. I knew I should clamp my eyes shut and never open them again, but I couldn't. I had to *see;* I had to *know*. I slowly opened my eyes to find the dead, frozen eyes of Eli Goldman staring back at me.

I sat up so quickly that the momentum nearly knocked Louis across the room. Unfortunately, the sunlight streaming through my window was not comforting this time. Instead, the stream of gold felt like a knife stabbing me right through the eye. It was nauseating. So nauseating that I leaped from my bed and hurled myself into the bathroom while simultaneously hurling up the contents of my stomach. That turkey and avocado BLT did not taste so good coming back up. Neither did the entire bottle of Sazerac I'd consumed.

Once I'd finished throwing my guts up, I seriously considered making my bathroom floor my permanent place of residence. It was cool, barely wobbly, and it had some pretty blue tile I was fond of, even though I knew it was a bit dated. I was debating the pros and cons of my new living arrangement when my cellphone began screeching from my bedroom floor—shattering the little bit of peace I'd managed to find.

I crawled into my bedroom, grabbed the phone, and answered it before looking at the name on the screen just to make the ringing stop. "Hello?" I grumbled.

"What the hell do you mean you quit?"

"Hey, Burke. Yeah, it's not working out. You can have your case back."

Instead of launching into a string of creative curse words as I expected, Burke paused. When he spoke again, his tone was softer. "What happened last night?"

"I just—I made a mistake."

"What did you do?"

"I took this job. That was the mistake."

Burke was quiet for another moment, clearly trying to get a read on the situation. If there's one thing a detective hates, it's not having enough information. "Chase, last night, you said you'd been hit by a car ...did you ... are you hurt?"

"Just a few scrapes." And a terrible hangover, but Burke didn't need to know *that*.

"Chase, if you think getting hit by that car has anything to do with the case, you need to tell me. We can figure this out."

"I don't *want* to figure this out, Burke," I hissed.

"But, why quit? You never quit."

I sighed. My head hurt far too much to deal with explanations. "Because you were right, Burke. It's too violent for me."

"I never—"

"You saw me yesterday with Tarant. I get around violence; I become violent."

"That's not—"

"It's fine. I'm sure you can do this on your own. I gotta go puke again."

On that note, I hung up and returned to my porcelain throne to empty my guts once more. After I was done, I cleaned up the residual mess with a towel and tried lying back down on my bed. It didn't work out. My phone kept ringing. I knew it was Burke, so I turned it off and laid back down again. It was impossibly brighter outside my windows, so I'd either slept longer or I'd been throwing up longer than I'd thought. Based on the fact that I was still exhausted and nauseous, I knew it was more likely to be the latter. I felt so sick, in fact, that the only thing I knew that might cure it was another drink. I was desperate for just a sip of something to dull the ache in my chest and the burning in my throat. I climbed out of bed and walked down to the kitchen.

I knew at once that the kid had been by at some point that morning because there was a stale pot of coffee and four aspirins on my counter, along with a hand-written grocery list. Remembering Reese and the things her alcoholic foster father had put her through made me hate myself a little. I remembered the look on her face when I walked through the courtyard gate, and all I could feel was shame—bone-deep, organ-twisting shame. I didn't want that drink anymore.

The coffee was stale and lukewarm, but I downed it and the aspirin in one gulp. Then I took the stupid shopping list along with my hangover from Hades and went to get groceries. I even went by the hardware store and had a spare key made. I told myself it wasn't for the kid. I just needed a spare in case I, you know, lost mine.

I was surprised—and if I'm honest, a little sad—that said kid wasn't sitting on my sofa when I made it back home later in the afternoon. I needed someone to distract me now that I'd officially quit the case. I knew I should call Father Nolan to give him the bad news, but I didn't have the strength. I had already disappointed too many people that day, so I gathered Louis into my lap and watched some show about British people racing cars.

The next day was Sunday, so feeling a little guilty, I got up, put on a plain gray dress, and headed to First Baptist New Orleans for the 9:30 a.m. service. I entered the considerably modern sanctuary right before the sermon began, taking my place on the row furthest from the front. I gazed across the pews at the other churchgoers as I listened to Brother Chad read from the gospel of Matthew—about the old being made new. A few rows in front of me, a little girl was coloring in her church bulletin. Occasionally, she'd look up and smile at her father or ask her mother for another crayon. I wondered if I'd ever been that innocent. I suppose I had. I was sure Regina Doyle had and probably Goldman and Lackey, too.

Sitting on that cushioned pew, listening to the familiar voice of the pastor, I breathed easy for the first time in a week. This was where I came to stock up on hope—something I have so little of myself. Someone in my line of work needs to find hope somewhere, and it's better to find it at the pulpit than at the bottom of a bottle. I'd learned that the hard way.

As the sermon ended and the music began to play, I slipped out like a shadow through the back door and walked out to the parking lot, feeling lighter than I had that morning. One of the ushers waved at me from the door but made no attempt to speak. Good. After two years, most people at the church had given up trying to get to know me, and I appreciated it. They'd finally realized that I don't go to church to socialize. I'm not one to explain myself to others or let anyone past my defenses. Fortunately, most of those people seemed fine with my behavior and simply waved and smiled.

Reese Kelley is not one of those people, which was evident to me when I returned from church to find her sitting on my sofa watching my special edition copy of *Robin Hood: Prince of Thieves* with Louis coiled leisurely in her lap. Thanks to my pop, I'd always had a thing for older movies. I kept DVDs instead of signing my soul to streaming companies so I wouldn't have to worry about the movies disappearing from my library. I feigned shock when I saw her there in the living room eating my cereal.

"I could have shot you," I warned.

"But you didn't." She didn't even bother to look away from the television to see if I was aiming a gun in her direction. Darn kids these days just can't be fooled.

I briefly toyed with the idea of investing in a security system before I remembered that I couldn't afford one. I could get a dog, but it would probably like the kid more than me, and the whole thing would blow up in my face. Besides, Louis would likely hate the dog, and I can't make my emotional support animal unhappy. I sat my purse down on the counter and walked up to my bedroom, changing out of my church clothes and into my usual jeans and T-shirt, avoiding looking at my scars in the mirror. I grabbed the key I'd had made from the dresser and slipped it into my pocket before re-entering the living room.

"This movie is terrible," Reese told me through a mouthful of my cornflakes. "Where've you been?"

"At church, where good Christian girls go on Sunday," I told her as I plopped down in the chair beside the sofa. "You should come. You might learn how sinful it is to break into someone's apartment."

"I don't remember that being one of the Ten Commandments. It's not like I'm stealing anything."

"You're eating my food right now," I pointed out.

"Didn't Jesus say in Luke, 'Whoever has two tunics is to share with him who has none, and whoever has food is to do likewise?'" she asked, looking at me for the first time and batting her eyelashes innocently.

I felt my eyebrows shoot into my hairline. "You know your scripture."

She shrugged and took another bite of cornflakes. "My dad made sure of that. We were in church every time the doors were open, and I was the Vacation Bible School memorization champ."

"Your dad sounds like a pretty cool guy," I said. I didn't ask what had happened to him. The dad she'd described wouldn't have let his daughter end up in foster care, not if he were still alive. Judging by her suddenly rigid posture, I had the feeling this wound was fresh.

She nodded but didn't speak. Instead, she focused on the "terrible" movie. It was at Alan Rickman's classic "I'll carve your heart out with a spoon" line.

"Is that Snape?" she asked, changing the subject.

"If by Snape, you mean Alan Rickman, one of the best actors of all time," I said, "then yes. You are correct."

Reese rolled her eyes. That was when I noticed the case file lying open on the couch beside her.

"Doing some light reading?" I asked, snatching the file from the sofa and snapping it closed.

"Hey!" she protested by pointing her spoon at me and spilling milk on my floor.

"These are private police documents," I told her.

"Then why do you have them?"

"I took them from Burke," I admitted. "But do as I say and not as I do, and I say don't go through my private police documents. Not that these matter much, anyway."

"What are you talking about? I think they prove that the killer was the 407 number."

"Why do you think that?"

"Because he said, 'If that jockstrap ever hurts you, I'll kill him.'" The kid had a point, and I'd noticed the text myself back before I was sure Chris Bryce sent it.

"I'm sure Burke will piece that together all by himself."

Reese stopped shoveling cornflakes into her mouth and stared at me. "Why would he need to do that by himself? Aren't you best friends? I mean, he was here looking for you an hour ago."

Of course he was. "That's because I quit."

Reese could not have looked more offended if I'd punched her in the face. "What? You can't quit."

I shrugged. "I already have. I guess violent crime isn't really my thing anymore."

"Is it because you were hit by a car?"

"That's part of it."

"Do you think it was the killer who hit you with a car?"

"That's a definite maybe."

"Isn't that a good thing?"

"I'm sorry?"

"The killer is coming for you now. That means you're getting close."

Her words echoed in my head like a song on repeat. *The killer is coming for you now.* Wasn't that the truth? Was history doomed to repeat itself every time I grappled with darkness? I could feel my chest tighten, and I knew I had to do something. "You done with that?" I asked, taking the bowl from Reese's hands and heading to the sink. I dumped out what was left of the milk, squirted the soap on the sponge, and began washing the bowl. As I washed, I counted my breaths—breathing in for two counts and breathing out for four. I was not about to have a panic attack in front of my teenage intruder.

After a moment, I heard Reese get up from the couch and step toward the kitchen area behind me. "You're—are you scared?"

I dropped the bowl in the sink and turned the water off. "Of *course* I'm scared. Only an idiot would be chill after a murderer tried to run them over with a car." My hands were gripping the sink so hard my knuckles were turning white.

"But ... but you can't give up," Reese said, voice barely above a whisper—almost pleading. "Someone was *murdered*, and the cops arrested the wrong guy. What if they send that guy to prison instead of the real killer? Don't you want to do something?"

"I'm not the only one who can solve this case," I reminded her through gritted teeth.

"It looks to me like you're the only one who has."

I sucked in a breath and pushed away from the counter. My heart was beating so fast it sounded like ocean waves crashing in my ears, and my stomach was twisting like tangled snakes. I had to get out.

"Do you like po'boys?" I asked, moving across the room and grabbing my keys, my body having shifted into autopilot.

Reese stammered incoherently.

"What do you prefer? Fish, shrimp, crawfish, oyster?"

"Fish?" she murmured.

"Sure, pick the lamest thing on the menu," I told her and made my escape.

Deuce Marlboro did not work on Sundays. I'm not sure when I memorized his work schedule, and I had no intention of thinking about that fact too much as I walked into The Gambler. I was surprised to see a few patrons sitting around. Noon on a Sunday isn't exactly happy hour. Then I noticed the football game on the flat-screen televisions. I suddenly remembered why I usually avoided any and all bars on Sundays, other than the questionable moral standard indicated by going to a drinking establishment on the Sabbath.

I looked around the small interior for a familiar face. Ace was working the bar for once while Dice moved from table to table, serving alcohol and the typical pub food. Meanwhile, Domino was watching the Saints play.

I took a deep breath and strode up to the bar. Given my stature, I had to hop a little to sit on the tall stool, but I'd like to pretend that I did so with all the grace of a classy debutante.

Ace noticed me almost immediately and made his way over, flashing me a perfect dimpled smile. "Hey there," he said. "Chase, isn't it?"

"You must like it when Deuce beats you to a bloody pulp." I turned to see Dice leaning on the bar to my right, her hazel eyes glaring at Ace.

"What are you talking about?" Ace played innocent.

Dice's glare intensified. "Go deal with the tables, you shameless flirt. I'll handle this order."

"Oh, come now, baby. You know I only have eyes for you."

Dice shooed him away with a flick of her wrist, then hopped over the bar and turned to me. I noticed with dread that she had not lost the glare.

"I told you not to break my brother's heart," she said. "I should pull out my earrings and fight you right here, but judging by the way you look like warmed-over garbage, I don't think the fight would be worth my time."

"Thanks for that," I grumbled. Honestly, I thought I had cleaned up pretty well for someone who still felt slightly hungover.

"Seriously, Chase, how much did you drink last night?"

"I didn't drink last night. *Friday* night, however, I had the largest bottle of whisky money could buy. Speaking of, mind making me a Sazerac? I could really use a drink."

Dice scoffed. "You're on a case."

"Haven't you heard? I quit."

Dice studied me for a moment, her sharp eyes analyzing every part of me—from my disheveled mop of hair to my red Converse. "You gonna give up when there's still a murderer out there?"

"Not my problem. I'm not the law," I said, but even I knew that argument was weak.

Dice shook her head, and I could see her disappointment stamping a line between her two perfect brows. Great. I added her to my growing list of people I'd disappointed. "No wonder Deuce has been acting like a kicked pup. You're not at all who we thought you were."

"You're right. I'm no use to anyone. Now, can I please get a Sazerac and two po'boys? One shrimp and one fish."

Dice shook her head. "No to the Sazerac. Time to deal with your mistakes sober."

"I could just go somewhere else."

"Then your sandwiches would get cold." With that, Dice walked through the door behind the oversized bar and into the kitchen.

I'd be lying if I told you I enjoyed any part of the football game playing on the television. Sure, the Saints were winning, but that meant that everyone was extra boisterous and cheering every time the quarterback stepped onto the field. It was so loud it gave me a headache, as if the rolling in my stomach wasn't bad enough.

True to her word, Dice didn't take long at all. She came out with my po'boys about fifteen minutes later. I paid her in cash, then got up from my seat at the bar.

"You really think I broke his heart?" I asked, unable to step away without knowing the full weight of my sins.

Dice leaned on the bar and looked me in the eyes. "I think it was always gonna play out like this. You're too broken to do anything other than break other people."

I have never agreed with Dice more.

Chapter 23

God Bless the Child

I tried to cheer myself up on the walk back to my apartment. I had let down everyone, including myself, and failed to get any spirits to help lift *my* spirit. I didn't want to take my funky mood out on the kid, so I tried to think positive thoughts as I ambled through the courtyard. To be honest, I kept coming up short.

When I walked into the kitchen with the sandwiches, it was to discover Reese unloading the dishwasher. I'd been living in that apartment for years, and I didn't even know the dishwasher worked. I just hand-washed the dishes I needed and let the rest sit in filth until they were needed again.

"That for me?" Reese Kelly asked me when I dropped the fish po'boy on the table and tried to keep track of where the kid was putting my cups, bowls, plates, and assorted cutlery.

"Where's Louis?" I asked.

Reese pointed over to his cage in answer. "I went ahead and fed him. He's been snoozing ever since," she said.

"Did you like the movie?" I asked.

She shrugged. "It was all right. Super corny, and Kevin Costner couldn't do a British accent to save his life, but it wasn't awful. I mean,

Men in Tights and the Disney version are both better, but the version with Russell Crowe is still the worst."

"You think the Disney version with the animated fox is better than Alan Rickman?" Seriously? This extreme error in judgment made me consider how many times this kid had broken into my apartment again. I even briefly considered changing the locks, but I figured it wouldn't work. Besides, Burke would find out about it and make me feel guilty. That's the issue with having a grade-A detective with a strong moral compass as your best friend.

On top of that, I'd already had an extra key made, which I had surreptitiously left on the coffee table when we were talking earlier—before I got all freaked out by literally everything she was saying. I glanced over at the living room area and saw that the key was gone, so the kid had taken the hint—and the key.

Reese didn't bother answering the question. She finished with the dishes then picked her po'boy up from the table and unwrapped it, taking a huge bite and letting out some guttural noise that I wouldn't have thought a kid her size was capable of making.

I smiled. "It's good, right?"

She nodded her head vigorously. "This is the best po'boy I've ever had."

"It's not as good as the barbeque shrimp," I told her, opening my own sandwich, "but it's good. The Gambler has the best po'boys in town. They won the Oak Street Po'boy Festival four years in a row."

"I'm fairly sure that festival is just a charity event and not an actual competition," Reese hit me with that truth, "but it's still the best po'boy I've ever had." She took another huge bite and made her way over to my lumpy sofa, propping her feet up on my homemade coffee table, which I still hadn't forgotten that she'd insulted. "So, The Gambler?" she continued. "Is that where your hot Cajun boyfriend works?"

I started choking on my barbecue shrimp. A shrimp literally got caught in my windpipe. It took me fifteen whole seconds to dislodge it with painful coughing, and did the kid help? No. She laughed at my pain.

"He's not," I gasped between coughs, "not my boyfriend."

"He was here until past midnight Friday bandaging your road rash." She indicated the crisp white bandages on my arms. "He may not be your boyfriend, but he's definitely something."

I shrugged. The po'boy was suddenly not settling so well in my stomach. "He could've been, I guess."

"You two get in a fight?"

No, I just dumped all my tragic life history on him in the course of an evening, but I wasn't about to tell the kid that.

"I'm sure you'll work it out," Reese said.

I laughed. "You know, I'm the investigator here. Maybe you should leave the psychoanalysis to me."

"Actually, I've been meaning to talk to you about that." She hopped up and strode toward my refrigerator to get herself a can of Coke before returning to the couch to eat more food. "I was thinking you might need some help around here."

"Excuse me?"

"I mean, you're a fine investigator, I'm sure, but—"

"I'm far better than just *fine*, thank you very much," I told her, all my insecurity transitioning into false bravado.

"Yeah, I'm sure, but wouldn't it be easier to detect stuff if you worked in a clean office and apartment?"

I looked around my dusty apartment and lied, "It's not that bad."

"This entire place is completely disorganized."

"I have filing cabinets."

"Yes. Empty filing cabinets and a desk full of files that date back to July of last year. You literally can't see your desk because of those files."

I scoffed. "You can totally see my desk."

"What color is it?"

Crap. This kid was calling me on everything. I'm pretty sure the desk is a dark oak, but it might be redwood. Either way, I got it from a thrift store. "I've been meaning to get around to cleaning it, actually."

"But you haven't had time because you're too busy solving cases," she gave me an excuse.

Seriously? Now the kid was trying to charm me. She was manipulating me and might have been doing a good job. "Okay, wipe the brown off your nose and tell me what you want," I told her.

She finished the last bite of her po'boy, wiped her hands on a napkin, and sat straight up on the couch so that she was looking me in the eye. "I want to come work for you."

"No."

"Why not?" There was a hint of a whine in her voice that made me cringe.

"I can't pay you," I said as I finished my own delicious sandwich. It was the truth. Private investigating isn't lucrative. I could barely afford the apartment I lived in, not with all my college debts to pay. I was also looking into getting a new camera and a telephoto lens. I couldn't afford to pay anyone but me.

"I'll work for free," she said.

"What would you do?" I asked.

"Your filing, your cleaning, and I'd even cook for you if you needed me to."

"So, you're asking to be my free butler. What's the catch?"

"All you have to do is teach me the craft."

"The craft?" What exactly did she think I was doing for a living? "You want to be a private investigator?"

She nodded.

"Why?"

She paused, and I could tell she was thinking over her answer. That was a pretty good sign of lying most of the time. Finally, she shrugged and answered, "Because it's cool."

Those sounded like famous last words to my ears.

"Oh no. No way, little bird," I said. "You will not be the Robin to my Batman. I do not need a sidekick, and my life is *not* a comic book."

"I already know what you're gonna say, and yes, I know it's dangerous—but I'll be fine. I'll do what you tell me and stay out of trouble."

I had recently been reminded of why I usually avoided danger myself. Still, I couldn't let the kid know she was right. "Actually, what I was going to say is that it's usually pretty boring, and you'll end up hating it within a week."

"Then give me a shot," she reasoned. "If you're so sure I'll quit in a week, then what do you have to lose?"

I stood up and walked into the kitchen, throwing the wax paper my sandwich had been wrapped in into the trash can. "Do you want a Coke or something?" I asked her.

"You're changing the subject," she accused, "and I already got a Coke, remember?" She waved the can at me.

"I'm not changing the subject," I told her. "I gave you my answer, and I'm sticking to it."

"But why? I could help you. Especially with this current case. I mean, your undercover thing failed, and I could totally pass as a college student and—"

"What current case?" I said, raising my voice. "I told you. I quit the Goldman case. I am officially case-free."

"So you say, but if you have me helping out—"

"You want me to let you go undercover on a case involving someone who tried to *murder me with his car*?" I asked. "That's *not* happening. This case is too dangerous. For both of us."

"Just hear me out." Reese got up from her place on the couch and went over to my office area, grabbing my laptop and bringing it over to me despite my protests. She typed something and then turned the screen toward me. On it was a video of none other than Regina Doyle performing a musical ballad I'd never heard before. She really was talented and had a powerful voice that reminded me of Cynthia Erivo.

"Stop it," I demanded when my heart couldn't handle it anymore.

"Wait," Reese said, retaking control of the computer and pulling up a video interview of Reggie and Goldman. The two of them had gone to one of the local elementary schools together to read to children with disabilities, and a reporter had shown up to film them for a human-interest piece. The young couple gushed over the children they had met and over each other. They were happy, vibrant, and in love. It was just one more reminder of why I'd joined the FBI all those years ago—to chase down the worst of humanity, the kind that destroys everything beautiful.

But then I'd been chased down and butchered—destroyed to my very core. I was no good to anyone anymore.

"Turn it off," I told Reese through gritted teeth.

Reese stopped the video and sat the open laptop on the coffee table, sitting down in the chair across from me. "Don't you see how beautiful she was?" Reese asked. "She was going to be the next big thing, and she died scared and alone. You read those texts. You *know* how scared she was. Why don't you do something?"

"Because nothing I do will change anything," I told her. *I can't save everyone.* "And all this—this that you're doing, it's not going to change anything either. I quit that case because I know I'm a loser, and it's about time you got over this idealized image you have of me and realize that. While you're at it, stop thinking you're so smart just because you drew some conclusions from a string of text messages. If you were smart, you'd never have pulled up those videos. That alone tells me you'd make a lousy detective because you made this personal. Go find someone else's time to waste."

I turned back toward the kid and immediately wished I hadn't. Her eyes were wet with tears. I could tell she was struggling to hold them back, and I scrambled for something to say, knowing that I'd already taken a step too far.

"I just," she muttered, and her voice was thick, "I just wanted the chance." She turned on her heel and made her escape before I could say another word, slamming the apartment door so hard that it woke Louis up. He shot out of his cage, clambered up to the top of my refrigerator, and chittered at me angrily. I stood there in shock, going over all that I had said in my mind. I had shouted at her, and I hadn't listened to her.

I told myself that she wouldn't speak to me again.

I told myself that was for the best.

I told myself I didn't care.

As soon as the kid left, I tossed her leftover sandwich in the refrigerator. Our entire conversation had made me too queasy to eat it myself. I then went to my kitchen and began rummaging through my cabinets, looking for something to drink. I was desperate. In a matter of days, I'd managed to fail every single one of my friends, and now I'd turned the kid against me too. It was worse than being fired from the FBI.

As I was rummaging for the only friend I'd managed not to fail—whisky—I heard a video on my laptop suddenly begin playing. I looked over to see Louis off the refrigerator and sitting on top of my keyboard.

I walked over to my laptop and picked up my traitorous ferret. Despite my desire to slam the laptop closed, I found myself mesmerized by the screen. The video of Goldman and Regina had switched over to another video from Tulane University's Theatre Department. Regina was again featured in this video, wearing the traditional peasant costume worn by Cinderella in Rogers and Hammerstein's classic musical. She was laughing—as charming as always—and then she began to spin. On her second turn around, the dress transformed into a beautiful golden ballgown—a magical costume change if I'd ever seen one.

"Changing costumes," I muttered as something clicked inside my brain. Of course! It all made sense now. I sat down on my couch, my excitement waging war with the anxious pit in my stomach. I had solved the case—of that I was certain—but I'd also quit the case. Could Burke figure it out without me? Probably. Did I desperately want to prove to him and myself that I wasn't completely useless and broken? Definitely.

I hopped to my feet, held the ferret up, and kissed him on the nose before plopping him on the couch, closing my laptop, and heading out the door to break into a dorm room.

Chapter 24

Crazy He Calls Me

B reaking into a dorm room is not my ideal way to spend a Sunday night, but after checking Candace's latest Twitter update and realizing that she'd be at a football party at the Sigma Chi fraternity house all night, I knew I might have a chance. Besides, it is better than watching geriatric ladies practice swing dancing—to be fair, almost anything is better than watching geriatric ladies practice swing dancing. I considered climbing through Candace's bedroom window, but the odds of free climbing up to the second floor and guessing the correct window really did not appear to be in my favor. Therefore, I rethought my strategy and settled on stealing the master key from the Residential Assistant's office at the main entrance.

I would like to take the time to detail a super high-stakes espionage sequence in which I snuck past multiple security officers and manipulated the RA into giving me the key, but that just wouldn't be accurate. It was far from exciting when I walked into the RA's office to discover that the poor college kid on duty had dozed off while reading through Plato's *Republic*. I mean, the only thing even marginally dramatic about the whole situation was that I pulled my hood over my head to make myself slightly less recognizable. The spare master key was hanging on a small hook on the wall. I quickly snagged it and left the office without being spotted by a single security person.

I mean, do colleges even have security people? I thought they did, but now that I consider it, I have never actually seen one. What the heck did they spend that inordinate amount of tuition on anyway?

Back on track, I made my way up the stairwell to Candace's hall, which was blessedly deserted. I really shouldn't have been surprised. It was a Sunday night in New Orleans the weekend after Halloween.

Despite my luck, I remained cautious and waited outside Candace's door for a minute to see if I heard anything inside. Once I was sure the coast was clear, I slipped on my latex gloves and let myself in. After securing the door behind me, I took a risk and turned on the light. Everything was as it had been before, with half the room awash in color and the other half empty.

I checked the closet first because I knew that was where Candace had tossed her catsuit. I found it hanging up, right where she had put it that Friday. I picked it up carefully and examined it for any damage or evidence. Other than the fact that it was an impossibly tight catsuit, there was absolutely nothing remarkable about it at all. I put it back where I had found it and focused my attention on the other clothes hanging up on the rack. At the very end, I saw what I had only glimpsed before; it was a purple, pin-striped blazer hanging on a plastic hanger with a pair of matching pants and a green button-up shirt. The whole costume clearly belonged to a man.

I quickly took it out of the closet and looked closer at it. It was exactly what I had suspected. I took it off the rack and laid it across the empty bed—Regina's bed—to examine it. The green flower sewn onto the lapel was slightly damaged, and a button was missing from the green shirt. I examined it further to find pasty-white, oil-based makeup on the collar of the shirt and jacket, as well as on the cuffs of the sleeves. It wasn't completely crusted over yet, so it had likely been worn that week, and the wearer had also been wearing what appeared to be a thicker, cake-like makeup—clown makeup. After pulling the collar close to my face to give it a whiff—it smelled like booze and sweat, as most things do in a college dorm room—I noticed that there was another red stain on the shirt, just to the side of where the lapel would sit. I thought at first that it might be blood, but after smelling it, I determined it was lipstick.

I quickly pulled out my phone and snapped a few pictures of the suit. Burke needed to get a search warrant for this place ASAP, and in order to get him to do that, I needed to show him some evidence. Of course, I couldn't just text him the pictures. That would prove bad for both of us if he knew I'd broken into her dorm. I'd have to meet up with him. I'd started to call him right then, but something stopped me.

I turned toward the door leading out into the hall and saw two shadows just under it. Then I heard a key being forced into a lock. "Just a sec," I heard Candace's muffled voice from the other side of the door. Well, crap.

I had seconds, but I somehow managed to gather up the suit from the bare mattress and dive underneath the bed and behind the chest of drawers before Candace re-entered her room. When she did, I heard her stumble to a stop just inside the door. Another set of footsteps stumbled in behind her. She was not alone —double crap.

"Huh," I heard Candace mutter. "I thought I turned the light off."

Triple crap and a big ole' pile of shit.

"Does it matter?" another female voice answered. I was super glad that it was just some other college girl with her and not Chris Bryce, the drug dealer.

"I guess not," Candace answered. If they were going to a party, Candace had obviously been pre-gaming; her words were already slurring together.

"Would you just get your wallet so we can go?" the other college girl asked. "The guys are waiting."

"Right," Candace said, and I heard her make her way toward her desk and start going through drawers looking for her wallet.

You know how when you're in church or marching in a parade or anywhere you shouldn't move, and you suddenly have the most unbearable urge to scratch *everything*? Yes, well, that was what was going on with me at that exact moment. It didn't help that I was cramped behind a chest of drawers in a place that hadn't been dusted since move-in day, *and* my biggest fear is spiders. First, my toes started to itch. Then, my nose started to itch. Next, my ear, followed soon after by the back of my head and my lower back. Pretty soon, I was itching all over. I didn't think it would ever end, but then I felt something—a light brush of fabric right under the tips of my fingers. I had found something, and now that I had that to concentrate on, the itching faded to the back of my mind.

"I can't find it," Candace whined.

I heard the annoyed clack of heels as her companion marched across the room toward Candace, followed by the unzipping of a bag. "It's right here in your purse, you slut. Now, let's go."

High heels left the room with a long-legged stride, and Candace shuffled behind her, seemingly less eager to leave. When she got to the door, I heard her pause, and I couldn't see her, but I swear she looked right over to where I was hiding. Then the lights went out, and I heard the door shut and the bolt click into place.

I waited a few minutes before scrambling out from my hiding place. Without daring to turn on the light, I hung the suit back in the closet. The fabric I had found under the bed was still clutched tightly in my hand. I hesitated a moment before reaching over and turning on Candace's desk lamp to see what it was I had found. As soon as the light hit it, the air rushed out of me. I stared at the clue. Then I took several pictures before tucking it back beneath the chest of drawers where I'd found it.

As soon as I got to my Isuzu Rodeo and started off campus, I called Burke.

He didn't answer because, of course he didn't answer. Nobody ever answers their phone when you need them to. I finally had evidence enough to clear Lackey's name and solve his case, and Burke wasn't answering his damn phone. I called him three more times before I'd even made it all the way off campus. I briefly considered going by the station, but I didn't think it was worth the risk of seeing Captain Chihuahua. Besides, it was Sunday. Surely, he wasn't at work, right? I might have gone by his house, but I didn't want to risk crashing some family night function. I was suddenly very aware of how one-sided our relationship seemed to be, and by that, I mean that I should at least be able to use police equipment to look up his address like he did mine.

Burke wasn't much for checking his text messages, but I sent him one anyway as soon as I had parked my car back on my side of town. I then grabbed my black purse and headed up to my apartment. Just as I made it to my door and pulled out my keys, the cellphone I'd stuffed into my back pocket began to ring. I managed to answer it only after a bit of scrambling around with my keys, purse, and phone.

"You called me eight times," I heard Burke's bass voice grumble over the phone, "and sent me a text I don't want to read." See what I mean about the texting?

"You know, you could sound more grateful," I told him, trying to single out my apartment key from the ring. "I just solved your case for you."

"I thought you quit."

"You can thank Louis for changing my mind."

"I'm not thanking your ferret."

"Rude."

I heard him sigh through the phone. To anyone else, it would have sounded like he was annoyed, but I knew he was simply overwhelmed by the good news. "What's the catch?" he asked, his voice sounding strangely weary.

"There's no catch." I finally snagged the correct key from my key-chain. "Actually, you do need to get a search warrant for Candace Moon's dorm room."

Burke was silent for a moment, and I realized that not all my actions that day had been above the bar and that I was talking to a cop. "Chase, what did you do?"

"That doesn't matter," I told him, "and believe me when I say you don't actually want to know."

"Chase ..." There was an actual warning in his voice. It was cute.

I was trying to get my key into the keyhole, and it was proving difficult. "You'll find a purple suit in her closet and—"

"Why do I care about a purple suit?"

I finally managed to sink the key into the doorknob. "You'll know when you see it, but the most important thing is what's left of Chris's Scarecrow costume hiding under Regina's chest of drawers."

"Detective Harlem," I heard an accented voice call just as Burke let out his standard two swear words per annoyance. I turned to see Rose Baker standing at the threshold of her apartment door.

"Hang on, Burke," I told him because putting a cursing detective on hold is a good plan. I then asked her, "May I help you, Mrs. Baker?'

Her cheek was still swollen and bruised, and she moved like a mouse who would rather not be noticed. She shuffled toward me but did not look up enough to look me in the eyes.

"Is Reese ... is Reese with you?"

I nearly dropped the phone. "What? N-no. She slammed her way out of my apartment hours ago. Why would you think she's with me?"

Mrs. Baker fidgeted uncomfortably, still not meeting my gaze. "She ... she said she was going to be helping you tonight, Detective."

I stared at her and blinked. "H-helping me?" I stammered. Of course! Of frickin' course! This kid, the one who acted way too much like me for her own good, had run out of my apartment in a huff because I had told her she couldn't be my junior private investigator. What would I have done if someone had told fourteen-year-old me that I couldn't do something? Heck, what did I do every time someone told *adult* me I couldn't do something? I proved them wrong, and of course, that's exactly what my newly found mini-me had done. I felt the acid in my stomach bubble up, and I recognized it as a sign of tightly controlled panic.

"Burke," I said into the phone.

"Oh, so you're talking to *me* now? You know I hate it when you talk to someone else while I'm on the phone."

"I need a favor."

"What?" Burke asked, his tone calming as he sensed something was wrong.

"While someone else files for the warrant, which we'll need *tonight*, I need you to bring a group down to the fraternity party at Tulane."

"What? Why?"

"My kid is about to go to a party with a murderer."

There was only a moment's pause when Burke said, "I'm on it," and hung up.

I then turned to Mrs. Baker, who looked terrified, which was likely due to my "partying with a murderer" comment. I should really learn to think before I talk. "She'll be fine, Mrs. Baker," I promised. "I'll be back with her as soon as possible."

Chapter 25

Dance Me to the End

Three minutes later, Burke called me back. "You at your place?" he asked.

"Kind of. I had to go in and get my other gun," I explained.

"You didn't have your gun on you?"

"I said, my *other* gun. I'm not an idiot. I always keep a piece in my car."

"I'll come get you."

"I'm almost at my car right now. I'll meet you at the Sigma Chi fraternity house on Tulane's campus."

"Sigma Chi?" Burke questioned.

"Chris's fraternity."

"How would Reese know that?"

"Instagram, Twitter, Facebook—some kind of social media," I explained.

"Chase," Burke's voice turned suddenly preachy, and I knew what was coming, "I'm on my way right now. Wait until I get there."

"Like hell," I huffed.

"Chase, you're already on thin ice with Morris, and you don't know what that kid's walked into—"

"First of all, I've been to a fraternity party before, believe it or not, and I know *exactly* what that kid is walking into, which is why I'm getting to campus as quickly as possible. Secondly, shove a Xanax into a doggie treat and give it to that chihuahua if you want her to calm down."

I could hear Burke's frustrated sigh over the phone before he answered, "Seriously, you have an issue keeping your temper when the case gets personal."

"What are you talking about?"

"You remember Bianca and Tarant?"

"I don't know what you're talking about." I did know.

"I'm serious, Harlem." Ooh, he'd started calling me by my last name. That meant he was *really* serious.

I hopped in my car, jammed the key into the ignition, and pulled out in the direction of the fraternity house. "I'll meet you there, Burke. Don't be late." I hung up and shoved my phone into my pocket.

All the way to the party, I kept going through my last conversation with Reese. It made me realize I was, without a doubt, an idiot. The kid was asking for attention; she was asking for a mentor, and instead of stopping to think about why she might be reaching out, I shut her out. I let myself think that I was shutting her out to keep her safe. Then, with the utmost ironic flare, she decided to prove herself by going to a party with a murderer. I was by far the worst role model ever. I was also a terrible liar. I'd almost convinced myself that I was protecting her by keeping her away from me. Really, I was just trying to protect myself.

I couldn't stop berating myself while thinking of all the terrible things that could happen to the kid if I didn't get to her on time. I can't save everyone, but I was damn sure gonna save her.

I pulled into the already crowded fraternity parking lot at a speed that made any question about my driving prowess null and void. I hopped out of my car, shoved my .38 into the shoulder holster under my brown leather jacket, and marched up to the front door of the large fraternity house. Of course, some jockstrap was standing there in a bedsheet.

"Hey," he called to me, but I silenced him by holding my open palm right in his face.

"I'm looking for a girl," I told him.

"You're the only girl I see." Oh ick. The Neanderthal smelled like he'd been swimming in alcohol, and he was hitting on me? I considered breaking his clavicle just to see if he'd feel it, but then I thought of Burke and changed my mind. I could control myself. I could behave professionally and not lose my temper, even if this guy was preventing me from finding a fourteen-year-old girl who didn't know she was in over her head. I could behave even if I were taking this entire situation quite personally.

So, I shoved the guy into a nearby bush and hustled through the front doors.

The house was packed. So packed, in fact, that someone my height couldn't move without getting a shoulder to the face at every step. Sometimes being short sucked. I finally made my way through the sweaty crowd and over to the soberest guy I could find.

"Hey, you!" I shouted over the live band, playing something that sounded like an evil bastardization of a jazz standard that had been put into a blender with gangster rap. The semi-sober guy was right in front of me, so I reached out and tapped him on the shoulder. He turned to look at me, and I waved. "I'm looking for a girl. She's about my height with brown skin and curly black hair. You seen her?"

"You just described half the girls here," he told me, and he was mostly right. I needed a new strategy. If I were Reese, what would I do to prove myself to the sleuth next door?

"Fine," I shouted. "Do you know Chris Bryce?"

"Yeah!" the guy told me. "He's the life of the party."

"Do you know where I could find him?"

"He's probably upstairs with his girlfriend—room 208. I don't know if you wanna go in there, though. Chris gets pretty crazy after a few drinks."

I smiled and nodded. I really hoped that Chris would get crazy. That way, I would have every right to get a little crazy myself.

I quickly located the stairs across the room and started to make my way to them. That was when the dumbest thing possible happened: Candace Moon spotted me.

"Hey, you bitch!" I heard her shout from just a few people away. She'd clearly had a few more drinks since her pre-gaming experience. "You're that detective *slut*." She slurred the last word. Slurring profanity makes it sound so much less insulting.

"Sorry, Miss Moon, but I don't have the time to be anybody's slut. Maybe you should consider dropping that habit yourself while I walk away."

"Hold it!" she shouted and grabbed the collar of my leather jacket, spinning me around to face her. On a normal day, I would say that Candace is about my size, but with her in six-inch heels and me in flat sneakers, she was towering half a foot above me. "You got no right here." So, proper grammar went out the window when she was drunk. That was fine. I have the habit of ending my sentences with prepositions.

"I came to pick up something that belongs to me," I told her. "As soon as I get it, I'm out." I turned to walk away from her again.

"Christopher is *mine!*" she shouted at me from behind.

"Keep him." I could get my own, and he'd be far more attractive and less creepy. I tried to keep my stride consistent as I approached the staircase.

Then Candace Moon pulled my hair.

She sank her gaudy nails into the back of my scalp and yanked my hair hard enough to spin me around to face her. Just like that, years of martial arts and self-defense training kicked in, and my muscle memory took over. My hand shot out, and a loud crack resounded throughout the room as my knuckles connected with her face in an epic backhand. The room fell silent, and I could see everyone looking our way.

We glared at each other for a moment until someone finally called out "catfight" as a joke, and the party around us commenced once again with laughter.

I should probably have stopped there, but I couldn't help but step toward the girl who was now holding her cheek and looking more than a little embarrassed and confused. I got up beside her and whispered in her ear, "Let me make this clear, precious. I don't want your man for myself. I want him behind bars. Get in my way again, and you'll get more than a scratched face."

She probably didn't even get the jab at her stupid Catwoman costume. She simply turned a little pale and retreated back to her posse of drunk college girls.

I stomped away in a huff, taking the stairs two at a time until I reached the second floor. Then I pushed by every canoodling couple I came across, until I made it to room 208. I didn't knock. I threw open the door and marched in. There on the bed was Chris Bryce, fully clothed and sitting right next to Reese Kelley. *My* fourteen-year-old, self-appointed apprentice.

I must have looked some shade of scary because Bryce jumped up as soon as he saw me, hands up and palms facing toward me. "We're just talkin'," he said. "She came in askin' for me, so the guys sent her up."

Reese jumped up as well. "He's right," she said. "Just talkin'. Apparently, I don't look old enough to be here."

"I got a kid sister at home," Bryce claimed. "I ain't no pedophile, but some guys here wouldn't care."

I glared at both of them. I really just wanted to launch myself at Bryce and tear him limb from limb, but dammit, I was going to prove Burke wrong this time.

I pointed at Reese. "You," I growled, "get to the car."

Without a word, she edged past me and out the door. I could hear her taking the stairs two or three at a time as I continued to glare at Bryce.

"I swear I didn't touch her," he told me.

I turned to walk away before my temper got the best of me, but his next words stopped me.

"I didn't kill Reggie either—or her meathead boyfriend."

I turned toward him, not even trying to hide the disbelief on my face.

He nodded, but it wasn't confident. He was still scared, looking at me like I was some kind of wild animal that would attack at any moment.

"Yeah, I know who you are, and I know what you think," he told me. "I didn't kill anybody."

"Why should I believe you?" I asked.

He shrugged, but the action was far from nonchalant. This guy looked like he was ready to squirm out of his own skin. "I didn't touch your kid."

"So, you're not a pedophile," I hissed. "Good for you."

"I'm not a good guy," he admitted, "but I'm not that bad either."

"You were Regina Doyle's drug dealer. Drugs are what killed her, so her blood's on your hands," I hissed.

He shook his head vigorously, still not lowering his hands. "I sell drugs, sure, but I never sold no coke to her. She was my friend. I-I *cared* about her."

Of course he did. Every straight guy who'd ever seen her in a show probably thought himself in love with Regina Doyle.

"If I'd known she was on the take, I'd ... I'd have—"

"What? You'd have stopped her? Stopped selling her the dope?"

He shook his head, still looking antsy. "Maybe we could go somewhere—talk?"

"Do I look stupid to you? Seriously, is the word scrawled across my forehead, and I just missed it somehow?"

He shook his head, shuffling his feet, his eyes darting all around the room before finally landing on mine again, only to grow large and round. "Don't—" he started, and that's when I realized, too late, that the guy wasn't scared of me. Not that it mattered because that was also the moment when I felt a sharp thwack at the back of my head, and the world went dark.

Chapter 26

Baby, I Don't Cry Over You

I opened my eyes, and the world was dark—frozen, unyielding darkness. I couldn't move. The coppery smell of blood was overwhelming, and a sticky wetness slid down my neck. My chest constricted, and I couldn't breathe. I tried to catch my breath, but it was so cold and so dark and so—

"What the *hell*, Candy?!" I heard a male voice shout. It sounded like it was coming from mere paces away.

"Shut *up*," a female voice responded, so close I felt like I could reach out and touch her.

I opened my eyes to find the annoying glow of a fluorescent light shining down on a linoleum floor. I wasn't locked in the dark, I wasn't freezing to death, and I wasn't alone.

"She's a *cop!*" the boy, Bryce, hissed.

I took a slow breath and forced my heart to slow down, trying to get my eyes to focus. I could see the legs of a desk chair directly in front of me and two sets of human legs standing just beyond that. Everything was fuzzy at the edges, moving in a way that made my stomach roll, and somewhere in my mind, I realized that this was because I likely had a concussion.

I focused on the male pair of legs. Those had to belong to Chris Bryce, meaning the other set of legs belonged to...

"She's a private investigator; that's not the same thing." I would recognize the voice of that stupid little slut-shaming bitch anywhere.

I tried to move, my whole body tensing as if ready for a fight, but my head hurt too much. The room spun, and time lurched to a near standstill for what felt like hours. I took a breath, fighting the nausea, and slid my hand slowly to the gun under my jacket—only to find the holster empty. I let out an involuntary groan, shutting my eyes, and the voices stopped arguing momentarily.

"Thank God." Bryce sighed in relief. "She's alive."

I heard a shuffling of feet before Candace called out, "Let me go."

"No way. You're not killing a cop in my dorm room."

Well, crap. This psycho girl was planning to kill me. Sweet little me!

"She could ruin *everything*," she hissed.

"You really don't get it, do you?" he asked, but I was pretty sure the question was rhetorical. "You stupid bitch, *you've* ruined everything already."

I used their heated discussion as a distraction, reaching into my back pocket for my phone. My head still felt broken, and I knew the screen was too bright to search for Burke's number and give him a call. But I'd recently figured out the S.O.S. feature thanks to Geraldine's instructions. Also, Burke, being the total helicopter parent that he is, had emailed me an article and told me to list him and any "close friends" as my emergency contacts. I pressed the appropriate buttons and slid the S.O.S. into place, sending out a notification to emergency services as well as to all my emergency contacts.

The two college idiots were still arguing when I slid the phone back underneath me and attempted to sit up. The world lurched a little, and I was super worried that I'd throw up everywhere for a minute, but it passed. Too bad it didn't take the pain in my head with it. Even still, I wasn't going down without a fight. Concussion or not, I was going to use this little incident to my advantage.

"Excuse me," I called out, "could you two maybe stop shouting? I've got this unbelievable headache."

"You should really learn when to shut your slutty mouth," Candace hissed.

"Is that what you said to the Golden Boy before you stabbed him?" I shifted my gaze to Bryce as best I could, considering his image kept swimming around in my vision. "Or did *you* keep him distracted while she did the killing?"

His eyes widened, and I knew I'd struck a chord.

"Leave him out of this, bitch," Candace hissed. I smiled as best I could, though it probably looked more like a grimace, considering the pain I was in. "That's right," I said. "You love him. You couldn't stand the way he worshiped Reggie. Is that why *she* had to die? Because you were jealous?"

Bryce stepped away from Candace, staring at her in horror. "I thought you said it was an accident—that she did it to herself."

"Christopher, don't listen to her," Candace's voice turned to caramel as she spoke to him. Suddenly, it all made sense. Candace was the brain; Bryce just helped her move the product.

I laughed despite the pain. "I'm sure Candy here *accidentally* shoved Reggie's face into a pile of tainted cocaine and then failed to call the paramedics when she went into cardiac arrest."

"Is that true?" Bryce asked.

"Shut up, you freak!" Candace shrieked. I looked up to see her pointing my gun at my head, her hands shaking with fury. So, that's where it had disappeared to.

Maybe it was the pain in my head. Maybe I have a serious death wish, or maybe it was a bit of both. Either way, the gun pointed at my head didn't scare me. It just pissed me off. I glared at her as much as I could through the pain in my head and goaded her, "You know how to use that, precious?"

She cackled a laugh that would have rivaled the Witch of the West and said, "I think I can figure it out" She aimed.

I smirked. "The safety's on."

It was a lie—that gun doesn't even have a safety—but it worked. Just as Candace glanced down at the gun, Bryce grabbed a lamp from the desk and brought it down on her arms. The gun flew out of her hands, clattering across the floor and under the bed. Candace screeched, launching herself at me from across the room.

I was just about to admit to myself that I might have miscalculated my whole escape plan when Burke stepped through the door and between me and my would-be murderer.

"Easy there, Miss Moon," he said, flashing his badge in one hand while aiming his gun with the other. "You and your boyfriend are under arrest."

Three more officers came through the door behind him. They each looked familiar, but the only one I could name was Chandler. Guess I'd have to forgive him for blowing my cover since he came in as part of the "save Chase from imminent danger" team. Also, I'm pretty sure he tightened Bryce's cuffs way too tight, judging by the guy's shriek, and that type of pettiness is commendable.

While I was focusing my energy on the various arrests around me, Burke moved to situate himself right in front of me. He said my name, and judging by his tone, he had already said it several times before I noticed.

"Where's Reese?" I asked, trying to make my eyes focus on his.

"She's fine," he said. "Your head's bleeding."

I reached up and touched the back of my head. When I pulled my hand away, it was wet and covered with blood. "Damn," I grumbled. "Bitch hit me. Guess I'm lucky it wasn't with her car this time." If I had to have my head shaved and get stitches because of her, I was going to be pissed. "Took my gun, too. I think it's... it slid somewhere."

"Paramedics are on their way," he said, and he was doing that thing with his voice where he was trying to sound calm when he wasn't really calm at all. "Try to stay awake."

"You hear what they said?" I asked, trying to comply with his rather stupid orders because, of course, I understood the importance of staying awake if I had a concussion.

He nodded.

"Think it'll be enough?"

"I dunno," he admitted. "Depends on what my guys find in her dorm room, but at least now they have probable cause to search it."

Probable cause. That sounded good. It sounded so good that it put me straight to sleep.

Chapter 27

So Insensitive

When I woke again, I couldn't move. It was dark, it was cold, I was alone, and I knew with heart-dropping clarity that I would *die* alone. I tried to call out, but my words didn't come, as my tongue was frozen to the roof of my mouth. I tried to open my eyes, but they were frozen shut, my tears having welded my eyelashes together in a gruesome trap. Footsteps in the distance broke through the silence; I had to wake up, I had to be heard, I needed to *move*. I filled my lungs with stale, frigid air and *screamed*.

I woke up with a yelp, cold sweat dripping down my forehead, and the smell of blood and sterile alcohol burning my nostrils. Even if I hadn't noticed the cold air, uncomfortable bed, and annoying beeping machinery, I'd have been able to tell by the smell permeating throughout the place that I was in a hospital. I opened my eyes to see a green curtain hanging to my left and concluded that my location was, in fact, a New Orleans emergency room. Great. As a self-employed person, my health insurance is total garbage, and based on the fact that my head felt like it was floating rather than exploding, I was pretty sure they'd given me the good drugs.

"You're awake."

My eyes followed that voice until Reese Kelley swam into my vision. Her dark hair had become more frizzy than curly, and her eyes were bloodshot. Poor kid was probably freaked out, but there was another emotion in her dark eyes that I couldn't quite identify. Honestly, it wasn't my top priority at that moment.

"Did they shave my head?" I asked.

That confused her. "What?"

"To stitch me up," I explained, and even I could tell my words were slightly slurred, "did they shave my head?"

"Um, no?" she answered. "If they did, you can't tell it."

"Oh. Good." I glanced down at myself, noticing the hospital gown for the first time. I guessed that my shirt had been too covered with blood to salvage. "Where's my jacket?" I asked.

"Burke took it," she told me. "It had a lot of, um, blood on it, and he didn't want the hospital to throw it away or something."

I started to nod, but that hurt. "That jacket's important. Love that jacket."

My brain was being annoyingly slow. I knew there was something I should be doing, but I couldn't quite figure it out. I reviewed what Reese had told me before landing on my next question. "Where's Burke?"

"He had to go to the station," she said. "He wanted to make sure Bryce and Moon were booked right. I think he was pretty pissed."

"Nah," I said, "that's just Burke. Where's—"

"I'm sorry," Reese cut me off, and I was surprised at the desperate crack in her voice and the tears in her eyes.

I said something classy like, "Huh?" before she continued.

"You told me not to go, and I got mad about it even though I shouldn't have been mad about it; I just wanted you to see that I was capable or something, but I'm not capable." She was pacing across the linoleum floor, her hands gesticulating wildly. "Nobody thought I was old enough to be there—some of the guys offered to *teach* me things, and that was *super* sketchy—then Bryce wasn't a *total* jerk, but he was still kinda scary because I think someone had told him that cops were asking questions. Then you showed up to rescue me because I'm apparently the type of girl that needs rescuing, and you got hit in the head and almost died after being hit by a car, like, yesterday, and it's all my fault because if I'd just listened you wouldn't have been there and—"

"Whoa, whoa, whoa," I interrupted. "I'm going to stop you right there. How the hell is *any* of this your fault?"

"Because ... because I went to the party when you told me not to. Don't get me wrong, I have a pretty good excuse."

I raised an eyebrow at that.

"I'm a teenager," she explained, "so the frontal lobe of my brain isn't fully formed, and I make bad decisions all the time, which I know you'll say is why I shouldn't spend *all* my time around you because you don't need *any* help making bad decisions, but—"

"Stop!" I cut her off again. Honestly, she was making my head hurt more. "Okay, yeah, going to the party was a bad plan," I admitted.

"Please don't send me away!" she shouted before I could continue. "I promise to listen next time. I won't mess up, really—"

There was real teen panic in her voice, so I found it necessary to cut her off yet again. "I'm not sending you away, kid. Seriously, where would I send you? You live across the hall."

My petty version of sarcasm at least made her smile.

"Besides," I continued, "I was the one who stayed behind in Bryce's room and let my guard down. I'm the one that let some sorority girl knock me out. None of that is on you." I took a deep breath and leaned back on the pillows. "And I could have been nicer when you asked about helping out."

"You were right, though," she said with such a helpless tone that I might have hugged her if I'd had the strength.

"Yeah, well, so were you."

That confused the kid. "What?"

"When you said I couldn't give up on the case. You were right."

"Oh. Thanks." She chewed on her bottom lip, still not making eye contact. "And thanks for showing up—when I was in trouble, you know."

I raised an eyebrow at that.

"Nobody's ever done that before," she told me. "Not for me."

That can't be true—I almost said that out loud before remembering who I was talking to. There was still so much I didn't know about the kid, but the idea that nobody had ever shown up for her broke my cold, dead heart just a little.

I reached out and put my hand on top of hers, searching for something to say that wouldn't make our situation sound like some sort of after-school special. Finally, I settled on, "Their loss. You're worth showing up for."

She smiled at that. "Is that the head injury talkin'?"

"What head injury?"

She nodded and coughed out a laugh at my poor attempt at humor. I guess she figured she owed me that much. I was nervous about having her around me. My life was not exactly safe, but I knew that she needed someone—not a mom, not even a sister, but a someone. I hoped I could handle being a someone.

"So," she changed the subject, "how long have you known Chris was the murderer?"

"He's not."

She looked at me with wide eyes.

"You were right," I told her. "It was the girlfriend. It was all right there in those texts."

Reese let out a victorious laugh. "Now you have to hire me."

I shrugged. "Still can't pay you, but we'll see."

"Seriously?" she asked, all that annoying teenage pride back in her voice. "You couldn't have solved this one without me."

"Well, technically, we were both right. I knew it was Reggie's drug dealer; I just had the wrong drug dealer in mind."

"And I'm the one who told you about the right drug dealer."

"I'd have worked it out eventually," I countered, "but yeah, you did okay up until you stopped listening to me."

She blushed like she was ashamed, and I hated myself a little for saying it.

"You've apologized, though," I added quickly, "so let's just put that behind us."

She nodded and allowed herself a small smile.

"Now, where's my phone? And my pants? Time to head out."

"That would be a hard pass, ma chérie." I turned to see Deuce Marlboro standing at the curtain, my cellphone in his hand.

"What are you doing here?" I asked.

He smiled, putting the phone in his pocket and coming to sit beside me on the bed. "Seems you put me in as an emergency contact."

I rolled my eyes. Of course. I'd forgotten about doing that the night Deuce walked me back to my apartment. I honestly forgot I even had his number. "Sorry for taking you away from work."

"It's Sunday," he reminded me. "You know Sunday's my day off." He reached over and slid a hair out of my face, his proximity making me blush. "You gave me a real scare. 'Specially when Dice tracked your phone here."

"Why'd they even let you in?" I asked. "Don't they have a family-only rule?"

"He told them he's your husband," Reese answered for him, and I swear the kid had hearts in her eyes.

I raised both brows at him.

He shrugged. "I'm yo 'husband; she's our daughter. It's fine."

"Right," I mumbled, pretending not to be embarrassed by how casually he referred to himself as my spouse. "Well, I appreciate you showing up, but I'm fine. I need to make sure that the bad guys get what's coming to them, so please give me my phone."

He shook his head. "Not until the doctor says it's okay."

"I'm mildly concussed, not dead," I grumbled.

"I think it's more than *mildly* concussed. The CT scan will tell us for sure," Reese spoke up. "In the meantime, the doctor said staring at a phone screen won't help your headache."

They were teaming up on me, and it was not fair. "I don't *plan* on staring at the screen," I told her through gritted teeth. "I *plan* to call Burke."

"Speaking of the case," Deuce said, kicking his feet up on the bed and slipping his arm behind me, careful to avoid my wounded head, "when did you know it was the drug dealer and not the athlete?"

Reese sat in the chair by the bed and scooted closer. They were clearly playing me, but I was too concussed to pick Deuce's pocket for my phone, so I really had nothing better to do than talk about work.

I sighed. "Since Burke filled me in on the case."

Reese's eyes widened. "No way."

I cleared my throat. "Can I at least have some coffee?"

"No," they said in unison because, *of course,* they did.

I rolled my eyes and answered Reese's question. "I wasn't one hundred percent sure, obviously, but given the facts, it was the only explanation I could think of."

I laid back on my pillows, explaining the case to them as best I could, given my concussion. Reese's clear interest kept me talking, and the way she lit up when I admitted to my time in the FBI made me simultaneously proud of my former career and ashamed of how it ended.

"So, how did Candace do it?" Reese asked after I finished my story.

I shrugged. "I'm a detective, not a psychic. That's why I need to interrogate her."

"Like, torture her?" Reese asked.

"Hardly," I told her. "I was FBI. Not CIA."

Deuce shifted beside me, bringing his hand next to mine and intertwining our fingers. To Reese, it probably seemed innocent enough, but I knew it meant that he'd noticed me trying to slip my phone out of his stupidly deep pocket. "Good to know."

At that moment, my phone started ringing. I turned quickly to Deuce and held out my hand.

"No," he told me.

"Dude, it could be my *mom*," I told him. "What if she got the alert and she's been trying to reach me this whole time? She probably thinks I'm dead or human-trafficked or part of some crazy New Orleans cult!"

The urgency in my voice prompted Deuce to act, and when he pulled out the phone and noticed that it did, in fact, say "mom" on the call screen, he handed it right over.

I took it and answered, "Hey Burke, gimme the deets."

I heard Reese let out a sound between a laugh and a snort, and Deuce rolled his eyes. I ignored them both as Burke said, "Rumor has it that the lawyer you hate from the D.A.'s office wants to offer Moon a deal if she flips on Bryce."

"What?" I asked.

"You think Moon will take it?"

I cursed creatively, pushing Deuce out of my way and moving to get off the bed. "Where the hell are my pants?" I asked, ignoring the strong way the room tilted to the left.

I also ignored Burke's deep, dumb, placating voice calling my name as Reese threw me my pants.

"She did it, Burke," I said as I tried to get my foot into my pant leg. "She practically admitted it to me."

"I know," he said.

"Gimme five minutes with her," I demanded, after finally getting my right leg into my pants.

"Chase, no," Burke said.

"Chase, yes! She bashed me in the back of the head; I think I deserve some time with her." I was really struggling with the pants situation when Deuce snagged my phone and hung up. It was rude, but it allowed me to finally get my jeans up and snapped into place. I stood up. Sure, I was dizzy, and my head felt like it had been hit by a bowling ball, but I figured I could manage.

I turned to Deuce and demanded, "Drive me to the station."

"You ain't been discharged," he reminded me. He crossed his arms across his chest and looked down at me. Had it been any other time, I'd have found it unsettlingly attractive.

I rolled my eyes and walked over to the curtain, calling for a nurse. As soon as I had one nurse's attention I said, "Please call Dr. Braswell here and tell him that Chase Harlem needs to see him."

She nodded and walked off—far too slowly, in my opinion.

"I think your doctor was called Smith," Reese told me.

"Don't care," I snapped as I paced back and forth.

I snatched my phone back from Deuce and sent Burke a quick text asking him to get a copy of Goldman's autopsy report and Regina's tox screen ready for me. I was still consulting with him on this case, even if it wasn't in an official capacity.

Finally, Dr. Desmond Braswell came in through the curtain. His skin was perfect, practically pore-less, and it was such a dark shade of brown that it looked almost onyx. He was a beautiful man, and on the weekends and every other Thursday, he was a *gorgeous* woman.

"Hey, Queen!" I greeted him with a smile and a hug around the neck.

"Oh, don't you even talk to me like that," he said. "You ain't seen one of my shows in *weeks*."

"I know, I know," I told him. "I'm sorry about that. Work's been chaos."

"I can see that," he said, opening the manila folder he'd carted in, which I assume had my file in it. He then eyed Deuce over the chart. "This his doing?"

"You think he'd still be standing if he'd done something like this to me?" I asked.

Desmond laughed at that.

"Actually, this was done by a murderous psycho-bitch, who I need to make sure faces all the prison time, so sign me out, doc."

Desmond gave me a 'mom' look that fit so much better on his other persona, but I let it slide. "You can't let the police handle this?"

I crossed my arms over my chest and raised an eyebrow. Desmond knows how I feel about the Chihuahua.

"You at least plan to change and shower? Because, girl, you got blood in your hair and on your jeans, *and* your shirt is a hospital gown."

"We can't all be as stylish as Desdemona," I told him.

He smiled at that. "No, *you* certainly can't," he said before going into serious doctor mode and adding, "Now, this concussion is pretty serious. The CT scan shows no lasting damage, but I suggest you don't sleep for twelve hours."

Deuce spoke up at that, "I'll make sure she stays awake, doc."

Desmond eyed me with a smirk. "I'm sure you will. Now, get out of here, go save the day, and I better see you next Thursday."

"You can count on it," I told him as I grabbed my kid and my sorta boyfriend and headed for the exit.

"You got your Jeep?" I asked Deuce as soon as we stepped out into the parking lot, and I realized that my car was probably still back at the fraternity house.

"This way, chère," he said, taking my hand.

"Wait, how'd you know that doctor?" Reese asked.

"I met him at a show," I told her.

"You called him a Queen," she pointed out.

I motioned for her to start walking and answered, "It's New Orleans, baby."

Chapter 28

Mad About the Boy

When we got to the station, I walked Reese in, sat her down beside Burke's desk, and told her to stay put. Deuce had stayed in the Jeep—further cementing my theory that he's probably on the run from the law, at least in some capacity.

I then set off to find coffee. I knew I wouldn't have to search for Burke. In about five minutes, he found me.

"What took you so long?" he asked as I poured my first cup of coffee in the breakroom.

"I had a teenager in the car with me," I said. "So, you know, I had to adhere to traffic laws and be a good example to the future of America."

He looked at me like he knew my story was malarkey.

I rolled my eyes. "Deuce was driving, and surprisingly, he's a stickler about traffic laws."

"The criminal from the bar you like?" Burke asked.

"That's the one," I confirmed. "I think we're dating."

"Since when?"

"Tonight. This is our first date. What can I say? I know how to treat a guy."

I started to sip the coffee I'd brewed and poured for myself, but Burke swiped the cup from my hands, drinking it himself. I relented without a fight considering it was Burke's coffee cup that I was attempting to drink from. I searched the cabinet under the coffee maker to find another cup, reluctantly settling for a Styrofoam one from the stack.

"Speaking of crazy date nights," I continued, pouring some hot java into my sad, un-recyclable cup, "did you get the warrant to check out Candace's dorm?"

He nodded. "We got a team there now."

"Chihuahua wouldn't happen to be there, would she?"

He let out a snort of laughter. "Field work ain't really her thing," he reminded me, as if I needed a reminder.

"Right, which is why they promoted her."

Burke rolled his eyes. "Your private war with the woman in charge is not doing you any favors."

I sighed. "Any word where Candy might have kept her product?"

Burke shook his head. "She admitted to having given Regina the drugs, but that's all she'd say. It's the D.A.'s understanding that Bryce was the one supplying the drugs on campus, but Moon still hasn't made an official statement with the D.A. We didn't find any drugs at Bryce's place either."

"He swears he never sold anything to Reggie," I told him. "You believe him now?"

I shrugged. "The more I think about it, the more I'm sure that he's just not smart enough to hide the fact that he's supplying drugs to the student body. Maybe he had something on him the night I failed at going undercover, but he's not the dealer. Even if he is *a* dealer, he's small-time." And that was when it hit me. "He had drugs in his car. That night at the club—I *know* he had drugs in his car."

"We've already checked it," Burke said.

"No, you don't understand; *that's* why there were no drugs in Candace's dorm. He moved them. They probably suspected that someone would find the stash soon, so he *moved* them."

"Okay," Burke said. "I'm not sure it matters. I mean, drugs or no drugs, they're both in hot water for the death of Eli Goldman."

"But the drugs were the motivation—at least for Goldman's murder. Reggie's death was caused by a completely different green-eyed monster. You can't prove who was the murderer and who was the accomplice without the drugs," I told him. "Unless you let me talk to Moon and get a confession."

"You think I should let you anywhere near Moon?"

I took a sip of my coffee. It was still too hot, and it burned my tongue. I wasn't sure how Burke was chugging his with no hesitation. "I'm not going to beat her bloody, if that's what you mean."

"You did try to fight her at the party," Burke reminded me, glaring with an annoying 'I told you so' look over his nice coffee cup. "Don't think she hasn't told everyone about your little fight."

"If by 'fight' you mean she pulled my hair, so I slapped her face off, then yes, that was a thing that happened, but I have a good excuse."

It was Burke's turn to sigh, and he did that annoying thing he does when he squeezes the bridge of his nose between his thumb and forefinger. "What's that?"

"She hit me with a car. I still have road rash."

Burke took another gulp of his coffee, which should have still been as piping hot as my own. "Okay. Morris isn't here, so I guess it doesn't matter. What's your plan?"

"You're going to offer Moon the D.A.'s deal."

"Sounds counterproductive. What are *you* gonna do?"

I blew on my still piping hot coffee. "Sulk. And play a bit of devil's advocate."

I walked into the interrogation room with Burke by my side because apparently interrogating a suspect who assaulted me without him, was not okay. Candace Moon was sitting on the other side of the table. She had her hands on the cool metal in front of her with her fingers interlaced, as if she could ignore the cuffs.

Even though she was keeping her head down, her eyes glued to her hands on the table, I could see that she had a slight bruise under her left eye from where I'd backhanded her. It made me feel pretty good until the pain in my head spiked, reminding me of the concussion she'd given me. I really hate the idea of losing any fight—ever.

She looked a bit like a whipped puppy, or at least she was trying to look like a whipped puppy. She was a murderer, possibly a drug dealer who laced her product with murderous intent, and she'd given me a knock on the head that I wouldn't soon forget, but she was also a girl in love. I could use that.

I flopped down in one of the two chairs across the table from her, having no trouble exuding frustration through every pore.

She looked up at me and then over at Burke, her expression mostly blank. "What's she doing here?" she asked him, voice as neutral as she could probably force it to be. It reminded me that she was an actress, having had the same training as Regina.

"I'm apparently here to offer you a deal," I grumbled.

I could see the surprise on her face slip past her mask as Burke cleared his throat and took the chair beside me. "The District Attorney's office has permitted me to offer you a deal."

She sat up straighter, looking between me and him. "What deal?"

Burke glanced at me, and I glared back. "We know that Bryce is our guy," he lied. "The text messages give us motive, and now that he's in custody, we're sure his fingerprints will match some found at the crime scene."

Her mouth plopped open like a fish out of water. "But ... Christopher wouldn't—he didn't kill anyone."

Burke sighed and leaned over the table closer to Moon. "I know this is hard for you, Miss Moon. You're an innocent girl who got caught up with the wrong guy. Bryce is just trying to cover his tracks, and he's willing to use you to do that."

Moon looked at me, her eyes wide, almost pleading. "You know he's innocent, though," she insisted. "You *have* to know."

I rolled my eyes so hard that it made my head hurt more. "I've read the texts, girlie. You don't have to cover for him."

"I'm *not* covering for him. He hasn't done anything."

I glanced at Burke then back at her. "I've heard love is blind, but aren't you being a little ridiculous? I mean, it's obvious he doesn't love you, so why protect him?"

Her face turned red, and for the first time since the interview began, I recognized the woman across from me as the one who'd attacked me in Bryce's dorm. "You don't know what you're talking about," she hissed.

I smirked. "I read the texts between Bryce and Reggie, and I know you did, too. That's why you deleted them from her phone. Anyone who read those would know Bryce was in love with her, and that gives him a motive for murdering her boyfriend. You covered for him then, and you're covering for him now."

"I'm not covering for anyone!"

"Was Bryce in love with Reggie or not?" I asked, making sure to keep my voice even in the face of her screaming.

She deflated a little and nodded. "But he didn't stand a chance, not with her superstar boyfriend to compete with. That's why Christopher is the way he is, sleeping with all these girls—it's because he can't get the *one* girl he wants. Did you know he stayed up all night making those costumes for the masquerade? He even made that extra Joker costume in case Eli ditched *again*."

I did not know that. "Did Reggie know how Chris felt? I mean, the texts are pretty clear to me, but she never sent him anything that would indicate she understood that."

She shook her head, but her face said she was unsure. "I don't know. I kinda think she might have known. That's why she set him up with me."

"Regina got you and Chris together?" Burke asked.

The girl nodded. "At first, I just thought it was, like, out of the goodness of her heart or something, but then I saw what everybody else had already seen—Christopher was crazy about Reggie. And it all made total sense. I mean, Reggie and I are incredibly similar. We're both theater girls, we both have dark hair and eyes, and we're both around the same size. I mean, we shared each other's clothes all the time. She probably thought that Christopher would see me and forget all about her—but that didn't happen. At the end of the day, I'm just an understudy, and she's a leading lady. How could I compete with that?"

"Were you jealous?" Burke asked.

"Well, duh, sure I was. Christopher is so talented and smart—"

"And a drug dealer," I murmured.

She glared at me then. "Who told you that?"

I shrugged. "We know Goldman's murderer was Reggie's dealer."

Her eyes widened at that. "You seriously think he killed Goldman? Like, really?"

"We're just following the evidence," Burke said. "We found a Scarecrow costume with Goldman's blood on it in your dorm room."

She shook her head as her eyes welled with tears. "You can't do this to him," she said. "He's *not* a murderer."

"Are you?" I asked.

She stared at me in shock.

"Tell me this, then," I continued. "When he found out what you'd done to Reggie, what'd he say? Do you honestly think he'll forgive you for murdering the woman he loved?"

"*I* love *him!* More than she ever could!" She screamed, sobbing and distraught. "I should have been the one he loved, not her! But I didn't mean to kill her; really, I didn't." She sucked in a breath. "She just wouldn't shut up about Goldman, so I gave her a little more coke than I usually did."

"What did you lace that coke with?" I asked.

She glared at me.

"I've seen the tox report. I know you gave her a little something extra."

"I gave her that when she saw the blood and was asking too many questions, and I made sure she sucked it all in."

"The blood on Bryce, you mean?" I asked. "Because he killed Goldman."

"*He* did not kill anyone!" She was shrieking now.

"Goldman was stabbed in the back and shoved in a freezer," Burke said. "Who else would've been able to do that?"

"Me!" she shouted. "He was threatening Christopher because he thought Christopher was the one giving Reggie the drugs. Christopher is a scholarship kid, and Goldman threatened to tell people he was a drug dealer. He'd have been kicked out of school. I couldn't let that happen, so I stepped up behind Goldman, and I stabbed him right in his meaty neck, and I kept stabbing him because I love Christopher Bryce, and no one will threaten him with me around." She sat back in her chair like a slowly deflating pool float. "Christopher just helped me move the body. If anyone should get a deal, it's him."

"I'll let our District Attorney's office know," Burke said. "And I'll need you to sign some paperwork if you're sure you want to protect him."

Moon began to sob.

I glanced at Burke, and he nodded.

As we walked away, I did the one thing I'd sworn I wouldn't do—I felt sorry for her. I'm not proud of that feeling, but it is what it is. She had loved someone past the point of sanity, and even though that guy definitely hadn't deserved that love, who of us actually does?

Seriously, in Candace Moon's mind, she'd probably done all of that, from killing Goldman to drugging Regina, for Bryce. Had I ever cared about anyone that much? Enough to lose my mind? I thought I had, but listening to her wailing as I walked away made me wonder.

Chapter 29

Cheek to Cheek

"How's your head?" Burke asked as he took a seat in the chair opposite his desk. I was sitting in his nice, comfortable desk chair, reading through the files he'd left out in the open.

"It hurts," I admitted.

He looked around. "Where's the kid?"

"Sent her home with Deuce an hour ago."

"Sorry for cutting your date short," he said.

"Me too. I was hoping to get lucky tonight," I joked.

"Didn't need to know that," Burke grumbled. "What's your name?"

I glanced up at him from the file in my lap, "Huh?"

"How old are you? Can you tell me what year it is? Who's our current president?" For a moment, I was beyond confused. Then, it clicked. "You're asking me concussion questions, aren't you?"

He shrugged. "I figured that girl must've really knocked you crazy since you're going through my files."

I closed the file in my lap and passed it to him across the desk. "It's the boyfriend," I said.

"Victim didn't have a boyfriend."

"No," I agreed, "but her husband did."

Burke opened the file and flipped through the pages, sighing at the witness statement I'd been reading. "I'll need evidence."

"Find it on your own. I don't work for free."

He chuckled at that.

I stood up and stretched, feeling my back crack before I sat back down. My head was killing me, but I still needed some answers before I could lay this case to rest.

"Did Candace sign all the appropriate paperwork?"

Burke yawned and nodded his head. "Yep," he told me, popping the "p." "That was one hell of a confession."

I shrugged. "All that FBI training had to be good for something. Bryce being charged?'

"He was an accessory. You want to beat a confession out of him, too?"

My head hurt, my eyes were burning, my hair was sticky and crusted with blood, and I stunk. All I wanted was to get home and take the hottest shower known to man. "Think I'll pass this time," I told him.

"Good. Let his lawyers deal with him." He stood up, grabbing his keys and his coat. "Let's go home."

"You mind driving me to my car?"

"Hell yes, I mind. You got a concussion. I'll take you home instead."

As he drove me back to my apartment, I asked Burke, "So, at what point do you plan to let Lackey go? I should probably tell my client."

Burke shook his head. "You know how long the bureaucratic system takes to work. Maybe he'll be released by tomorrow afternoon."

"Meaning I can tell my client now?"

"Do you really want to call your client at three in the morning?"

"Crap, really?" I glanced at my naked wrist. "I'm never going to have a normal sleep schedule."

"Has it been twelve hours since your concussion?"

I glared at him. "Technically, I have seven hours to go."

"I'd offer to stay up with you, but I want to spend some time with my own kid."

"She's adorable," I said. "Could you drop me off by my car first, though?"

He laughed at my question. "You really think I'm going to let you drive with a concussion?"

"How else am I going to get my car?"

"Ask your boyfriend," he told me as we pulled up to 911 St. Peter Street. I saw Deuce's Jeep illegally parked by the sidewalk and felt my face heat up. I guess he wasn't joking about keeping me company when he talked to Dr. Braswell.

"You know," Burke said, pulling his black Honda over to the curb, "this whole car thing wouldn't be an issue if you'd accepted my offer of a ride and backup earlier today. You probably wouldn't have such a headache, either."

I rolled my eyes. "I promise that next time I find myself in a time-sensitive, potentially disastrous situation, I'll listen to you."

"No, you won't."

"You're probably right." He was definitely right. It was time to extend an olive branch. "I tell you what, we can meet for dinner tomorrow, and by 'tomorrow,' I mean tonight."

Burke smiled. "See you soon. If I don't get caught up by reporters."

"Just leave my name out of it," I warned him.

Burke shrugged. "It could get you some work."

"That's what I have you for."

He shook his head. "You know she'll never let me hire you as a con-sultant."

It was my turn to shrug. He was right. The Chihuahua would literally roll over and die before she let anyone in her precinct hire me. "It was worth a shot."

I hopped out of the car and headed through the courtyard and up to my apartment. As expected, Deuce had let himself in and was sitting on my lumpy sofa with Louis lounging in his lap. Reese, on the other hand, was nowhere in sight.

"The girl went on home to her apartment, chère," he said as if he could read my mind. "Her mama was real grateful to you for helpin' her."

I nodded and dropped my purse on the coffee table before considering whether to sit down or have a shower first. The back of my head still hurt like hell, and my hair felt matted and crusty. I could smell blood, so I quickly determined that a shower was needed first and moved upstairs toward my bathroom.

"You not plannin' to sleep now, are ya?" Deuce asked. "Remember what yo'doctor said."

"I need a shower," I told him.

He smirked and cocked an eyebrow. I knew what he was planning to say before he said, "Want some comp'ny?"

I smiled despite my exhaustion. "Any other day, mon ami, but not today. I'm gross." I'd never called Deuce by a pet name before, though he had plenty for me. It must have caught him off guard because he straightened and stared at me for a moment.

The moment passed. He stood up and walked over to me, gently laying Louis on the couch as he did so. Then, Deuce cautiously placed a kiss on my forehead. It was so different from how he usually behaved around me—sweet instead of seductive—I admit it caught me off guard. He raised his hand to my face and gently stroked my cheek. His fingers were calloused, like a man who'd seen real work and more than one rowdy bar-fight. It seemed like a paradox that someone so rough and tough could be so gentle, and for a moment, I let myself believe that his gentleness was reserved for me and me alone. I closed my eyes and breathed him in. He smelled like mangos and Cajun spices, while I smelled like spilled blood and death. What a combination.

"Should I leave, ma chérie?" he asked, barely over a whisper.

"Stay," I murmured without opening my eyes. "Please."

I felt his lips brush my hairline again before he stepped away. I opened my eyes to find him smiling down at me.

"You hurry with that shower," he ordered, voice still gentle. "I got you a prize."

Well, *that* implication suddenly broke whatever trance I was under as I felt my stomach tighten. "Um, that's not necessary," I told him quickly. "I'm not that kind of girl."

He stared at me in confusion for a moment before laughing. "Get yo 'mind outta the gutter, chérie! I brought you beer since you finished yo 'case!"

"Oh." I glanced down at the floor and then up at him, my face heating from embarrassment. "Normally, that would be great," I told him, "but the last time I got drunk—I over-shared."

Deuce shrugged. "I don't mind the over-sharing."

"Yeah, well, I also quit my job, yelled at the kid, and was a complete jerk to everyone I cared about. I'm thinking my whole 'no drinking on the job' rule should be extended."

"No drinkin' at all, then?" he asked, no judgment in his voice.

"Maybe just on special occasions." I'm a realist, after all.

Deuce smiled. "Might be hard to do when yo' datin' a bartender."

"Are we dating now?" I asked.

"What you think this is?"

Before I could stop myself, I rose onto my tiptoes and kissed him on the cheek. Then I turned on my heel and booked it for the shower.

The shower took longer than I expected. The hot water felt so good on my tired body that I melted into it. As I washed, I was extra careful around the gash on my head. Apparently, it wasn't deep enough to warrant stitches, but it had bled something awful, as most head wounds do, and my hair was absolutely drenched in blood. It took me three handfuls of shampoo to get all the blood out, and by the time I was done, my drain looked like the shower scene in *Psycho*. I watched the brownish-red liquid circle and disappear into the darkness. For a moment, I allowed my eyes to travel up my legs and to the scars on my torso. I traced my fingers lightly over the slightly raised skin, a smattering of pale lines across my body, just under my breasts. Some things would never wash away.

For the first time in two years, I climbed out of my shower and faced the mirror. It was cloudy. Summoning all my courage, I wiped the fog away from the glass and stared at my naked reflection. I'd never looked at the scars while sober, but standing there in the privacy of my bathroom, the adrenaline from solving a case draining out of me, I could finally face what I'd become. I traced my fingers across the lines that'd been carved into my flesh, crossing and uncrossing to form six letters—letters that, when reflected in the mirror, formed one long word: VICTIM. I'd been a victim. I'd had no choice in that. What I did have was a choice in what I would become now.

I waited for my chest to tighten, for my pulse to pound, and my breath to become ragged, but it didn't happen. The woman in the mirror stared at me stoically. I grabbed a towel and wrapped it around myself before going into my bedroom and putting on my most comfortable sweatpants and a baggy T-shirt.

When I returned downstairs, Deuce was sitting on my couch watching a television show about home renovations and holding a package of Lindt Chocolate Truffles. Louis was lounging on the back of the couch around Deuce's shoulders. I sat down, pulling Louis into my lap and scratching him behind his ears. He huffed in delight and nuzzled into my thigh. Deuce offered me the bag of truffles, and I didn't hesitate before tearing the package and popping one in my mouth.

"Chocolate better than beer, chère?" Deuce asked, draping his arm around my shoulders.

"It is an acceptable alternative," I told him, talking around the chocolate in my mouth. After finishing two more truffles, I closed the package and leaned my head against Deuce's shoulder, letting out a long sigh.

"You got about five mo' hours 'fore you can rest," Deuce reminded me. "Don't let the chocolate get you too sleepy."

I didn't say anything but reached up and grabbed his hand, pulling his arm tighter around my shoulder and snuggling into his side. It'd been a while since I'd had a man on my couch, and I'd honestly thought I'd be more nervous. Deuce, however, was a different kind of man—the kind who knew all about my broken pieces but still showed up.

"You catch the bad guy?" he asked after a moment.

"You bet I did."

"That roommate, Candace Moon?"

"Yep." I popped the "p."

"Dammit," Deuce cursed.

Perhaps because I was delirious from sleep deprivation or maybe because I just wanted to, I released his hand and tapped him lightly on the tip of his nose with my index finger. He wiggled his nose in response, and that caused me to laugh. "You lost a bet, didn't you?" I asked.

He nodded reluctantly, but I saw the smile at the edge of his lips.

"Who won?" I asked.

"Dice, as usual," he said, taking another sip. "Well, she guessed that the roommate was probably the drug dealer. She figured the girl had help, but she never mentioned that Bryce guy."

I rolled my eyes. Of course, his brilliant sister had figured it out before me. "Maybe she won't take all your money."

"You know betta than that."

I laughed and stroked the soft, white fur on Louis's back. "If I can ever afford it, I will definitely hire her as my personal P.I."

"Not me?" he asked in mock offense.

"Only if I need a hot male bodyguard."

Deuce smiled, and I thought his teeth had never been so white or so feral. "You *do* think I'm hot, don't you, chère?"

Of course, that had slipped out. Had I been less exhausted, I probably would have just played it off. However, given the context, him sitting in my living room as if we were a real, domestic couple, Deuce's comment made my face heat up like a poorly made light bulb. I tried to cover it up by shoving more chocolate in my mouth, but I nearly choked on that.

Deuce, bless him, pretended not to notice that I'd almost gagged in embarrassment. Instead, his eyes trailed down to my right hand—the one I'd used to backhand Candace—and his fingers caressed the small tear across my knuckles where they'd connected with Candace's face. "What 'appened to yo 'knuckles?"

I took a deep breath and put the chocolate on the coffee table in front of me, jostling the grumpy ferret in my lap. I didn't think I was ready to discuss the fear I experienced when I thought my new protégé might be in danger. Honestly, I had only been that scared once before in my life. As I drove to that fraternity house, every worst-case scenario flashed before my eyes, and I couldn't help but think that the entire thing was my fault. On some logical level, I knew that it was not, but I also knew that I would always blame myself if something happened to that kid. I took a deep breath. I'd been open with Deuce before, so I might as well give it a go. You only live once, so the saying goes.

"I take it that Reese didn't fill you in on everything that happened?" I asked him.

"She don't know me like that," he said. "'Sides, I'd rather hear it from you."

I sighed and stroked Louis's fur again. Then, I told Deuce everything—including how scared I was when I realized Reese had gone to a party with the murderer, where she could have been hurt because of me. By the end of my tale, I was a mess of tears and snot.

Deuce scooted closer to me and wrapped his arms firmly around me, kissing me on my head. I felt Louis scramble out of my lap and watched him skitter across the room just as Deuce pulled me into his chest. Then—to my utter humiliation—a sob escaped, followed by another and another until I couldn't control them. The bad boy flirt just held me closer, letting me sob into his chest and totally drench his black T-shirt. I don't know how long I cried—not long, I hope—but Deuce kept his strong arms around me the whole time. I couldn't remember the last time anyone held me like that—just held me close without trying to kiss me or make me promise things. I still can't.

When I finally had myself under control, I pulled away from the warm comfort that was Deuce Marlboro and wiped my face. Good thing I'd already washed all my makeup off in the shower or I'd have had little black rivulets rolling down my cheeks. "Sorry," I murmured with a hiccup. "I don't know what happened. I don't cry often."

"That would explain why you bad at it," Deuce joked. "Girls that cry all the time have ugly cry faces. Yo's is cute."

I had to laugh at that. There I was, making an idiot of myself, and the hunk was still trying to flirt. "Thanks ... I think. It doesn't change the fact that everyone I get close to gets hurt. If it weren't for me, Reese would never have been at that party."

"Okay," he said, "but the cops'd still have that innocent kid locked up. Louisiana got the death penalty, so you prob'ly saved his life tonight, chère." He pulled me close to him again, tangling his big hand in my hair, miraculously missing the gash, as he pressed me to his chest. I could hear his heartbeat, and it sounded nearly as fast as mine. I tentatively put my arms around his waist, breathing in his warmth.

I wanted so badly just to let him comfort me, but sometimes, when the darkness comes calling, I can't help but be... confused. How can people who are so capable of *good* be so evil?

"I don't understand human beings," I muttered into his shirt. "When I was little—I was raised on a farm, and when summer came around, my cousins and brothers and I'd go out into the woods near the barn and hunt fireflies. I was one of the younger ones and the only girl, so you could imagine how determined I was to prove that I was just as good as those bigger, stronger, faster boys at, well, at everything." I laughed at my own stubbornness. "Yeah, I absolutely idolized my oldest cousin, Trent, possibly because he was so unlike my perfect big brother. Trent liked to break rules. So, when Trent started putting all the fireflies we'd collected into a mason jar, I didn't question it. I put the jar by my bed that night and fell asleep watching the little lights dance. When I woke up the next day, I was absolutely devastated to find a jar of dead bugs."

I laughed again, this time bitterly, and took another bite of chocolate before continuing, "Trent made fun of me for crying and said they were just bugs. That's how he saw them, and it makes sense, I guess. But now that I'm older and I've seen so much, I wonder if it's how murderers see the people they kill—like bugs. Is that how Candace saw Eli—as just some lightning bug threatening her boyfriend? Did she never register that Eli was a person who mattered?" I stopped for a moment, thinking briefly of all the other criminals I'd put behind bars, the thieves, the rapists, the murderers. "I mean, God, what does it take to make a person see the world that way? What kind of messed up mind views life as something so easily expendable? I don't get it."

"That's because you ain't nothin' like that," Deuce told me.

"If not, then why—why is it so easy for me to find people who are?" And there it was, all my self-doubt left out in the open. I try so hard to be a good person and to make some kind of difference in the world. But at the end of the day, after I've slapped a girl in the face and stormed in guns blazin' to help my kid, I wonder if I'm a lot more like the people I chase than I'd care to admit. I've killed before, and not always in self-defense. Had things been different—had I found Reese in a different situation,

I might very well have killed again. What does that say about me? Do I really have more in common with a serial killer than I do with regular people?

Deuce took my hand, maneuvering us both back to the couch and looking me in the eyes. "Chère, you care 'bout people more'n you care 'bout you. That's the difference. And that's a damned rare quality."

I shook my head, turning away from his distractingly large eyes. "Yeah, well, it shouldn't be. Kindness should not be rare. Sorry I'm being such a downer," I told him.

"You been up for hours, and you got a concussion. I think you can be a downer." He sat down beside me again, leaning his face close to mine and running his fingers through my hair. "I could always help distract you," he growled. There was a hint of playful suggestion in his voice, and I laughed because I knew what he was trying to do—to make me laugh.

"You're too tempting for me, Mr. Marlboro." I meant to reach up and caress his face playfully, but when I did it, it wasn't playful at all. His cheek was warm, and the feel of his stubble under my palm made my heart speed up in a dangerous sort of way. I could feel his strong, square jaw, and I was staring right at his perfect mouth, his lips with just the right amount of pout to stand out without looking effeminate. I wanted to kiss him. I wanted to kiss him, badly, so I did.

I turned my body toward him on the couch and softly planted my lips onto his warm mouth. I could feel his chest rumble like a purring cat as he gently wrapped his arms around my waist, pulling me nearly into his lap and deepening our kiss. His tongue asked for entry, and I allowed it, exploring his mouth with mine. He tasted of beer with a slight hint of spearmint. His teeth were perfectly straight, and our tongues danced slowly. I wrapped my arms around his thick neck. I felt his hands roaming down to my thighs, then over my butt, and up to the hem of my shirt, skin touching bare skin.

I froze. For a moment, all I could think of was how close his hands were to the scars I'd only recently been able to face myself. I abruptly shifted away.

Without me having to say a word Deuce released me, scooting to the far end of the couch and holding his hands up, palms out. "I'm sorry," he said quickly.

"It's not you," I said, knowing that I wouldn't have to add "it's me" because, of course, it was me. Like it or not, I was damaged goods. I wanted to explain, but what could I say? "Can you just—can you just hold me tonight?"

"A course I can, ma chérie. It would be my honor."

Louis came careening out of the kitchen, clambering up my leg and up to my shoulder, where he planted his front paws and chittered at Deuce in that annoyingly territorial way that all ferrets have.

"Hey!" Deuce shouted at the ferret, stepping away from me with a huff. "I thought we was on the same team?"

Louis chittered at him angrily, and I couldn't help but laugh. It was a raucous laugh—with no inhibitions—and it felt good. After a moment, Deuce laughed, too. Then we were both standing in the middle of the apartment, me with a ferret on my shoulder, laughing like idiots.

After my laughter had subsided enough to speak, I explained, "He-he wants some jazz."

"What?" Deuce asked, wiping the tears of laughter out of his eyes.

I shrugged. "It's what we do when I can't sleep," I said. "We listen to jazz and dance."

I pulled Louis off my shoulder and looked into his tiny pink eyes. "'Paper Moon' as sung by Ella Fitzgerald," I said suddenly.

The little fur ball chittered the affirmative.

I handed Louis to Deuce, grabbing my favorite gambler by the hand and guiding him up the stairs to my record player while continuing to ramble about a song that had just popped into my head. "Thanks to my furry friend here," I explained, "it's in my head on repeat, and I can't make it stop." We made it up the stairs, and I rounded the top rail, bending down to search for the vinyl in the cardboard box under my piano. "It doesn't matter what I try now. I've tried everything. I've tried thinking of other songs, doing math problems in my head, all that garbage, but it doesn't work." I triumphantly lifted Ella Fitzgerald's record in the air, waving it in Deuce's face. "The only solution to getting a song out of my head is to listen to it." I placed the record on the turn table and dropped the needle as close as I could to where I thought the song might be. Sweet musing emitted from the speaker, and I turned back to Deuce and Louis. "We either sing along or dance along," I told him.

"What?" He was a little baffled, to say the least. Maybe Dice would explain it to him later. Then she could explain it to me. I needed it explained to me.

"You can't just stand around and listen to great jazz," I explained as if I were telling it to a child. "You either sing along, or you dance, so which will it be?"

Deuce gave me a smile that was absolutely blinding and stepped toward me. "Whatever you wanna do, chère. You the boss here." It was exactly the right thing to say.

And that's how we ended up dancing to Ella Fitzgerald until my concussion safety watch was over, and I could finally go to bed. I didn't ask Deuce to stay the night with me, even though I wanted to. I knew one day I'd have the courage to do so.

Chapter 30

When You're Smiling

When I woke again, my bedroom was swathed in darkness, so I guessed I'd been asleep for at least seven hours. I rolled out of bed and scrambled into my bathroom without paying much attention to the state of my apartment.

It was only when I exited the bathroom that I noticed the lights on downstairs and the murmur of the television. I climbed down into the lower room to find Reese Kelley sitting on my sofa, bundled in my orange and blue blanket, legs pulled up to her chest and her chin resting on her knees. Good. I needed to talk to her anyway. I stepped into the room and turned on the light.

"Okay," I prompted. "What's up?"

Reese nearly jumped off the couch in surprise, then gave me a look that quite blatantly asked if I'd lost my mind. Then she seemed to really consider whether or not I'd lost my mind, and after she was satisfied that she would not be figuring me out on her own, she asked, "What?"

I reiterated, "What's with the junior investigator schtick?"

"Did you just curse ... badly?"

That caught me a bit off guard. "What? No, I said 'schtick.'"

She raised an eyebrow.

"It's synonymous with the word 'gimmick,'" I attempted to explain.

That did not help, and I couldn't help but shake my head in exasperation. Really, do kids not read anything other than Twitter anymore? "You don't have a very extensive vocabulary, do you?"

She scoffed—which is, ironically, another word she probably doesn't know the meaning of. "I'll have you know that I've memorized most of the Urban Dictionary."

"That doesn't count," I said, walking across the room and taking a seat beside her, "and don't think I didn't notice that you're trying to change the subject." I took the remote from the coffee table and turned off the television. "Now, why do you want to be my junior investigator?"

She crossed her arms and pointedly looked away from me, letting out what sounded like her own version of an exasperated sigh. I mean, really, do teenagers have any right to be exasperated? Aren't they too young for that sort of thing?

Eventually, the kid asked, "Will it make a difference if I tell you?"

"You mean, will I let you be my junior investigator?"

She nodded once.

"Probably not," I said a little too quickly. "I mean, you did the exact opposite of what I asked you to do and put your life in serious danger. It wouldn't be very adult of me to reward you for bad behavior."

"Yeah, but are you *really* an adult?"

"Legally, yes."

"Mentally?"

She had a point, but I damn sure wasn't going to let *her* know that. "Just answer the question, kid."

The kid sighed, and for a moment, I wondered if she'd win this round. But she finally admitted, "I need your help."

I was confused. "What? Like, you want to hire me?"

"Sort of. Maybe not. I don't know." She slumped down in her seat in pure adolescent fashion, biting her bottom lip as if it would help her keep quiet. After a moment, she let that lip out of its toothy trap and whispered, "I need to find my mom."

Well, damn. "Reese ..."

Reese cut me off, "She left me, and I know what that means, okay? I don't expect to, like, be reunited or whatever, but I just need—I need closure, you know?" She wiped something wet from the corner of her eye, and I turned away to give her some privacy. "It's stupid."

"How are your grades?" I asked, surprising the schtick out of myself.

"What?"

I ground my teeth. "Consider this your job interview," I explained. "You're already losing points for being dressed in pajamas. Now, tell me, how are your grades?"

"B's and C's and the occasional D."

"Make those A's and B's, keep out of trouble, jump when I say jump, and you've got yourself an unpaid internship."

"Seriously?"

"Keep asking stupid questions, and you're fired."

"Alright! Thank you!"

"Over-excitement also gets you fired."

She smiled, and for one horrifying moment, I thought she was going to hug me. Instead, she stuck out her hand. "Shake on it."

I did, knowing this whole thing was a stupid idea, but at least she'd stopped crying.

"Make sure to ask Rose for permission."

"Not Hank?"

"I don't give a flying fart what Hank says, and if he's made his way back into the apartment, you make sure to let me know." I picked up the remote again and turned on the TV.

"Will you handle it, or will you call your super-hot-but-intimidating boyfriend?"

I almost dropped the remote. "Boyfriend jokes will also get you fired," I warned.

Reese laughed in the delirious way people do when they really haven't gotten enough sleep. "You recognize that he is a hottie, right?"

"I'm neither blind nor stupid, but he's still not my boyfriend. Now, you have barely slept, so go get some sleep, and don't forget to ask Rose about the whole job thing. Oh, and in case you missed the whole 'unpaid' internship' part, I can't pay you, so if you were hoping for that, no dice."

She laughed. "It's, like, 8:00 p.m.," she said. "Way too early to go to bed."

"*I'm* going to bed."

"You just woke up?"

I nodded, "Yes, and I'm already tired. Concussions will do that to you."

Reese rolled her eyes but retreated from the couch and headed back to her own apartment. I didn't really know why I gave in and offered her a job. It was not like me to let people help me out. Plus, I still believed the job was too dangerous for a kid. Then again, if she was going to go around doing stupid stuff even without being a part of the investigation, it would probably be easier just to keep her close by.

I tried to convince myself that was the reason I'd said yes. I then tried to convince myself that it was just because I'm a sucker for a good sob story. I even tried to convince myself that it was all because I saw potential in the kid. All these things were technically true, but there was more to it than that. Truthfully, I let Reese Kelley work with me because she *mattered*, and if my bruised knuckles had taught me anything, it was that nothing was going to change that fact. She mattered to me, and I was someone to her. It was all really messed up.

I flipped off the TV, crawled back upstairs, and got into bed. This time, insomnia would not get in my way.

At 6:00 the following morning, I awakened to my phone buzzing. When I finally located the thing, I saw it was a text from Burke, letting me know that I'd missed dinner and that Lackey had been cleared of all charges. I assumed he got Chandler to send it.

I closed the message and dialed the priest. "They should be letting Lackey out later today," I told him after I'd explained that his son was, thankfully, innocent of murder.

"Thank you, P.I. Harlem," he said, his voice a calming baritone that probably sounded resoundingly comforting at mass. "You are an answer to prayer."

"You might want to talk to your kid about toning down on the party scene."

I heard him chuckle. "I'm afraid I'm not one to judge, and I have no power over him anyway. I never have."

"He knows you're his dad, doesn't he?" I asked. I was pretty sure the kid had referred to him as "bio dad" at some point, but I was concussed.

Father Nolan was quiet for a moment before he answered, "Yes. He discovered his stepfather, who raised him, couldn't possibly be his father when he took a freshman biology course and learned about dominant and recessive genes. When he asked his mother, she—well, she hadn't wanted to lie to him. He's even attended mass a couple of times." The priest sounded marginally proud about that last fact. "You know, people often argue that God and science are somehow in opposition to one another, but here is a pristine example of the Heavenly Father using science to achieve His will."

I smiled even though he couldn't see it. "The Lord works in mysterious ways."

"I knew you were a believer. You should come to mass."

I thought about my answer. I was raised Protestant and had never been to a Catholic mass, but I wasn't opposed to it. I considered answering that I'm Methodist, but honestly, I wouldn't mind visiting another church. We all believed in the same Christ, after all. Plus, I could get Burke to come with me since he was a practicing Catholic, and he wouldn't mind answering any questions I had. "I just might do that, Father Nolan," I told him. "I'll see you on a Sunday."

"I'll make sure to have your paycheck to you well before then," he said. "God be with you, Chase Harlem."

"And you as well," I said and hung up the phone.

I pushed myself out of my bed, my head hurting with only a dull throb instead of a full-on jackhammer of pain. Walking over to the record player, I saw the Ella Fitzgerald album Deuce and I had danced to the night before and turned it on. He'd be stopping by to check on me later, so I might as well get ready.

Instead, I walked to the door leading out to my balcony overlooking the courtyard and stepped out into the New Orleans sunshine.

I'm not one for superstition, but if anywhere in the world has magic, it's my city, and despite the danger it posed, it felt like it was healing my broken soul. Whatever the future held, I'd do my best to return the favor.

Epilogue

Serendipity

Months passed, and a new routine emerged consisting of me, Reese and Deuce rotating around in each other's lives. Burke would occasionally drop by to pick my brain over a case like some annoying cousin, and I admit that I was beginning to get comfortable in my new life. Then, one day, I came home from solving a case to find my assistant waiting for me in the courtyard with an important message.

We'd had to have many serious conversations about what constituted an 'important message' in the time since I solved the Nolan case, because she was taking her job as my office associate way too seriously. She had me returning calls to every single person who made an effort to contact me, including a little girl whose kitten had gone missing. Yes, that's right. I went from chasing murderers to chasing kittens. I caught that stupid cat, too. I fell out of two trees catching that stupid cat, and I was covered in splinters and had leaves in my hair, but I caught that mangy animal.

That's how I looked as I approached my apartment building that day to find Reese waiting for me on the stairs. She stood up as I approached, and I handed her my camera so that she could print some of the pictures I'd taken for another case. There was nothing too traumatizing on that particular memory card, so I didn't feel bad handing it off to a kid.

"He's here," she greeted me.

"If by 'he' you mean that idiot podcaster, tell him I'm out of town. I'll go take a nap on a park bench while you get rid of him."

Since the Nolan case had been so high-profile and the noble Detective Burke had been willing to share the fame and my name with the reporters at his last press conference, business had been booming. I'd also had a certain young podcaster, who goes by the unfortunate name of Barry Bobo, popping up uninvited at the most inconvenient times, in hopes of my granting him an exclusive. I'd turned him down three times, but just like my high school boyfriend, the guy couldn't take a hint. I'd taken to having Reese give him the run-around anytime he called.

However, Bobo did not appear to be the man Reese meant when she implied that someone was waiting for me in my office. She shook her head, then looked me up and down with that judgmental look that only teenagers can master, curling her lip and squinting her eyes. "You look like trash," she told me.

"Um, yeah, because I was looking for that stupid cat you sent me after," I told her.

"I take it you found Mr. Freckles?"

"Yeah, and that name makes no sense. Mr. Freckles was completely gray and also a girl."

Reese shrugged. "Pretty sure it was named by a five-year-old, so ..."

"Forget the stupid cat. Who is hanging out in my office?" I asked her.

Reese smiled so widely that it showed off both dimples. I don't think I'd ever seen her so excited. "Richard Baxter," she said the name slowly, enunciating every consonant with a precision I didn't know she had.

If you were paying attention, you might remember my run-in with one Richard Baxter that night at the Blue Nile. In case you've forgotten all about him, let me refresh your memory: right after the last major hurricane hit the Big Easy, billionaire Richard Baxter came to the rescue. He donated millions to help rebuild and relocated his company's home base here to support and give jobs to the people who had lost everything. Moreover, he kept many of his charitable donations a secret, and they were only revealed years later when one of the charities awarded him with a Philanthropist of the Year award. You can't walk down the streets of New Orleans today without hearing the name Richard Baxter, and that is a wonderful fact.

It also doesn't hurt that he's incredibly attractive. Like, imagine the best-looking guy you've seen; fix all perceived flaws, and then you'll have Richard Baxter. He has ice-blue eyes. and a jawline that I'm pretty sure is considered a lethal weapon in most countries. He's also in that vague age range between thirty and forty where men seem to thrive.

"Is this a practical joke?" I asked, wondering where my mini-me might have picked up a sense of humor. Last I checked, she was organizing everything in my office, from my refrigerator to my DVDs, so I doubted that anything other than her typical teenage snark would have manifested overnight. However, there was absolutely no way that I was going to believe that a multi-billionaire was sitting in my office asking me to take a case. Didn't he have people for that sort of thing? Heck, didn't the guy have people for every sort of thing?

"I'm *not* joking. I *never* joke about business. You *know* that."

"Stop emphasizing your words like that. It's unsettling. Also, why the heck would Richard freaking Baxter be in my office?"

"He wants to hire you for a case. Also, he liked the coffee. Didn't I tell you that brand was superior?"

"You gave Richard Baxter coffee?" That question was not important, so I didn't give her time to answer. "I'm fairly sure a guy in his position would have a PI on his payroll already. Besides, how would he have even found out about me? It's been months since that newspaper article, and I keep refusing to give that unfortunately named podcaster guy an interview."

She rolled her eyes. "Clearly, my social media campaign has been effective."

I paused and stared at her. "What social media campaign?"

"The Private Investigator Chase Harlem business pages I made online, with links to digital copies of every article of every case you've ever been a part of."

So, here's the truth: I like my privacy. I like my privacy a lot, so I don't go out of my way to get any more attention than what I need to make a living. I started to lose my temper, but Reese didn't deserve that. After all, I knew she meant well. I also knew why most self-proclaimed hermits never invited nosey teenagers into their lives.

"We'll talk about this later," I said. "I've got to go talk to a handsome billionaire while looking like roadkill." I walked past her and headed up to my office.

"Remember, you already have a boyfriend!" she shouted after me.

I waved a hand in response. I'd stopped denying it. Not that I'm admitting it, but I'm not denying it.

Even though Reese had told me he'd be there, it still took my breath away to see Richard Baxter sitting on my raggedy sofa with his ankle crossed elegantly over his knee, casually leafing through a magazine. He was just as handsome as he had looked on the cover of *Men's Health*, and I'm fairly sure the suit he was wearing cost more than my trusted Isuzu.

"Mr. Baxter," I greeted him. He looked up, and as I locked eyes with his ice-blue saucers, I almost forgot how to speak. Good thing I had years of training. "Sorry for the late entrance. I had a case."

He smiled at me, and I momentarily forgot that oxygen is essential to higher brain function as well as, you know, life.

"It's fine," he told me. "I hope the case was solved." His voice was so deep and resonant that it echoed around my small apartment like it was stuck on a continuous loop.

I cleared my throat. "Of course." I then motioned to my desk and chairs under the stairs—my makeshift office. "Would you like to speak in there?"

"Yes, that would be satisfactory." He stood up and walked into the office with more grace than a dancer. Of course, he was a head taller than any dancer I'd seen, and it hurt my neck to look up at him. I tried not to think of this as I followed him into the office, which was really just a nook with a desk.

Thank Jesus that the nosey little protégé had cleaned my office for me. I motioned to the two chairs in front of my desk before moving behind the desk myself. He sat down, somehow managing not to grimace at sitting in what had to be the cheapest chair he'd ever seen.

"Your daughter is quite the hostess, P.I. Harlem," he told me. "You know, she's about the same age as my youngest son."

That caught me off guard. "Yeah, she's not my daughter." We literally look nothing alike. "She's my ... assistant." After getting over my shock, I moved to my own chair and sat across from him.

"I see. I take it she took care of the social media campaign?"

"Yes, she did do that."

"Very professional work."

"I'll let her know you think so," I told him with a smile. "Now, how may I help you, Mr. Baxter?"

He crossed his legs in an exceedingly elegant way. I could tell he was sweating under his incredibly expensive silk collar, so he was nervous. "P.I. Harlem," he started, but then he stopped and examined me for a moment. I felt a little awkward under his icy stare. "I'm sorry. Have we met somewhere before?"

I thought back to that night at the Blue Nile when I was chasing Chris and answered confidently, "No. No sir, I think I'd remember meeting you."

He smiled again, but he didn't seem entirely convinced. I really needed to work on my lying skills.

"I see. My mistake. You see," he continued, "I need to engage your services."

Of course. "Let me guess, your family pet is missing? Someone is embezzling from your company? Or worse, someone is embezzling from one of your charities? Please tell me you're not hiding a dead body somewhere."

"No." He paused, steepling his fingers and bringing his lips to his fingertips. "P.I. Harlem, I think someone is trying to kill me."

Acknowledgments

Writing a book is a solitary effort, but getting said book into the hands of readers takes a whole army. I completed what became this version of *Chase Harlem* back in 2020, when so many wonderful people were suddenly finding time to finish the novel they'd always dreamed of writing. I knew when I chose to go the traditional publishing route that it would be an uphill battle. You would not have the book you're reading now if it weren't for some of these amazing people who helped me through the ups and downs of the editing process and then through the world of publishing.

First, I have to thank my parents and my family. I continue to use my maiden name, Burke, because I'm proud of where I came from. My parents always made sure I had exactly what I needed. They bought me books and fed my love of reading. They paid for my college education and encouraged me to work toward my goals. My brother is Burke, so I must thank him for that bit of inspiration, and his wife, Katie, is the coolest sister I could ask for. She's always giving me new books to read and learn from.

My Mawmaw bought me a book every time we went shopping. My Meemaw and Grandaddy kept every silly ghost story I wrote in second grade and beyond, and my Granny gave me access to books that I was "too young to read." (But are we mystery authors ever too young for Sue Grafton?) My Poppa made me think everything I did was magic, and I selfishly wish he was still here to tell me how proud of me he is. My Aunt Lisa and Uncle Ray have always encouraged me in school, coming to every event I was a part of, and I know they'll be in the front of line at my book launch. My Aunt Judy has already thrown all the book parties for me, and as one of the most amazing women I've ever met, inspired me to write strong women who can take care of business. My Pawpaw, my Uncle Jerry, and my father-in-law, Wayne, are the cops I based all my cops on. These men helped me to understand what it is detectives live with every day.

My Aunt Libby and Uncle Chris get their own paragraph because Libby is the real-life Chase Harlem (she can find anyone) and Chris had the good sense to marry her.

I'm incredibly blessed to have been born into such a family.

Next, I have to thank the love of my life and my personal Deuce Marlboro, Beau Brown, who encouraged me to keep writing even when I was sure I'd never be a "real author." He's a writer and an artist who has been my sounding board and most talented confidant. When I started getting serious about finishing this novel, he kept our very young children occupied so I could work. When I finished the first draft, he let me read every word out loud to him (it's the best way to edit) and gave me feedback and tips along the way. Then he made time to listen to the next draft and the draft after that. By the end, my man listened to at least five versions of this book. I hope every day to be as supportive and loving of a spouse to him as he's been to me.

If you follow my blog () or chat with me on my socials, I know you're waiting for me to thank my book review partner and unofficial publicist, Becky Brown. I dare you to name a single person who has a better relationship with their mother-in-law than I do. She's read every manuscript I've ever written, even that wild thing I keep in the drawer. She's gone to conferences with me, promoted my work to her friends,

(The Sisters) and colleagues, and even helped me set up and organize events. This writing career of ours would not exist without her support. I must also thank my unofficial doppelgänger and official photographer, Shannon Dille Porter. She took my headshots for all of my media, and she's the only person who can get a real smile out of me. She's a talented artist and photographer, and the absolute best mother of three I've ever seen in action. I don't know what I'd do without her as a sounding board, prayer partner, and interchangeable skirt-wearer.

In my eleven-year teaching career, I had the opportunity to work with some amazing people. There were times when I started this writing journey that I was a hot mess. Every rejection hurt, and I had that one friend I shared a classroom with who I vented to constantly. Thank you, Bradley Wilson for putting up with me. I'm definitely naming a character after you in the sequel!

I also had the opportunity to teach some marvelous students during that time, but there was one family I want to mention who taught me way more than I taught them. Thank you to Ava, Faith, Sofia, and Traci Theros. Thank you to Sofia, who was the first person outside my family to read this manuscript, and for convincing me not to kill off the ferret. She also made me the most amazing artwork of these characters that I love. Thank you to Faith, my personal assistant and a real American hero, for swiping a copy of my manuscript and handing it to a real-life editor, Carole Byars, who gave me a free line edit because you mowed her yard. I honestly would never have landed a deal without your support of my "badass" character. Thank you to Ava, my fellow writer, for taking me seriously, for joining me in writing workshops, and for being wise beyond her years. Finally, thank you to Traci who raised the three coolest ladies I've ever met, and in doing so, taught me to be a better mom.

(Mike and Jason are also really cool, and they're blessed to live with such awesome women.)

My current work environment also can't go without a mention. My bosses and colleagues have been amazingly supportive of my "other" career. I need to give a special thank you to Christy Hayden, who drags me out of my office on days where I've spent my entire lunch break writing and makes sure I eat food and touch grass. She also gave me the idea for Chase's self-defense class, and I'll always be grateful to her for the characters that developed from that subplot. She also reads every book I throw at her and keeps me sane on the insane days.

Now on to the professional organizations who took me in and taught me how to tread water in the sea that is publishing. I want to thank Brian Klems and Writing Day Workshops for introducing me to both of my literary agents and helping me to grow a writing platform. I've met so many fellow writers through these workshops, and I hope to continue to support them as they've supported me.

I want to thank the Birmingham Writing Workshop, especially my amazing critique partners who called out every mistake with kindness and built up every success: Aimee Hardy, Octavia Kuransky, Corinne Flickinger, Rolly Jackins, Barry DeLozier, Michael Yusko, Rick Geiger, David Hammond, and Drew Kizer. They cheered me on when I thought my career was going nowhere, and their advice made me a better author.

Thank you to my Sister's in Crime, especially my critique partners Isabella Zimmerman and Barbara Allyn, I thank you for the advice you've given me both as a writer and as a business person.

Thank you also to Clay Stafford and Killer Nashville for the Claymore Award and the conference that allowed me to meet my amazing publisher.

Finally, thank you to Alexandria Brown and Tina Beier for believing in this book from the beginning and making it better than it ever could have been. When I met Alex at Killer Nashville, I had accepted the fact that it would never be professionally published. I'd been told that nobody wanted this book. She did. She understood Chase's sense of humor, her drive, her trauma and everything I needed Chase to be. Alex and Tina took a chance on me and this mystery series when nobody else would, and I will be forever grateful.

I'm sure I've already destroyed the word count here, yet I'm equally sure I missed someone. To the someone(s) I missed, I'll catch you in the sequel.

About the Author

Elise Burke Brown comes from a family of detectives, including a grandfather who filled her childhood with true crime stories she learned not to repeat at daycare. Her debut novel won 2023 Killer Nashville Claymore Award for best unpublished investigator manuscript as well as the 2021 Monroe-Walton Award for best new author. She's had stories and poetry published in Sojourn Literary Magazine, Dewpoint Literary Magazine, The Moonlit Road, The Dark Sire Literary Magazine, and Southern Quill. She's also sold stories to the podcast, Chilling Tales for Dark Nights. She runs the popular book blog, https://coupleofbeesre ad.com/

Can't part with Chase just yet? Check out the sneak peek of Chasing Phantoms!

Chapter 1

I've Got the World on a String

Whoever said that diamonds are a girl's best friend never witnessed the ferocity of a woman with a taser. Maybe girls prefer diamonds, but women know better.

Philanthropist and all-around nice guy Richard Baxter didn't really understand this fact before he met me, but the day a truckload of goons slipped a cloth sack over his head and dragged him out of a charity event and into a dark alley, he learned quickly. In his temporarily induced blindness, he was probably wondering where the pocket-sized private investigator he'd hired to protect him had gotten off to, but I'll try not to hold his doubts against him. As I am a private investigator, not a bodyguard, I knew that I'd have to come up with a plan to catch his kidnappers in the act fast.

Which is why when said kidnappers opened the sliding door to their cliché white van, I was standing inside with my trusty taser in my right hand and my cell phone live-streaming the attempted kidnapping in my left.

"Hey morons!" I greeted the four men surrounding the only billionaire I know of who has a shred of decency. "Who's ready to go viral?"

The goons were not amused. The one who'd opened the door lunged toward me, snatching at my phone—not the smartest move considering it put his neck within tasing distance. He hit the alley's concrete ground with a crunch.

The goon with the gun suddenly remembered he was armed and raised his weapon at me with a shout. I round-house kicked the weapon out of his hand–purely for theatrical purposes–then leapt from the side of the van, wrapping my legs around his chest and tasing him in the temple. My momentum and the zap from the taser knocked the now unarmed goon backwards, and I rolled off him and up onto my knee just in time to zap goon number three right in the gonads, leaving just one more goon to consider.

Thinking that fourth goon would have sense enough to go for the gun, I got to my feet quickly. Instead of arming himself, the idiot ran back toward the building he and his friends had dragged Baxter out of.

"Hey!" I shouted. "Get back here so I can tase you!" As much as I enjoy a good jog through the graveyard, I'm not a fan of physically chasing criminals, but there was no way I was letting this jerk get away. I handed my phone to a still hooded Richard Baxter and took off after goon number four.

Before I could reach him, however, the emergency exit door opened and my teenage sidekick, Reese Kelley, stepped out, taser in hand. She leapt over the banister by the door, pouncing on goon number four and tasing him in the neck, just as I'd taught her.

Another teenager exited the building: Baxter's youngest son, Tim. "Dad!" he shouted when he saw his father, who'd managed to get the cloth hood off his head. Tim launched himself down the steps and through the alley right into his dad's arms.

I turned to my own teenage protégé, expecting a similar greeting. Instead of being concerned for my health, however, she was looking perplexed as she glanced between the taser in her hand and the man groaning on the ground at her feet.

"What's wrong?" I asked.

"I don't think the voltage is high enough," she answered. "He didn't piss himself."

I shrugged. "They don't always do that."

Stupidly, the goon at her feet tried to stand up. Reese casually leaned down and tased him again.

"Ha! That did it," she said, standing up and grinning at me.

I rolled my eyes. "Gimme your phone. I should call this in."

She tossed me her phone but asked, "Where's yours?"

I nodded over to Richard Baxter, who was still hugging his son. "It's still livestreaming. Baxter's got it."

Reese grinned maniacally. "We're gonna get so many likes."

I ignored her disturbing obsession with internet fame and called the New Orleans Police Department's non-emergency line. Honestly, with the livestream going, cops were likely already on their way, but I figured a call to dispatch would make things a lot less confusing upon their arrival.

"You've reached the NOPD's non-emergency line," Geraldine answered on the third ring. "How may I direct your call?"

"Hey Geraldine, this is Chase."

"Well, hey there, honey." Geraldine gushed, always happy to hear from me. "Did you tase somebody again?"

I laughed. "Honestly, Geraldine, I tased a lot of somebodies."

"I tased one, too!" Reese shouted from beside me.

"We've got four in total," I told Geraldine.

Geraldine let out a low whistle over the phone. "Sounds like you ladies had quite the catch. Everybody okay?"

I looked over at Richard, who gave me a thumbs up. "We're all fine here, ma'am," I told Geraldine. In the distance, sirens began to peal.

"Well, honey, the boys are on their way," Geraldine said. "You girls hang tight."

"Thanks, Geraldine," I said, then hung up.

I made my way across the alley to where Richard stood. Tim raced past me, and I turned to see him talking excitedly to Reese and inspecting her taser. I thought about shouting out a warning for him not to tase himself in the face, but I didn't want to embarrass either kid. I grinned at Richard. "How you doin'? They didn't rough you up too bad, did they?"

The sounds of sirens were getting closer, and I needed to make sure my client didn't need a ride to the hospital.

He shook his head. "Nothing I haven't experienced before," he assured me. "I expected them to at least poison me."

"They've been watching you a while," I told him. "They knew that all they'd have to do is threaten the people at the charity and your son to make you do whatever they wanted. If I'd been worried about them poisoning you, I'd have had another plan."

He looked around at the groaning bodies on the ground. "They certainly didn't give you any trouble," he told me. "What about the driver?"

The sirens were so close that I could hear the tires squealing.

I shrugged. I'd pretended to be a cheap sex worker just to get him out of the van, but I wasn't about to divulge that to a client. "He's hog-tied in the back."

Richard raised a perfectly arched eyebrow.

"I lived on a farm," I explained. "I know how to tie up a hog."

At that moment, three cop cars finally arrived on the scene, careening into the alley one right after the other. Reese scrambled over to my side. Despite her many friendships within the NOPD, years as a Black girl on the streets of New Orleans had taught her to be cautious around cops she didn't know. I slung my arm around her shoulder to let her.

"Chase." I startled at the sound of my first name on Richard's lips. He'd been utterly professional throughout my time working for him. I turned toward him to see a slight blush painting his high cheekbones. "Now that you are no longer working for me, I was wondering if you would be interested in joining me for dinner one evening."

My jaw hit the dirty alley floor as I stared at the world's most eligible bachelor in stunned silence. Reese elbowed me hard in the ribs to get me to talking, but I was still too stunned to move.

"Miss Kelley is welcome to come along," Richard told me. "She gets along well with Tim, and we do really miss having a full table at family dinner."

"P.I. Harlem," one of the cops called to me as he was cuffing one of the kidnappers.

Finally, I got the nerve to speak up. "One sec Briggs," I called to the cop, before returning my attention to the startlingly blue eyes of Richard Baxter. "I'm really honored that you'd ask me, Mr. Baxter—"

"Please," he interrupted, gently. "You're not working for me anymore. Call me Richard."

I cleared my throat. "Richard, I'm really flattered by your offer, but I'm kind of, that is, I have a boyfriend, and as nice as he is, I'm not sure he would approve of me having dinner with Louisiana's hottest and most eligible bachelor." It was only the second time I'd referred to Deuce as my boyfriend, and I was embarrassed to have stumbled over the childish word.

Richard, bless his heart, didn't hide his disappointment, but he tried to cover it with a smile. "I completely understand, but if you or Reese ever need me for anything, please consider me a friend to call. I've grown quite fond of both of you."

"Harlem!" Officer Briggs called to me again, his voice rough and impatient. He's never really been a fan of the way I make criminals pee their pants before handing them over to the cops.

I made my way to him, fully aware that he was going to bitch at me about having to put a piss-covered criminal into his squad car again, but I honestly didn't care. I'd just made nice with New Orleans's hottest billionaire *and* I had a hot date to get to. What could possibly go wrong?

Need to expand your TBR? Check out
Rising Action's upcoming titles!

And don't forget to follow us on our socials for cover
reveals, giveaways, and announcements:
Instagram: @risingactionpublishingco
TikTok: @risingactionpublishingco
Website: http://www.risingactionpublishingco.com

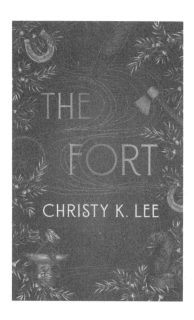

It's the height of the fur trade in Canada, and Abigail Williams leaves her home in England and travels deep within the rugged wilderness to escape her scandalous past. With her young son in tow, Abby imagines a life on the banks of the North Saskatchewan River, in the rugged but beautiful Fort Edmonton, where she can mend horseshoes in her father's blacksmith shop and her past will not be a hindrance to her happiness.

Life has other plans. The interest of Henry, an officer at the fort, and Gabriel, a French trapper, are not what she expected. While she wrestles with what future either man can give her, her past comes to haunt her, and she and her son must flee with a ragtag group of voyageurs to Montreal. The winter journey is fraught with dangers, from raging rivers to the chaos that is Lake Superior. But Abby is determined to create a new life for herself, whatever the barriers.

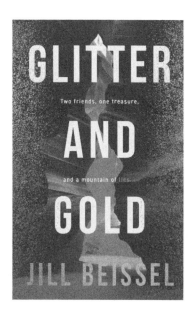

After her mother's death, Delaney Byrne faces escalating debts and a sister to support. Their home is burglarized, hinting at her mother's obsession with a hidden treasure in Arizona's mountains. When her estranged best friend, Joss, proposes one final treasure hunt, Delaney is skeptical but desperate.

As they delve into the wilderness, Delaney and Joss navigate a maze of old betrayals and hidden dangers. Each clue they uncover draws them closer to the treasure but deeper into risk. Delaney vows not to repeat her mother's mistakes, but the mountain's perils are relentless, and trust is scarce.

Blending the gripping suspense of Erica Ferencik's The River at Night with the psychological depth of Andrea Bartz's We Were Never Here, Glitter & Gold is a tale of survival, secrets, and the lengths we go to for family and fortune.

SOME DREAMS COST MORE THAN OTHERS.
HERS MIGHT COST HER HEART...

SEA SALT
and
COFFEE
BEANS

Grace
Santamaria

When Sofia loses her coveted job, her American dream is on the line. With her U.S. work visa hanging by a thread, a job interview at a top Miami marketing firm is her last shot at staying in the country. But as she navigates the high-stakes competition, she finds herself irresistibly drawn to her chief rival for the position—charming and ambitious Esteban.

Esteban embodies the glamorous Miami lifestyle Sofia has always admired, and he's unbothered by their rivalry. But for Sofia, everything is at stake. She can't bring herself to tell him how much this job means to her, nor that her future depends on securing it. With her visa expiring, mounting family pressures, and bills piling up, Sofia faces an impossible choice: win the job, or risk returning to a life she fought so hard to leave behind.

Can Sofia claim the career—and the love—she longs for, or will her dreams slip through her fingers just as they're within reach?

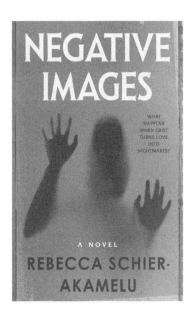

NEGATIVE IMAGES

WHAT HAPPENS WHEN GRIEF TURNS LOVE INTO NIGHTMARES?

A NOVEL

REBECCA SCHIER-AKAMELU

Anita Walsh, still reeling from her husband's sudden death, finds herself haunted not only by grief, but his Negative Image, a new phenomenon where the deceased prey on those they loved in life, turning intimate memories into nightmares. This spectral figure uses their shared past as a weapon, systematically dismantling her friendships, career, and self-worth. Desperate for escape, Anita plunges into a quest to sever the ghostly bonds that tie her to her tormentor.

As society grapples with the rising terror of NIs, a charismatic extremist proposes a radical solution to isolate the haunted from the unafflicted, gaining dangerous followers. Anita, alongside another victim of this spectral affliction, must navigate their personal hauntings and societal threats to prevent the breakdown of their community.

With its gripping narrative and eerie exploration of love and betrayal, Negative Images delves deep into the psychological horrors of grief and the supernatural, making it a must-read for fans of horror and ghost stories alike.